A
Woman's War

Marjorie Daley

Printed in the United States of America

100% Human Generated Content

Library of Congress Control Number: TXu-2-434-325
Paperback ISBN: 979-8-9885653-2-1
Epub ISBN: 979-8-9885653-3-8
Audiobook ISBN: 979-8-9885653-4-5

Publisher's Cataloging-in-Publication data

Names: Daley, Marjorie, author.
Title: A woman's war / Marjorie Daley.
Description: First trade paperback original edition. | Daley Book. | Laramie, WY; 2024.
Identifiers: LCCN: TXu-2-434-325 | ISBN: 979-8-9885653-2-1
Subjects: LCSH: History--Fiction. | World war 1; 1914-1918. | War—Women's work. | War--Fiction.
BISAC: FICTION / Historical/ 20th century/ World War I.

"On the face of it, no one could have been less equipped for the job than these gently nurtured girls who walked straight out of the Edwardian drawing rooms and into the manifold horrors of the First World War."

From The Roses of No Man's Land by Lyn Macdonald

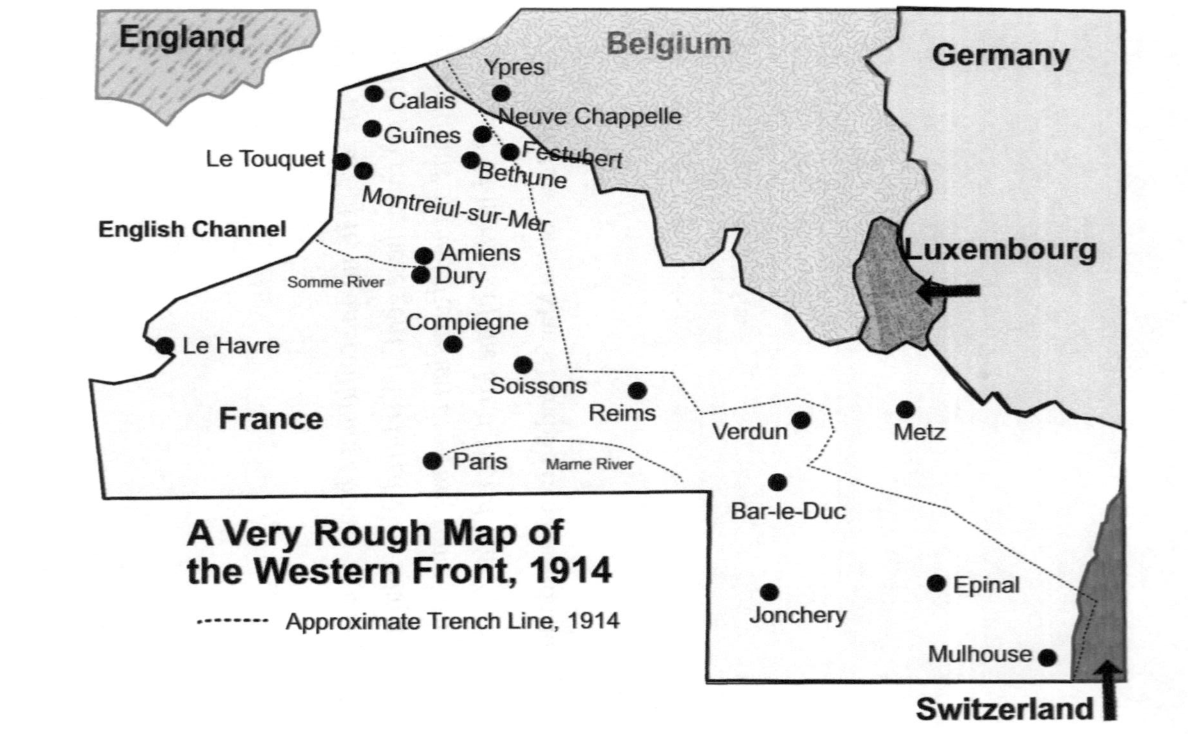

England
Belgium
Germany
Ypres
Calais
Neuve Chappelle
Guînes
Festubert
Le Touquet
Bethune
Montreiul-sur-Mer
English Channel
Luxembourg
Amiens
Dury
Somme River
Compiegne
Le Havre
Soissons
Reims
Verdun
Metz
France
Paris
Marne River
Bar-le-Duc
Epinal
Jonchery
Mulhouse
Switzerland
A Very Rough Map of
the Western Front, 1914
-------- Approximate Trench Line, 1914

Foreword

Documentation of women's activities in WWI was, in most cases, contradictory. One military source claimed that only the Russians had problems with typhoid. In her memoir, Beauchamp detailed a horrendous form of typhoid rampaging through the Entente trenches. British military sites declared that women did not serve in the trenches. I found documentation of both nurses and FANYs in the trenches, including the British ones.

Women's roles in the war were downplayed or even suppressed. The best instance of this is the story of Marie and Irene Curie's contributions during World War I. One 21st-century physician arrogantly stated that 'even Marie and Irene Curie helped' develop the science of radiography. In reality, the Curies could, without much hyperbole, be declared the mothers of radiography.

All this is to say that while this book is fiction, it draws very heavily on real events and real people. When there were conflicting opinions or events, I looked for two or more sources that collaborated with what I wrote. In very minute instances, details were changed slightly, for instance, the Canadian hospital at Dury became French. This historical fiction does not detract from the very real story of women's service from the front lines to the home front as they waged A Woman's War.

Chapter 1: August 1914

"The lamps are going out all over Europe; we shall not see them lit again in our lifetime" - *Sir Edward Grey, British foreign secretary. August 1914*

July 31, 1914
Outside Reims, France

"It's a squirrel, you coward," Elodie Fabien laughed at the big brown Norman Cob who had shied sideways at the angry chittering above him. "If he throws acorns, perhaps you have a reason, but this is just noise."

The horse shook his head, pawing in impatience. Under his thick mane, his too-short ears, frostbitten as a colt during a winter blizzard, flicked back and forth, setting his mane dancing. Elodie pressed her heels to his sides to drive him forward. He gave in with good grace, cantering toward a fence a few strides away. He gathered his hindquarters under him, powering up and over. He took a short step and settled. His rider petted his neck before picking up contact again and rounding toward another jump.

The early morning light filtered through the trees lining the jump alley that ran between vineyards to the west and pastureland to the east. Some long-ago ancestor decided that this road of trees would provide a windbreak for the precious grape vines. Successive generations had turned it into a pleasant bridle path. To the north lay the Belgian frontier. Behind the horse and rider, the tall steeple of Reims Cathedral was just visible as a distant suggestion.

Wherever a tree had aged and fallen, light stretched shadows across the lane and flickered as the leaves trembled overhead. It was going to be a hot morning. A few more jumps and the pair had reached the end of the alley before horse and rider turned back to the farmhouse and breakfast. The horse settled into a long swinging walk, blowing as he caught his breath. Elodie pulled at the cotton of her jodhpurs, trying to work air onto hot legs. Her calves were wrapped in cloth puttees, now dark with horsehair and sweat. She settled back into the saddle and, feeling guilty at the sloppiness, loosed her linen jacket's buttons. The faint breeze cooled the silk of her riding blouse, at least.

She sometimes wondered at the British and their love of hot clothing. Paris might rule the fashion world, but the British set the standards for proper riding dress. She knew very well her mother preferred her to ride sidesaddle. Elodie grimaced. This particular horse hated skirts flapping against his sides and was spooky and difficult to ride aside rather than astride. Of course, Elodie tossed her head unconsciously, she rode sidesaddle as well as she did astride. She had, in fact, ridden aside over every obstacle in the alley, but it was the principle. Riding habits might be chic, but she preferred to mount without a groom's help.

Pulling off her velvet cap, she welcomed the suddenly cool breeze in her sweaty hair. She wiped her face, dropping her reins as she did so. Another complaint Maman would have - this sweating like a farm hand. But soon, all those complaints would be behind her. Ahead of her lay a year in Paris at the Sorbonne. She twirled her chestnut hair and then tucked it back under the cap. Of course, while the complaints would end, so too would early morning rides through the countryside around Reims. She sighed and picked up the reins again.

As they neared the stables, the sound of the stableman shaking out buckets brought the horse's head up, his ears pricked in eagerness for his breakfast. He jigged a bit but settled obediently. Elodie slid off, dropping gently to her toes and petting his shoulder. He nuzzled her absent-mindedly and then focused on the sound of grain rattling into feed pans. She slid the reins over his neck and led him into the still-cool stables.

"Miss Elodie, I thought it was you who took

Brûlée out," the stableman, Alain, greeted her. "How was he?"

"Fresh enough to spook at squirrels," Elodie replied, slipping off the bridle and handing it to Alain before she haltered the horse. "He is such a jumper. I am going to miss him when I go to university." Brûlée sneezed and then rubbed his head against her jacket. She pushed him away and brushed ineffectively at the brown hairs he left behind. Together, the two of them untacked the horse and put him up, where he lost interest in them, burying his nose in his feed pan. Elodie gave him an affectionate pat and locked the stall door behind her.

"I'll see you tomorrow," she called out and left the stables. She contemplated the house. The trick was to get to her room before her mother noticed that she was wearing jodhpurs. Elodie dusted at her jacket again.

She was just passing the big oak tree that graced their farmyard when her mother's voice rang out, calling Elodie's younger brother Theo to breakfast. Elodie frowned and backed up to keep the oak between her and the house. She looked up into the tree she used to climb when she was Theo's age. Perhaps she still could climb it and wait until her mother left the back of the house? She could then creep in unseen. The slick soles of her boots put paid to that idea.

Instead, Elodie sat down at the base of the tree

and pulled off her velvet cap again. Her hair tumbled down, parts of it stuck flat with sweat and parts wild from the gallop. She pulled out what remained of the braid and finger-combed the tresses. It dried quickly in the heat and she rebraided it. Perhaps if she were neater, her mother would be less critical. Elodie started as the kitchen door slammed.

Theo came around the tree, carefully balancing a cup of coffee on a saucer, a small roll beside it. His cheerful ten-year-old face was set in concentration to keep from spilling his burden and his cheek was stained with strawberry jelly that had escaped a cursory wipe with a napkin. He handed her the saucer and cup and stood looking down at her with a serious expression. The comforting smell of hot coffee and freshly cooked bread made her stomach growl.

"Thank you, Theo." Elodie settled the cup and took a sip.

"Maman says if you went out riding this morning in men's clothing, she is going to beat you," Theo said gravely. "Can I watch?"

"Don't be silly. You know Maman would never do that," Elodie chided him.

"It's because Tante Grete is here, and Maman wants you to make a good impression on her and give up on going to university and marry Lothar." Theo did not pause for a breath. Elodie chewed on the roll to keep rude words from tumbling out.

Elodie had gone to convent school, learning the

art of running a proper Catholic household. At fifteen, she had gone on to the girls' lycée which was an extension of the convent, focused on turning out good homemakers. A year ago, at eighteen, she had graduated. Her parents had sent her on a modest tour with an Englishwoman and then the bargaining had begun. Isabeau wished her daughter to marry by twenty. The daughter wished to attend university first. There were too many interesting things to do and see out in the world beyond the farm gates.

Her father had listened gravely and after six months of pleading, he had handed down his decision. Elodie could attend one year of university. She would then return and marry after she reached twenty-one. As with all Solomonic decisions, it left neither party completely happy nor completely injured.

"I'm not going to marry Lothar," Elodie said finally. "Not now or ever." Theo sat down beside her.

"I should hope not. He's *chiant*," Theo stated. Elodie giggled at her little brother recognizing that Lothar was dull. "And you didn't seem to enjoy kissing him last summer," Theo went on with a hint of mischief in his eyes.

"Theodore!" Elodie gasped.

"I wasn't spying. Honest, Elodie. I was just avoiding Stephan. I ran around the stables and there you were."

Elodie could hardly blame him for trying to avoid Stephan, and that brought her back to the problems of the day: getting into the house and why her mother was more prickly than usual. Her mother, Isabeau, was hosting her best friend, Grete Rohr. They had been close since their school days in Switzerland and the women and their children had spent a good deal of time together over the years. Grete was on her way to put her youngest son, Stephan, on a ship from France to England for his fifth year at Eton. They could have sailed from a German port, but this gave Grete and Isabeau a chance to gossip.

Elodie found the entire family a trial. Stephan, the youngest boy of fifteen, was a monster. Elodie wholeheartedly loathed him. The daughter, Mathilde, was two years younger than Elodie and nice enough, but staid and dull. Then there was Lothar. She had imagined him as a German prince in an opera when she was younger, with herself as the heroine. In reality, he was only marginally better than his little brother. Lother had two interests in life: himself and the German army. He was at the *Preußische Kriegsakademie,* the German military academy, becoming more of a pompous bore.

Tante Grete was, all things considered, not too bad – just stuffy. At least her husband, the Colonel, had not come on this trip. Colonel Rohr barely tolerated his wife's French friend and spent most of his time angering Elodie's father with pronouncements of German greatness.

"How do you always manage to be

everywhere and overhearing everything?" Elodie asked mildly. Theo's face took on such a look of mischief that Elodie laughed.

"I am going to miss you when you leave for university." He changed the subject.

"I'll miss you too, *mon vilain*. But I will be home for holidays."

"Bring me something good."

"I will." Elodie drained her coffee cup and climbed to her feet. "Go see if I can make it through the kitchen without Maman seeing me."

Perhaps sensitive to his children's feelings about the guests, Elodie's father woke them very early the next morning, a clear and beautiful Saturday. They slipped out of the house and across to the stables where Alain had the horses ready. In respect for her father's sensibilities, Elodie wore a dark green riding habit knowing her father would ride Brûlée. Instead, she would be mounted on a handsome gray gelding. She liked him well enough, but he was not her favorite. Theo groaned at the prospect of riding his pony. Alain helped Elodie to mount as Roland swung onto Brûlée with a grin at his daughter's discomfort. He had purchased the Norman Cob as his riding horse, only to have his daughter commandeer him as her own.

Theo rode in front on his pony, making mad circles and leaping over small fences, showing off in the hopes that he would soon move up to a full-sized horse. Elodie eyed him critically. He'd soon need a bigger mount if his legs grew much longer.

As the local magistrate, Roland Fabien was constantly busy and this was a rare opportunity to spend time with his children. He watched his son tolerantly. He admired his elegant daughter on the gray horse, thinking it was only yesterday that Elodie had been tearing around on the same pony. Soon, Elodie would be in Paris and Theo... perhaps he should find somewhere safe to send Theo.

The peacefulness of the farm was at odds with the rumblings coming out of Germany. Perhaps that was why Colonel Rohr had not come with his wife on this visit. Roland shifted uneasily. But no, he shook his head, surely in a new century, war should be inconceivable to civilized men. He put all thought of political conflict as far from his mind as he could.

By mid-morning, horses and humans alike were very hungry. They turned for home, chattering happily. As they neared the stables, a bowler-hatted man dressed in a formal morning suit ran toward the trio. Behind him, the stableman Alain stood in the shadow of the barn, his body rigid and fists clenched at his sides.

"Judge, judge. Bad news," the man gasped. "The Germans have declared war on Russia."

Brûlée tossed his head against the suddenly tightened reins.

"You know it is only a matter of time until..."

His words petered out as Roland threw up a hand. Elodie looked from man to man. Her father's face was grim, all the joy of the morning gone. The stranger's face was pale and chilled. Alain was frozen, eyes fixed on something very far away. He started as the judge dismounted and came forward to catch the reins from him. Roland turned to help Elodie down and gripped her arms very hard as her feet steadied on the ground.

"No word to your mother. Let her enjoy Grete's company. Tell her I will be back for supper." He frowned and Elodie nodded, a frisson of fear running through her. He looked over at Theo. "Do you hear me, Theo? Not a word to your mother." Roland turned to go and then spun back to hug his children tightly.

"Guillaume!" Roland called for his chauffeur, who came running. In moments the three men were gone, Guillaume and the judge in his green and cream Roi des Belges and the bowler-hatted man in his horse-drawn shay. Elodie glanced at her little brother.

"Help Alain put up the horses," she said sternly. Theo nodded; his face gone white. Elodie turned on her heel and went to the house to change out of her riding habit and think in silence. Germany was looking eastward, but how long would it take for them to turn their attention west toward their historic enemy, France? Was that what her father's man had meant to say?

Sunday passed quietly for the Fabiens.

Unbeknownst to them, across the border, Luxembourg collapsed. With a token army of four hundred men, they stood no chance as ten thousand Germans marched across the tiny country. The army stopped at the French border, waiting for the next moves in this game as German and French troops began maneuvering like chess pieces.

On Monday, Elodie and Theo decided they would escape the house early, attempting to avoid Stephan. Theo just wanted well away but Elodie had decided on shopping. She wore a blue skirt that cleared the tops of her boots and a pale green blouse that accentuated her narrow waist. She would very much have liked to have left the S-bend corset at home, but she was willing to admit that it did make the shirtwaist drape nicely. Over it all was a jacket that fell to her knees, with elbow-length sleeves and a wide belt to keep it closed. And, of course, there was a wide-brimmed boater hat sporting a pale green silk rosette and light blue ribbon. Turning it in her hands, she pinned it to her stylishly drooping coiffure and examined herself with pleasure in the looking glass. She hoped to meet her friends in Reims and this outfit was very appropriate for a young lady shopping for university.

Roland glanced at their pleading faces as he readied to leave and then gave in with a snort. Theo and Elodie piled in beside their father in his pride and joy, the open-topped Roi des Belges, and motored out into the lane. Theo chattered to Guillaume on the drive and once in the center of Reims, near the great cathedral and their father's office, he darted from the car toward a group of his friends, a backward wave to his father's reminder to be home before dark.

"I should be here all day, Elodie. Guillaume can give you a lift home if you are ready to leave after noon." Roland smiled at his daughter.

"Thank you, Papa." She kissed his cheek and started off into town. Roland watched her go. It was hard to see his firstborn on the edge of flight. Perhaps university would allow a gentler admittance to adulthood. It would certainly not be a kind introduction in a military German household with Lothar, especially not if it was also an enemy household. He shook his head, wondering at his wife's wishes, then looked up at his office and felt the weight of the day fall on his shoulders. He went on to his own cares and worries about the larger world.

Elodie met with her gaggle of friends for a gossipy, breathless run through the shops and then a slightly giggly luncheon. A few of her friends were destined for marriage and others for the classroom, as teachers rather than students. One or two had taken a secretarial course and would soon be working girls. Elodie looked at them with faint awe, knowing that option was completely out of her reach. University had been enough of a stretch for her father. For a moment, she felt cold. Looking down at her plate, she realized this might be the last time they would all be together. Then witty Jasmine made one of her observations and in the laughter, that premonition slipped away.

After lunch, the girls broke apart into smaller groups, each heading to their afternoon responsibilities. Elodie hurried toward her father's office, juggling a few packages that she dumped into the Roi des Belges' backseat. Guillaume was storing purchases for the farm in the trunk.

"Are you leaving with me, Miss Elodie?" he asked.

"We have time for a drive," Elodie declared, climbing up on the driver's side running board and looking at him archly.

"Miss Elodie, you know the judge doesn't want you to drive," Guillaume protested weakly.

"But I am such a good driver. You start the car, Guillaume. I'll drive," Elodie insisted. Elodie reached into the back seat, finding a long scarf tucked in one of the door pockets. She then sat down sideways, gathering in her skirts so the door would not close on them before turning to face forward. She resettled her hat, making certain that the pins were in place, and tied the scarf over the top and brim, fastening it securely beneath her chin. Under Guillaume's nimble fingers, the car coughed to life, and he took his seat beside her. Then she let out the clutch, decorously driving the car, roof down to take advantage of the sun, out of Reims.

Guillaume relaxed fractionally as Elodie drove with uncharacteristic restraint. The roads outside of Reims were little more than paved cart tracks and they occasionally motored past horse- or oxen-drawn carts. The animals were growing more accustomed to cars, but many eyed them sideways, threatening to spook at the noise of the engines. When the traffic thinned, Elodie pressed on the accelerator and the car leaped forward. Guillaume clenched his fists on his legs.

The wind pouring over the windshield caught the edges of Elodie's wide hat and pulled it upward, hatpins and ribbon straining to keep it in place. She clapped one hand to the top of her head, eliciting a squeak of dismay from Guillaume. Elodie glanced over at him and laughed as she noted his fists.

"Don't worry, Guillaume, I haven't wrecked yet. I am a better driver than you are," she called over the noise of the engine and the wind.

"I know that, but your father will have me for dog meat if this car gets a scratch," the chauffeur replied.

"Why buy a car that can go fifty miles an hour and then drive it at twenty-five?" Elodie shouted back. "It's like putting Brûlée over fences a foal could jump."

"Brûlée has more sense than you do," Guillaume protested. Elodie laughed again. She loved to drive with the top down and the wind racing past her. It was almost as exciting as riding a powerful horse.

As she drove, she thought about not stopping and instead escaping into the world. But as a side road approached, she turned onto it, starting a circle that would bring them back into Reims. As they neared the outskirts of the city, Elodie slowed the car. The last thing she wanted was reports getting back to her father of the judge's distinctive automobile racing through town. And someone would certainly complain.

A crowd flowed through the streets toward the cathedral, drawn in by the insistent roll of a drum. The brisk rat-a-tat echoed off the biscuit-colored buildings. Elodie's eyes met Guillaume's. The drum meant news - important news - carried by the *commissaire*, the most senior police officer in Reims. Elodie's mind flashed back to the Saturday before and the bowler-hatted man. *It's only a matter of time…*

She stopped the car and, as one, driver and passenger exited, joining the streaming crowd following the drum's command.

The noise echoed off the church and reverberated around the *Square du Palais de Justice*. The buildings surrounding the square were governmental offices and their windows were filled with white faces. Her father was surely among them. The *commissaire* in his blue uniform and red cap stood in the center of the square, a continuous roll of sound coming from the drum hanging from his belt. When a significant crowd had gathered, he stopped, and the square fell silent. He unfurled a piece of paper, holding it up.

"The Germans have invaded Luxembourg." His words fell like bricks into the silence. A wave of mutters started, growing to yells and cries. The *commissaire* beat his drum again, demanding silence.

"The Kaiser has given the King of Belgium twelve hours to allow German troops to cross Belgium to invade France. We declare war on Germany if they cross our borders." A sudden explosion of cheers rang off the stones around the square. The *commissaire* beat on his drum until silence fell again. "If this occurs, there will be a general mobilization of all men enrolled in the reserves. You are to report to your assigned garrison by Sunday."

All around Elodie and Guillaume, people cheered, and boys threw their hats in the air. Elodie covered her mouth with one hand, not certain if it was excitement or dread she felt. War. Her country could soon be at war. The Germans would not allow tiny Belgium to stand in their way. And Belgium, with its smaller army, would not be able to withstand the Germans. She looked at Guillaume, shocked to see his face drawn and eyes stricken with horror.

"Are you all right, Guillaume? Is this not a glorious announcement?" She had to shake his arm to get his attention.

"No, Miss Elodie. I served in the 1904 uprising in Madagascar. This is not a glorious day. We must get you home before things get out of control." He took her arm, offering shelter from the surging crowd.

"What will you do?"

"I will have to report. This is terrible news, and it changes everything. I was going to ask Jeannie to marry me."

"You must ask her anyway. Surely this will be over soon. The Germans will certainly see reason," Elodie said hopefully. The chauffeur shook his head, ushering her toward the car. It took a long time to wend their way through the celebrating crowds.

Elodie sat silently in the passenger seat on the drive home. Wiser heads would prevail. This was the twentieth century and war was a thing of the past. The Germans were just, well, just being German. Her heart caught when she remembered university… would her father still let her go? Another, more cheerful thought occurred to her.

"I hope this means that Grete Rohr and that little monster she spawned leave soon," Elodie said as they turned into the farm gates. "Either England or Germany, I really don't care."

"If they can get to Germany, Miss Elodie. England may not allow them entry," Guillaume said. "The roads may be closed, and trains will stop running soon." Elodie shuddered at the thought that the pair might stay longer.

A forlorn figure was slumped against one of the hitching posts. Elodie frowned. It was Alain the stableman's youngest boy, Jere.

"What on earth? Guillaume, let me out here, please. I need to see what is wrong with Jere."

"Yes, Miss Elodie."

Elodie stepped down from the car, hearing heartbroken sobs coming from the little boy. Surely word had not yet reached the farm and his father had not already left for the reserves. The child was holding a scrap of gray fur in his bloody hands.

"Jere? What is going on?" Elodie knelt down beside him. The bruised, bloody, and snot-streaked face turned up to hers made her reach out to him in sympathy. One hand pointed toward the barn, finger trembling. The gray fur, she realized, was the corpse of one of the barn kittens.

"The Boche," he whimpered. Elodie scowled as she stood up, heading for the stable. Stephan was not allowed in there, or pretty much anywhere there wasn't someone to keep an eye on him.

It was dim and cool inside but the horses in their stalls were upset, eyes rolling and heads tossing. Elodie paused, listening and letting her vision adjust. There was no one on the ground floor and the tack was still neatly hung. Stephan had not then reenacted last year's vandalism. A hint of sound drifted down from the loft. Elodie crossed the barn floor with swift steps, cursing the corset that hindered her movements. She was short of breath as she reached the top of the ladder to peer around.

In the dimness of the loft, with light filtering through cracks, she could see a teenage boy. Stephan Rohr had not yet started to grow tall and show a man's form. Instead, he was short and chubby. His blonde hair fell over his forehead as he hunched over something in the hay - the bloody corpse of a kitten in his hands and another twitching at his feet.

"You little *morveux!*" Elodie darted forward and grabbed his collar, yanking him backward onto his rear end. Stephan was not small, but Elodie had handled horses for years and she was very angry. "Get out of this barn, you brat." She pulled him to his feet and shoved him towards the ladder.

Stephan turned toward her, hands raised in fists and face scarlet with

. He lunged forward, grabbing Elodie's sleeve, ripping it loose from under the jacket. For a split second, both were shocked by the violence.

"That's my favorite blouse," she hissed. Stephan held up the sleeve, tearing it at the seam.

"This is what I will do to you," he growled, his voice breaking. He threw the scraps aside and started toward her again. Elodie jumped backward, feeling her heel connect with something hard. Reaching back to catch her balance, her hand fell on a long wooden handle. Where there was hay, there were pitchforks. Elodie snatched it up, holding the sharp tines toward

Stephan. He retreated and Elodie pushed her advantage, driving him down the ladder one rung at a time. She jumped the last few rungs to the ground, throwing the pitchfork to one side and grabbing his ear, twisting it hard. His face was white with fury, and he swung at her, almost making her break her grip. He pressed on, kicking. She felt the other sleeve rip and her hat was knocked sideways.

Elodie wrapped her free hand in his hair, clenching her fingers and jerking his head back. He barely had enough hair to grasp so she boxed his ear hard and pulled again. His hands came up to catch at hers.

"My father should whip you. Enough." She managed to land another blow across his ear. "You are an absolute beast." With Stephan now mostly under control, she dragged him toward the house. As they passed Jere, Elodie jerked Stephan to a stop.

"Jere. Find your father and tell him to take care of… of the thing in the loft. Run now." The little boy scrambled up and ran towards the field. Elodie and her prisoner went up to the house and into the kitchen. Just then, she heard the front door slam and feet race down the hallway -- Theo coming from town to bring the news. Theo loved the barn cats. He would want to fight Stephan and her beloved brother would possibly get hurt. She would let her father deal with the situation.

She shoved Stephan through the cellar door,

slamming and locking it behind him. Let him stew for a while. There was a spate of screaming, thankfully muffled by the thick door. Elodie leaned against the wall, suddenly realizing she was out of breath. Gasping for a moment and wanting to loosen her corset, she dropped the key into her jacket pocket before realizing the jacket was ruined.

"Maman! Maman!" Theodore yelled as he ran. Elodie hurried into the parlor as her brother burst through from the other door to where their mother and Grete were seated, Grete embroidering and Isabeau mending clothes.

"Theo, don't yell," Isabeau Fabien admonished gently.

"Maman. The news. The *commissaire* was in the square. We are at war. The Boche invaded at Joncherey this morning, and Luxembourg too." He bent over, trying to catch his breath. Isabeau sat very still, eyes on her best friend. Grete Rohr's face paled. Finally, Isabeau put down her work and looked at her son, her gray eyes sharp.

"You will apologize to Tante Grete for using vulgar slang," Isabeau said sternly. The boy looked at his mother in shock. She had not reacted to the momentous news.

"I apologize, Tante. It was rude of me. But Maman..." Theo caught sight of his sister standing in the doorway and stared at her.

"Elodie, what is going on?" Isabeau peered in

the direction of the kitchen as if she could see through walls. Elodie smoothed down her skirt, feeling the ghost of a breeze up her torn shirtwaist. She stepped into her mother's field of view and the older woman gasped at her daughter's appearance. Elodie's hair hung down wildly and the hat brim was crushed. Her skirt and jacket were torn and filthy and there was blood on the breast of her blouse.

"Elodie, what happened? Are you all right?"

"I found Stephan in the barn. I am sorry, Tante, but he was killing the barn kittens. I'm afraid I hit him several times and then I locked him in the cellar." Elodie took the key out of her pocket and set it beside Grete.

Grete's face paled and for a moment she looked sick. Theo turned on one heel and charged out of the room toward the barn. Elodie winced.

"Oh, dear." Isabeau vented a small and completely inadequate sigh.

Outside, the Roi des Belges flashed by the windows, Guillaume at the wheel.

"He has gone to collect your father. Elodie, perhaps… perhaps you would be good enough to look in the railroad timetable for a train for Tante Grete. To Germany, if you please." Isabeau's voice was thin. She looked at Elodie's rumpled appearance and missing sleeve. "After you change your clothing, please."

"Yes, Maman," Elodie excused herself.

By evening, the Roi des Belges had returned at a more sedate pace. Elodie looked down from her bedroom window as Guillaume opened the passenger door for her father. The chauffeur looked to have aged in the few hours since she had seen him last.

Elodie's father strode into the house and Elodie went down the stairs and into the parlor. Her father stood at the cold fireplace, a glass of cognac in one hand and a cigar in the other. Isabeau's face was gray and Grete's face was hidden in a handkerchief.

"Papa?" Elodie spoke softly.

"The Germans took Luxembourg yesterday and they invaded Joncherey this morning. We beat them back. I'm afraid it's not over." His voice was quiet.

"Yes, papa. What do we do?" The silence was broken only by the incongruous sound of chickens in the farmyard. Finally, her father's eyes fell on their guest.

"Grete, you and Stephan must prepare to leave in the morning. If the trains are running, you will go back to Germany. If they are not, Guillaume will take you to Esch-Sur-Alzette and the German troops in Luxembourg should be able to help you make your way home."

"Yes, Roland." The woman drew in a shaky breath and lifted her face from the handkerchief. "Elodie was kind enough to look up times for me. Perhaps I should pack now. Excuse me, my friends."

She stood up, shakily leaving the room. They heard her footsteps going slowly up the stairs.

"And us, Roland, what shall we do?" Isabeau's voice trembled. Elodie glanced at her normally self-assured and confident mother in dismay. Her father threw back the drink and poured another.

"For now, you will write my mother in Le Havre and make arrangements for you, Elodie, and Theo to stay with her if need be. We shall know shortly if the Germans are planning more than just threats."

"But, Papa, I am to go to the Sorbonne in three weeks!" Elodie protested.

"If the Germans invade, Paris will be their target. You will not be safe there."

"But…" Elodie fell silent as her mother reached out a hand to hers and squeezed gently.

The Fabiens and Grete had gathered quietly in the dining room when the cook entered, her face red. She glared fiercely at Elodie and then addressed Isabeau.

"Madame, the German boy is still in the cellar where Miss Elodie put him."

Elodie started guiltily and Grete stood up so quickly her chair fell back. Roland glanced at Elodie with a raised eyebrow and went to the kitchen, followed by the others. Elodie darted into the sitting room to get the key and brought it to her father. She retreated to stand next to Theo as Roland opened the door. Stephan stalked out, shading his eyes from the sudden light. He was covered with mud and cobwebs streaked his hair, face, and clothing, the evidence of his crimes still on his blood-stained hands.

"Oh, Stephan, I am so sorry," his mother pleaded with him, but the boy only had furious eyes for Elodie. Beside her, Theo snorted, trying hard not to laugh.

"Theo," Roland snapped as his son lost the battle. "Remove yourself until you can act properly." Gales of laughter followed the boy's exit.

"Germany and France are at war, and we must return home," Grete told him.

"Good. We shall crush France," Stephan snarled. Roland raised his hand as if to slap Stephan but dropped his hand to his side. Instead, he spoke calmly.

"Stephan, perhaps you will care to wash up and join us for dinner. Ladies, if you will return to the dining room. Except you, Elodie." He stopped his daughter. When the room had emptied, Roland asked "What was that about?"

"Oh, Papa. Stephan was torturing and killing the barn kittens and he thrashed Jere." Elodie gripped her hands together. Roland looked over her shoulder with a long sigh.

"Perhaps good will come of this war if it saves us from visits by that… that boy," he said finally.

"Consider yourself scolded and sleep with your door locked tonight."

"Theo and I always do when he is in the house," Elodie whispered. She hurried back to the dining room and sat down somberly, not looking at anyone. That night, Elodie said her prayers with extra fervor.

In the morning, German troops swarmed over the Belgian frontier.

Chapter 2: August 1914

"The war will be over before the leaves fall from the trees." *Kaiser Wilhelm II to his troops on the eve of battle, 1914*

Elodie awoke with an aching head and crept downstairs to find aspirin powder and a cup of coffee. The people clustered around the breakfast table were a silent, grim bunch. Isabeau and Grete sat together at one end while Roland hid behind a newspaper. Next to him, Theo ate with single-minded determination. Stephan sat in solitary aloofness, keeping a chair between himself and the next person. He had gathered breakfast items around him, guarding them. Theo appeared to have collected a decent amount before the confiscation started because his plate showed signs of having been full. The icy glitter in Stephan's eyes barely penetrated Elodie's headache. She slid into the cramped space next to Theo and reached for the coffee pot. Stephan made to move it out of her grasp, but a wordless growl from behind her father's newspaper stopped him. Elodie smirked.

The aspirin powder was bitter, but she swallowed it with determination, chasing it with coffee. Her father looked at her sympathetically around the edge of the paper but made no comment, eventually folding it up and laying it down beside his plate.

"Elodie, I need you to drive Grete to the train station this morning," Roland said after a few moments. Elodie blanched at the thought of being stuck in the tiny horse trap with the Rohrs.

"Me, Papa? In the trap?"

"No, child. You may take the Roi des Belges." He smiled at her confusion.

"But…"

"Surely you did not think your driving lessons were a secret? Guillaume kept me quite reliably informed." Roland snorted at his daughter's red face. "There are duties only he can attend to on the farm today, so you must drive."

"Yes, Papa." Elodie dropped her head as she ate. So, Guillaume had not been the victim of her charms but a proper servant to her father. She felt just a little betrayed and, on the whole, a bit silly. How Guillaume must have laughed at her attempts to bribe him with pieces of pie.

After breakfast, Elodie changed out of her

wrapper and into an old shirtwaist and black skirt. With a proper jacket, it would be suitable to take the Rohrs to the train station. She was quite certain her mother would be marshaling the house in preparation for their departure and Elodie would be hard at work as soon as she returned. She coiled her hair into a simple chignon and put on a hat with a red, white, and blue ribbon tied cheerfully around the crown. The French colors made her proud.

By mid-morning, Grete was ready to leave. Alain appeared from the stables to help carry luggage to the car. He shot Stephan a stiff glare that subsided after a glance from Roland. Only Elodie heard his hiss to Stephan.

"Touch my son again and I will kill you."

Stephan paled and straightened up. "*Paysan*," he breathed back. Alain's eyes narrowed at the insult.

"Thank you, Alain," Roland said calmly, dismissing the stableman. "Are you ready, Grete, Elodie? Good. In you go." Elodie set the switches and began cranking the engine. It caught with a roar, and she jumped back as the crank kicked. This was the one thing she hated about driving, but Guillaume insisted that if she was going to drive, she should start her own automobile.

She took her place in the driver's seat and waved to her parents as they watched the guests leave. Her mother seemed to have found a well of determination. Elodie had expected tears, but the older woman only lifted her hand in farewell. Her face held the same hard look that Elodie had seen in paintings of the women who marched on Versailles.

Reims was packed with people, men on their way to their stations, some Luxembourgish refugees, women in country dress, and seemingly thousands of young boys milling about in excitement. It was as if everyone from the department of Marne had descended on Reims.

The city's train station was complete chaos. Men in uniform embarked, bound for their assigned units, while women cheered them on. As each train departed in a cloud of steam, those remaining turned away to dry eyes wet with crying. As each group left it was replaced with another, brave faces at the onset and tears as the trains vanished.

Elodie looked for a porter, finally finding a teenage boy who whistled as he towed an empty wagon behind him. She hurried back through the crowd to find the Rohrs standing almost like stags at bay. The French had suddenly realized who these strangers were, and the mood was growing tense. The porter disappeared as he sensed the atmosphere and Elodie took a deep breath as she dove into the crowd toward Grete.

"Come on, Tante Grete. We've got to get you on the train." Elodie said cheerfully.

"My luggage? Where is the porter?" Grete asked. Elodie looked around, seeing only unfriendly faces.

"Take what you can carry. You'll have to leave the rest. Quickly." The people on the platform had recognized the Rohrs, but they also recognized Elodie. She had the terrifying feeling that only her father's position and family good name stood between the townspeople and this tangible face of the enemy. One train was still scheduled to head east to Metz and then north to the Luxembourg frontier. Elodie was determined to see the Rohrs on that train.

"The train is coming. Hurry." She chivied them along like a sheepdog. Steam rolled up from under the carriage, obscuring it from view. As the steam drifted away, the carriages were chalked with rude sayings about Germans, and a talented artist had drawn a picture of the Kaiser being kicked by a French soldier.

"You should board quickly, Tante Grete."

"Goodbye, Elodie. Thank you for your help. And tell your mother…"

"I will, Tante."

"We will destroy France," Stephan said with a nasty grin.

"One French soldier is worth ten German soldiers," Elodie replied stoutly. He climbed into the carriage.

"I hope you die." Stephan leaned out of the window to hiss at her.

"*Va au diable*," Elodie told him cheerfully, a bit

taken aback at herself for the profanity. A woman nearby looked at her in shock.

There was a long, mournful blast from the whistle and the train pulled slowly away. A new crowd swirled up onto the platform. Elodie did not bother to wait for the train to depart the station. The Rohrs were on their own and at the mercy of the angry French. She found herself not caring whether they arrived safely at the frontier.

In Elodie's absence, Isabeau had transformed Theo and the housemaid into a veritable army that rushed around the house. In the 1800s, Reims had been designated a buffer to protect Paris, and boasted a series of forts that stood in a ring between the city and the east. Like other fortress towns between Paris and their traditional enemy, Reims would be a target if the German army invaded.

Isabeau presented the tasks of packing and storing items as an early fall cleaning. If the war ended before it was well begun, there would be no harm done.

"Pack a trunk to take to Le Havre, Elodie. Then help Theo, otherwise, he'll bring all the barn cats and forget clothing," Isabeau commanded as Elodie went up to her room.

An empty trunk waited for her, and she sat down on her bed to contemplate it. It was not particularly large, not the steamer that she would have packed to go to the Sorbonne. She nudged it with her toe. And Le Havre, she thought with dismay. She did not mind her grandmother's house and life in the port city, but it was far more constrained. She knew no one there, so there would be no luncheons and no shopping.

Elodie threw herself back on her bed. It had taken so much persuasion to win one year at university and now it was taken from her. It just wasn't fair. Why did Germany have to take this moment to invade? She laughed at herself for the vanity of thinking the Kaiser cared about one French girl's dreams.

Slowly, she began to pack, choosing serviceable clothing. Disappointment rose in her chest, and she wiped away tears on the green riding habit that she put into the clothing pile to leave behind. There would be no horses in Le Havre. Mementos were not important, so she set aside carved wooden horses and trinkets from school. These could go into the cellar and if they survived, it would be good. Otherwise, she suspected she would not miss them.

Elodie sat on the lid of the trunk to close it and sniffled a little.

"Are you scared?" Theo popped up, startling her. She quickly wiped her eyes and nose.

"No. I'm just sad."

"I think this is a grand adventure."

"You would. Shall I help you with your room?"

"I'd rather go for a ride," Theo wheedled. "I can ride the gray and you can ride Brûlée."

"Not today, *mon vilain*, Maman would be quite angry. Perhaps tomorrow. If you can get out of bed early enough."

Theo agreed reluctantly, and brother and sister went to pack up the precious belongings of a ten-year-old.

Three days later, they finished Isabeau's demands and turned their attention to the vineyards and fields. By then, most of the farmhands had gone to join their regiments and their wives stepped up to care for the livestock and work the land. It was odd to see Suzette in the stables instead of Alain, and to drive the Roi de Belges instead of Guillaume.

Isabeau dispatched Elodie to take donations to the church in Reims, where she found changes in the city distressing. The number of soldiers shipping out had not noticeably diminished and the only men not in uniform were those over forty-five, the infirm, and the shirkers. She delivered the donations and then went to her father's office. Roland looked grimly out the window at the drunken men and insisted that Elodie return to the farm and stay there. She obeyed with uncharacteristic meekness, startled at the language the drunks were shouting in the street.

The next day, Elodie awoke with the dawn, a beautiful sunrise suggesting it was going to be another hot day. She lay for a moment in a bedroom empty of a girl's little knickknacks and dreams. Papa was getting more and more somber as news of the war rolled in. The Germans were amassing in Belgium and the tiny country was fighting back at a terrible cost. There had been skirmishes in Mulhouse, southeast of Reims, where the Germans were testing French defenses. Elodie expected Roland to order his family to Le Havre any day.

Perhaps she could at least feed the horses this morning and sneak in one last ride. She rolled out of bed, quickly pulling on jodhpurs, a loose silk blouse, and a linen jacket. She twisted her hair into a bun, forgoing any attempt to style it. Speed was necessary. Her riding boots and leg wraps were in the vestibule, so she crept silently downstairs in her stockinged feet, hearing the usual clatter from the kitchen. She finished dressing and stepped outside, taking a deep breath and stretching slightly.

Birds trilled from the trees around the farm. Somewhere above her, a lark sang its heart out in the sky. Inside the barn, the horses were already eating, and the surviving barn kittens were curled on saddle pads after a night of learning to hunt mice.

Brûlée looked up at her from his hay trough, eyes curious. She rubbed his broad seal-brown forehead and quickly tacked him up as he finished breakfast. His mouth was now stained greenish, and he enthusiastically rubbed against her jodhpurs.

"Stop, Brûlée," Elodie admonished him and

double-checked her tack. He stood rock steady at the mounting block, but the moment she was in the saddle, he was eagerly moving down the track, ears up and looking for adventure.

They were just approaching the first series of fences when he leaped straight upwards, all four feet off the ground, landing in a series of crow hops, not wanting to stand still. He leapt upward again, not in a rear but almost a capriole, lifting his front feet and springing into the air. She fought to control Brûlée's bizarre panic, but he seemed blind, unthinking and unhearing. For a second, she debated jumping to safety, but at that moment, he landed on his feet, knees almost buckling under him. Lathered sweat covered his shoulders and bloody froth dripped from his mouth.

Elodie stared in horror. He wore a gentle bit and she had not remembered snatching at it. Perhaps he had bitten his tongue in his panic. He trembled, head down, exhausted, shifting from hoof to hoof.

Thunder ripped through the air and Brûlée reared again. Immediately, Elodie threw her weight onto his neck. His feet came back down, and he made to bolt, but she pulled him around, eyes searching the clear blue sky. Then the thunder began in earnest, rolling across the landscape in volleys.

Elodie held one rein tight, keeping the horse's head turned toward her knee. He spun and protested as she tried to track the noise, birds flying in panicked spurts from the trees. When the thunder did not pause, Elodie turned Brûlée's head toward the barn and let him stretch into a gallop. He fled in terror, and she crouched low, riding this force of nature but not controlling it. He was flagging as they neared the stables and she pulled him around, bringing him to a trembling stop.

Her father appeared from the stable door, grabbing at the reins, and began soothing the anxious horse.

"Slip down, Elodie." She did as he bid and then took the reins on the other side. Together, they moved Brûlée into the barn where he stood in his familiar stall, shaking while sweat dripped from him. Roland handed her a rigid leather strap while he took handfuls of straw from the stall floor. The two began stripping sweat from the horse, trying to cool the overheated body. Lather piled at Elodie's feet. Roland frowned at the blood coming from the horse's mouth and began to wipe it away.

"What is that, Papa? That thunder?"

"Artillery. Turn him out and go up to the house."

"But he'll colic," Elodie said, shocked at the command.

"Elodie. Do as I say."

"Have the Germans invaded France?"

"Not yet. You sometimes hear artillery from a hundred miles away or more. You, your Maman, and

Theo will leave for Le Havre this morning."

"But Papa, are you not coming with us? What will you do?"

"I will stay here. I have my duties as judge."

"I will stay as well," Elodie decided instantly. "Who will take care of the farm? I can manage the vineyards and the horses."

"No, Elodie," Roland's voice was hard. He stopped, focusing on the horse for a moment and turning him out to pasture. The horse stumbled toward his herd, who milled around in agitation. Roland continued in a softer tone. "You must go. I must know you are safe. Away from the Boche." Elodie's eyes widened at the pejorative. She had never heard her father use that word. That, more than anything, frightened her.

"Come now. Your Maman needs you." He took her arm, gently escorting her from the stables. Elodie went without protest.

Her mother was seated at the table, eating quickly.

"Good morning, Maman." She touched her cheek to her mother's.

"You smell like horse," the older woman said, with more than a touch of irritation in her voice. Elodie flushed. "Go to your room and clean up. We leave on the noon train."

The four stood silently on the train platform at Reims, not knowing what to say. Their luggage had been loaded and they only needed to climb aboard. Finally, Isabeau kissed her husband and straightened his tie.

"Wear your warm boots."

"I will," Roland said softly. Isabeau patted him on the upper arm and turned away, but not before Elodie saw tears glitter in her eyes. Her little brother, stuck somewhere between a man in his gray tweed suit and a boy with his quivering lip, could not seem to move.

"Say goodbye, Theo, and help Maman settle in," Elodie whispered softly. He sniffled and cleared his throat.

"I'll see you before Christmas, Papa. That's what they are saying," Theo said bravely.

"Christmas it is, Theo," Roland promised. He hugged his son tightly. "Take good care of your Maman and sister."

"Yes, Papa." The boy pressed his face into the man's chest, then he ran for the train car before his father could see him cry.

"Please let me stay, Papa. You'll need me," Elodie begged.

"This will not be a place for a girl if the Germans invade."

"I'll be with you, Papa." Elodie felt her world spin at the grayness of his face. She wondered why the sound of war and all the news had not hit the very core of her being the way his face did.

"I won't be able to protect you here. Go now, Elodie. Please."

"Yes, Papa." She hugged him tightly, breathing in his scent so she could remember him. The train whistle sounded, and she reluctantly turned to climb into the carriage. All along the platform, the doors were closing, and the stairs were being lifted into their storage places. She leaned out the window to wave goodbye. Her last sight of her father, he was standing with his hat raised over his head so his family could see him in the crowd that thronged the platform.

Chapter 3:
September to October 1914

"Rise up, Frenchwomen, little children, sons and daughters of the fatherland! Take over the work of those who are on the battlefield." *French Prime Minister René Viviani, August 1914*

During the best of times, Le Havre was a busy port city. Through her wharves passed tons of coffee, cotton, and oil. The population was cosmopolitan, because Le Havre traded goods from northern Europe to the distant shores of Africa and even the Americas.

As the train neared the city, Elodie was tasked with keeping Theo from falling out the windows in excitement. Outside, the roads were filled with French soldiers in uniform, armaments, and a few automobiles. Teams of horses or mules pulled caissons while men, most looking as if they were on a grand adventure, walked behind carrying their rifles. They smiled and waved at the townspeople who gathered to cheer them eastward.

The train squealed to a stop and the passengers began to collect belongings and step down onto the platform. Isabeau cast a stern eye over her children. When they had gathered up their luggage, Elodie and Theo followed the upright form of their mother, the plumes on her hat bobbing defiantly. The bedlam at the station included an advance team of British Expeditionary Force soldiers, the BEF, in drab uniforms, as well as brightly red and blue uniformed French soldiers. Belgian refugees with their bundles looked weary and bewildered. The air was filled with Dutch, English, and French, lending to the general chaos. It had been a year since Elodie had spoken English and the language sounded as harsh as Dutch against the more melodic French.

Isabeau stopped, sorting through her reticule for luggage tickets. Around them, humanity ebbed and flowed. Finding the tickets, Isabeau dusted off her dark blue jacket and touched her hat brim to ensure it was sitting properly. Thus armored, she took a deep breath.

"Theo, stay with your sister. Elodie, hold on to him. I'll find a porter." Isabeau looked around in desperation before plunging into the crowd. Elodie held on to the protesting Theo, who wanted to see the passing troops.

"Be patient, Theo, you know you'll have time to roam around later. Maman is worried enough right now," Elodie insisted. Although he settled a bit, she kept a firm hand on her brother's shoulder. It took some time before Isabeau returned with a man in tow. He was pulling a cart loaded with their trunks, and Elodie and Theo fell in behind in an impromptu parade. The porter led the way to the taxi stand and shoved their baggage on the rear step of a hansom cab while the Fabiens settled themselves in the back seat. Isabeau pressed a few centimes into the porter's hand, and he vanished into the crowd.

The driver clucked to the horse and the hansom started at a decorous pace. There was no rushing through the streets. Instead, the journey was stop-and-go as soldiers took precedence. *Gendarmes* halted civilian traffic for every military vehicle and file. Even Theo had his fill of horses, guns, and artillery by the time they turned down the quiet, tree-lined street near the Parc de Rouelles where Grand-mère lived.

Their grandmother had moved to Le Havre when Elodie was very little, to stay with her daughter Emilie after Emilie's merchant husband had died. When Emilie died, Grand-mère had stayed, living in a three-story home overlooking a tidy garden. With only the old lady and her few servants living there, it was very quiet. The house was comfortable and elegant, rather like Grand-mère herself, Elodie reflected. And dull. Grand-mère was staunchly rooted in the nineteenth century.

Theo danced up to the doorbell, twisting it vigorously as his mother supervised the unloading of the trunks at the front gate and paid the cab driver. In moments, the door flew open, and their tiny grandmother stood in the doorway, dressed in dove gray. Louise Fabien's eyes darted from one child to the other and down the garden path, where Isabeau was coming up the steps. Her face almost crumpled into tears as the stocky figure of her son did not materialize beside his wife. Elodie hurried forward, reaching out her hands. Her grandmother hugged her tightly and regained her slipping composure. She admired Theo next, complimenting him on his height. Her longest embrace was reserved for her daughter-in-law.

"Will Roland be coming soon?" Louise Fabien asked.

"It depends on the war, Belle-mère." Isabeau turned to look back at the trunks with a sigh. Louise surveyed the small pile.

"My men servants have left for the Front. Elodie, can you and Theo manage the luggage with the help of Cook and the serving girl?" she asked.

"Of course, Grand-mère," Elodie said faintly, looking at the trunks with dismay. Cook and the serving girl had followed their mistress out to greet the visitors and await instructions. As Isabeau and Louise went into the house, the four struggled to get the heavy cases brought up the path.

"Why did we pack so much?" Elodie groaned.

"You just had to have all your dresses." Theo leaped back as a trunk fell heavily to the paving stones.

"Here, just grab the handles and we'll move each one. All four of us should manage."

Eventually, the trunks were inside and wrestled to each room. Elodie unpacked. From the window, she could see the trees of the park that backed the house. It was peaceful and green and gave no hint of the turmoil outside the park grounds. She sank down on the window seat, resting her forehead on the glass.

The trip had been exciting, but now she felt let down and empty. They had fled just the threat of war, not even the real event. She felt like a coward running from the first hint of trouble, and realized with a sudden shock that she was now a refugee. To be sure, she was not one of the few they had seen *en route* to Le Havre, with bundles of belongings on their backs and terror on their faces. At their grandmother's, she would be well-fed, safe, and warm. The disruption to her life was one of missing familiar creature comforts and her horses.

Elodie read the papers every morning and evening, engrossed in the stories. The artillery barrage that had precipitated the family's evacuation had been the opening salvo of the Battle of Liège, after King Albert of Belgium had refused Germany's demands. The

German army poured over Belgium's eastern border while Belgium fought to stop their encroachment. Their goal was Paris, and they had not thought Belgium would stand in their way. Belgian refugees flooded into Le Havre. There was work for them in the port and in Britain, with the munitions factories stepping up production.

Theo was able to escape the quiet confines of their grandmother's home and hear the talk on the streets while Elodie remained in the residence. The older women sternly squashed Theo's recitations of street gossip but he repeated the stories in private to his sister.

At first, the newspapers' horrifying reports about the atrocities - the Rape of Belgium - seemed vulgar propaganda, but the truth was borne by the refugees. Humanity had taken a back seat to war. The German soldiers were enraged at Belgium's failure to capitulate, and men, women, and children were slaughtered in the streets.

Elodie was forbidden to go into Le Havre without a chaperone, her grandmother's dictum enforced by her mother. Her mother and grandmother spent long hours edging handkerchiefs and embroidering impossibly complex patterns onto anything that could hold a stitch, Elodie thought uncharitably. Elodie lacked the patience to embroider and was put to work winding yarn into usable balls. She sat with the older women in the gloomy house, listening to gossip and feeling trapped.

As the BEF prepared to back their French allies, their ships rode off the Opal Coast, waiting to land their army. Le Havre bore the brunt of the influx as the first full shipload of BEF soldiers arrived.

Theo's face peeked around the parlor door. Seeing his sister alone, he came into the room, bringing with him the oily, fishy smell of wharves and street dust.

"Where?" He nodded at the empty chairs.

"Deciding what needs more needlework," Elodie said bitterly. "Where have you been?"

"The wharves. Elodie, a BEF ship docked. I went down and watched this morning. There are four infantry divisions and one cavalry division. You thought the streets were crowded when we arrived, they had nothing on what it's like today. They are full of the British in their green uniforms. Is there anything to eat?" Elodie gestured toward a bowl of fruit and Theo took an apple, sitting down to gnaw at it.

"Our military is so much more glorious," Theo continued, gleefully. "You can barely see those British uniforms and yet I overheard men saying they are the best army in Europe. They unloaded the men first. Elodie, they are so excited to be here and the singing and laughing. You should have heard them. Then the horses came down. There were millions of them."

"The newspaper said fifteen thousand

horses," Elodie corrected, her eyes busy on her winding.

"Surely, there were more. They poured off the ships. The cavalry left first, trotting out past the infantry. I should like to be in the cavalry. It is ever so much faster than walking. People were throwing flowers at them, and they waved. Then they started bringing down cannons and guns. There were so many, the Germans cannot have even half that many. The gunners left next and the rumble they made! Elodie, the windows shook. And even when they were gone, the wharves were still filled with men. The people said they are heading to Maubeuge and from there they join our army and defend us from the Huns." Theo should be a spy, Elodie thought. He certainly managed to be everywhere and hear everything. She gritted her teeth as her brother talked, wanting to be out there, hearing and seeing all the activity.

In the next few weeks, Theo's estimates proved as over-optimistic as the French and British commanders' expectations of victory. Defeat after defeat hit the Entente forces as they fought against the Germans. The British rally point of Maubeuge fell, as the Entente turned and ran for the Marne River, the German army hard on their heels. The papers called it the Great Retreat and moaned that Paris would be the next French stronghold to fall, but General Joffre had a plan.

"Listen to this, Theo. Joffre had all the taxi drivers in Paris transport soldiers to the Marne. Every single cab - round and round - and they made a difference. We stopped the Germans at the river. The papers are calling it the 'Miracle of the Marne,'" Elodie summarized the evening's papers for her little brother. "If the taxi drivers hadn't stepped up, we would have lost, but they arrived just in time." Her eyes scanned down the page, coming to an interview with an old French woman, one of the taxi drivers, who told the reporter, 'I only did my part. All true French women will do the same.' Those words burned into Elodie's soul. After everyone had read the newspaper, Elodie tore out the article, carrying it to her room to read over.

As the battles continued, casualties mounted by the thousands. Trains from the front lines carried injured BEF soldiers to hastily staffed hospitals, including ones in Le Havre. For the first time, there was talk of possible food shortages and calls for women to join the workforce.

Elodie had wound all her grandmother's yarn and had been set to crocheting delicate lace along the top of the bedsheets. As her mother and grandmother talked, Elodie practiced conversations in her head, each time successfully overwhelming the older women with her arguments. She said nothing, because any attempts to start a conversation that involved Elodie leaving the house were immediately shut down.

The slamming front door made Grand-mère start and press her lips together. Before she could call Theo into the parlor to scold him, he had appeared in the doorway, his face white and eyes wide.

"The Germans, they shelled the cathedral yesterday. The one in Reims. They say there is nothing left." His voice shook. "And Reims is behind enemy lines."

Isabeau immediately left the room. In her haste, she stumbled into a small table, ignoring the statuette that crashed to the floor. Elodie covered her face as Theo began to cry.

"Elodie," Grand-mère's voice cracked. She cleared her throat. "Elodie, please go to the newsstand and buy the most recent papers." She followed Isabeau out. With his mother and grandmother out of the room, Theo tried out some of the curse words he had heard on the wharves. Elodie ignored him, feeling much the same herself.

She brought back the papers, confirming Theo's report. In the bleak days that followed, Roland Fabien did not appear, and no letters came.

Finally, Elodie was unable to hold her impatience any longer. She had to do something to help her country. At dinner that night, she glanced around the table at her mother and grandmother, who seemed gray. The lack of news about Roland had aged both of them. Perhaps she should bide her time, but then she reminded herself of the taxi driver's words: 'All true French women...' She took a deep breath.

"Grand-mère, Maman. I should like your blessing to find work. I know there is somewhere that I can help with the war effort." She was pleased to hear that her voice remained steady.

"Your best place is here," Louise said sharply.

"With respect, Grand-mère, all women are stepping up to do their part. I shall do mine as well," Elodie said, implacably. "I have done nothing but run from this war."

"I have enough on my plate with your father missing, Elodie." Isabeau looked at her, eyes flashing and voice harsh.

"I want to help find him, but I can't, so the next best option is for me to help with the war effort. I am sick and tired of winding yarn and crocheting."

"Those are the safest options for you. You are only a girl and what can a girl do? The best thing would be to stay here and remain safe." Isabeau controlled her voice. Louise looked at her, lips pressed, and Elodie thought that perhaps the older woman disagreed with her daughter-in-law.

"Please excuse yourself, Elodie. No more of this nonsense," Grand-mère said coolly. Elodie flung down her napkin and stormed up to her room before she burst into tears of frustration. She threw herself down on her bed, cursing into her pillow.

As dark was falling, someone knocked on her door. Elodie sat up, straightening her hair.

"Come." It was not Theo as she expected, but her grandmother. The old woman smoothed down the front of her dress and then sat beside Elodie.

"I truly do understand your desires, Elodie. But this is a place and time where you must listen to your elders." There was a long silence. "My dear Elodie, I too wanted to help my country. I was with Coralie Cahen and the Red Cross in Metz. I went with her to Vendôme when Metz fell to the Prussians."

"You were in the Franco-Prussian War?" Elodie asked in surprise. No hint of this had ever reached her ears.

"Yes. And it is nothing glorious and it is not a thing of dreams. Of nightmares, perhaps." Her voice trailed off. Elodie stared at this elegant woman with her quiet manner and immaculate house. She could not imagine her working as a nurse in a war-torn city.

"I don't have to work in a hospital. Please let me do something. Teach refugee children or, I don't know, work in a shop."

"No, Elodie. Your mother is correct. Your place is here." Grand-mère got up. "Don't be bitter. You will see we are right. Sleep well, Elodie." She left the room, pulling the door closed behind her. Elodie sat in the dark for a long time after her grandmother had gone.

By morning, she had thought over all her

options. Her grandmother had shown her the way, so she might as well follow that path. Elodie dressed in a dark blue skirt and jacket with a white blouse underneath. She would forego the corset, she thought with relief. Sorting through the few pieces of jewelry she had, she pinned on a delicate cloisonne horse, then put on her wide-brimmed hat and slipped into the kitchen, eating quickly and trying to stay out of the cook's way. The old woman looked at her in dour amusement.

Her mother and grandmother were not awake yet and Elodie found her brother slouched on one of the chaise lounges, his shoes threatening the delicate fabric.

"Sit up before Maman sees you," she scolded gently. Theo straightened, his feet hitting the floor with a thump. He was making some childish preparations for the day's adventures. Her mother had not yet enrolled him in school, still hoping against hope that the war would end.

"Theo, tell Maman and Grand-mère that I am going to the British Number Two Hospital to volunteer. I will be home this evening, or I will send a note."

"Can I go with you?"

"Not today. I need you to tell Maman where I have gone."

"Coward," Theo said with a grin. Elodie shrugged.

"True. But Maman does not yell at you as much as she does me." Then she stepped out of the house, practicing her English in her head. She had not spoken English since her brief tour after graduating from the lycée, but it would surely come back.

The Number Two Hospital had been built in 1900 as the home of the Olympic Sailing Regatta and stood overlooking the ocean. Without the ambulances lined up outside, Elodie would have mistaken it for a grand hotel. The second floor boasted a wide veranda that wrapped around three sides, offering a panorama of the English Channel beyond. All in all, it was a glorious building.

Elodie wiped her hands on her jacket, reviewing what she would say. She thought she had the verbs and tenses all planned out. Slowly she went up the stairs to the doors, pausing to allow men in white coats to push past, then following them, looking around in curiosity. The grand windows let in light and sea reflection glittered on the walls. Four rows of beds filled the hall and nursing sisters in gray dresses and white aprons moved between them. Every bed was filled, some of the men sitting up and others seemingly asleep.

"Can I help you?" One of the sisters approached her, speaking in English.

"I'd like to volunteer."

"Are you a nurse? Do you have any training?"

"No."

The sister shook her head. "I'm afraid we aren't taking volunteers. We don't have time to train you," she said, perhaps more briskly than intended. "Maybe at a French hospital?" She eyed Elodie's horse pin.

"The French hospitals, there are none nearby. Only in Paris. Thank you." Elodie's shoulders sagged, and she turned to go.

"Miss…" The nurse followed her to the door. "Do you know anything about animals?"

"I know horses. My family lives on a horse farm close to Reims," Elodie replied.

"There is a BEF veterinary hospital at Usine Bundy on Boulevard Sadi Carnot. They are desperate for help," the sister suggested. Elodie's face lit up. Maybe nursing would not be her duty, but perhaps her mother would take more kindly to her helping with horses. She had not minded too much at home.

"Thank you." Elodie left with lighter feet than she had thought possible. She could catch an omnibus to Boulevard Sadi Carnot, a street that led north out of Le Havre.

The Usine Bundy was a former factory. The brick building rose up two stories and the windows were open to the street, giving out a smell of disinfectant and horse manure. The aroma was strong at first, but as with all horse people, it immediately ceased to bother Elodie. She opened the main doors and went into a sunlit room. The interior of the factory had been converted into rough stalls. Long horse faces peered over the door chains, while sicker horses presented their hind ends.

The usual horse accoutrements hung haphazardly or took up floor space in front of the stalls, which each boasted a head collar and rope. The whole scene was one of disorganization held together by determination. A man in a British uniform came out of an office, wiping his bloody hands on a rag. His hair was thinning, and he moved with the deliberateness of a horseman.

"Yes?"

"I have come to help. The nurse at Number Two said you require extra hands."

"This is no place for a woman."

"I grew up on a horse farm. I've done everything from breeding to, what is… *euthanasie.*" Elodie struggled for a term she had never heard in English.

"Euthanasia," he corrected. His tired face sagged. "You are French. Perhaps you can work with the French Army."

"They do not have a facility here. The British do, and I am here."

The man looked over her shoulder at the stalls. He wiped at a stubborn spot on one hand, taking some time to think.

"Truth be told, I do need a helper, and someone who can speak French at that. I'm short-staffed and my full complement of men won't be here until October. I've made do with locals, but sometimes… well, there have been some misunderstandings. I'll try you today and if you do know horses, you can come back tomorrow."

"Thank you. My name is Elodie Fabien."

"Captain Harris. Here, you can start with this horse. The farrier was a ham-handed fool and we've got a string with hoof abscesses. Hot water is in my office through that door and Epsom salts in the cupboard."

"Epsom salts?" Elodie understood most of what the vet had said, and she could see the horse's hoof obviously hurt. He stood with it cocked up and the leg above was starting to puff with retained fluid.

"Magnesium sulfate. I've a patient on the table who should be coming round from anesthetic. Excuse me, Miss Fabien."

Elodie approached the horse, talking quietly and looking over her patient. It shifted its weight onto the sore hoof and back again. Elodie petted its neck and then slid the halter over the long red head, leading it out of the dirty stall. She tied it up and went to find a bucket of water, iodine, and Epsom salts in the kitchen. As she searched through the cabinets, she found a cream-colored apron and put it on, covering her skirt and shirtwaist. Eventually, she located what she needed and collected hot water from the boiler.

Elodie went to the horse, first cleaning out the

hoof and then convincing the animal to put his foot in the bucket of warm water and Epsom salts. At first, he kept pulling the hoof out, but as the warm water soothed the pain, he relaxed in relief. Elodie was able to leave him long enough to clean out his stall.

"Now, *mon vilain*, this will hurt, but then you will feel better," she told him, kneeling down and awkwardly lifting his foot. Normally, she would have held it properly, between her knees, but her skirt got in the way. Captain Harris drifted over as she tested the hoof and then dug away with a knife until the abscess spurted a few teaspoons of green and yellow pus. She wiped it away and bathed the hoof in hot water.

"Ah good. That will ease the pain. What are you going to pack it with?" Harris leaned over, looking at the abscess. "Maybe dig there a bit." He pointed and Elodie complied.

"Iodine and magnesium sulfate. It is on that pad. Please hand it to me." The veterinarian handed her the pad covered with a thick layer of reddish powder that looked like icing. She used the hoof knife to pack the abscess with medication and put the entire pad over the wound. Harris handed her a long bandage and she wrapped up the hoof. As she put it down, the horse shifted weight onto it for a moment. The vet nodded in approval.

"He'll be happier now. Manure goes out that door." He pointed to the far side of the building. "I've lined up a farmer to take it away, or I think I have. We'll see if he shows up. There are four more horses with the same issue in the next four stalls. Fool of a farrier. When you've finished with them, find me and we can go to the pneumonia ward." He walked to a horse with stitches that held together one shoulder. Elodie winced at the injury and put away the horse she had just nursed.

By the end of the day, Elodie was exhausted, and her skirt was filthy, but she felt real pleasure looking down the stalls of horses, all tended and hopefully healing as they quietly ate. She had gone through the pneumonia ward with Harris, doing what little they could for the very sick horses. Crowded conditions in a ship's hold stressed the animals badly. Here they could recover in a quiet place before being sent east to the battlefields. She had also met the solitary man who was part of Captain Harris' detachment and organized French workers who would clean stalls and carry off the manure and dead horses. It had been a very satisfying day.

"Will you be back tomorrow?" Captain Harris seemed to materialize out of the slowly darkening barn.

"If you permit," Elodie smiled.

"I expect your patients would all go hooves up if I told you not to come back," he said as the first horse she had treated looked out of the stall and whuffled at her, his mouth full of hay. Elodie laughed.

"I'll be here as early as I can," she said, and left through the main doors. If she hurried, she could make it home before it was fully dark. As she rattled towards her grandmother's on the omnibus, she felt at peace for the first time. Perhaps working with horses was not going to help win or lose this war, but it did make the horses feel better and that was enough.

Theo was waiting in the front garden when she walked up to her grandmother's house.

"Where have you been, Elodie? Maman is very angry," he told her as she paused. "Whew. You smell like horse."

"I've been at a BEF veterinary hospital. Where are they?"

"In the parlor," Theo answered. Elodie sighed. She may as well get this over with.

Her mother sat in one of the wing chairs, furiously knitting at something gray. Her grandmother sat in the other, reading snippets from the newspaper out loud.

"Good evening, Grand-mère, Maman," Elodie said cheerfully as she bent over to kiss each woman.

"So, you have finally decided to come home," her mother said waspishly. "It was unkind of you to worry us. And not to let us know where you were."

"I apologize, Maman. I'll be going out again tomorrow."

"A military hospital is no place for a young

woman."

"I will not be going to the military hospital. I am working as a veterinary assistant for the next month. With horses, as you can see." She gestured to the generous horsehair and manure all over her skirt.

"What would your father say?"

"Maman, Grand-mère, not a week ago soldiers were taken to the Front in taxi cabs, by women taxi drivers. I know you both read that article because you discussed it. Remember the quote, 'All true Frenchwomen are doing their part'? This is my part." The two older women looked at each other for a long moment.

"Perhaps you are correct. Your grandmother spoke with the grocery delivery man. He is Belgian and he knows of a refugee school that needs help," her mother said. Elodie almost laughed. She decided not to point out that she had offered this very solution but had been turned down.

"Maman, I told the British captain that I would return every day until his men arrive in Le Havre. I know horses and I am good with them."

"Elodie. We do not approve," Grand-mère said.

"I mean no disrespect, Grand-mère, but this is my decision. This is my war, and I will serve France." She paused, trying to decide if she should mention her grandmother's confidences of the night before. "Grand-mère, I only want to do my part." She emphasized 'my' and touched her chest. The old woman's eyes flashed in understanding.

"May I be excused?" Elodie's mother waved her hand and Elodie took that as permission. She escaped quickly, breathing a sigh of relief.

After she had changed, the housemaid whisked away the filthy clothing with a sigh of protest. Elodie sorted through her belongings until she found an older skirt. Perhaps, she would run to a *marché aux puces* for old clothes she could wear without worrying about them. Someone might even have a pair of jodhpurs for sale. Elodie washed and collapsed exhaustedly into bed, feeling pleased with herself.

When she left in the early light of the next morning, she found a neatly packed luncheon wrapped in a cloth waiting for her. Her grandmother, of course. Her grandmother understood. She might be old-fashioned and strict, but she was not unreasonable. And where her mother-in-law led, Isabeau would soon follow.

Captain Harris looked up from the injured horse's shoulder, his face brightening as Elodie walked into the factory building. There was constant chatter as the workers cleaned stalls, because talk kept horses calm.

"Ah, Miss Fabien. Excellent. I've made the rounds, and our patients are fed. Will you check on the horses that you worked on yesterday? And remember to chart them."

"Ah, my written English is not the best," she confessed.

"Do what you can. Write in French if need be. We can fix it later." He moved on to the next horse. Elodie was unfazed by the veterinarian's brusque manner. He was a horseman, and the comfort of his charges came first. With more horses expected as more ships docked, there was no time to waste. One by one, she worked her way down the aisle, stopping occasionally to provide translation services between the English soldier and the French workers.

When church bells all over Le Havre rang out noon, she stopped and went toward Captain Harris' office, where she could wash her hands and eat without the constant flies. She found Captain Harris sitting at his desk, writing notes in a ledger.

"May I eat in here?"

"Of course." He looked up with a smile and shoved some papers to one side, making room for her wrapped lunch. "Do you, by any chance, read German?"

"No. I can recognize some words, but my English is better."

"Know anyone who can?"

"Not on this side of the Front," Elodie replied honestly.

"Well, yes. I have the same problem."

"Perhaps there is a Belgian refugee who can

help."

"It's not that important. When the Germans retreated from the Marne, I was sent a package of papers a veterinarian left behind." He shrugged. Elodie picked up one of the papers he tapped and examined it. She set it down with a shake of her head.

"Nothing. I suppose I could find a dictionary and translate it."

"No. I'll follow up on your Belgian idea. Surely one of them can make sense of these more easily than slogging through with a dictionary."

"I would think so." Elodie unwrapped a baguette. It had been sliced open and layered with cheese and butter. Captain Harris looked at the sandwich longingly out of the corner of his eye. Elodie tore the baguette in two and handed him half.

"Are you certain?" At Elodie's nod, he took a bite. "I'll provide the tea, shall I, and we can have a proper meal."

Within a few minutes, he had prepared a pot of tea using a Bunsen burner. Elodie was not fond of English tea made palatable with heavy doses of milk and sugar. She preferred coffee, but to turn down the offered drink would have been uncivil, and she was thirsty after handling her patients. They sat in companionable silence as they ate.

That evening, she asked the cook to prepare two baguettes and a bottle of water for the next day.

The days seemed to fly by, with new horses

coming and recovered horses going. A few went down the street to the slaughterhouse. Elodie hated that part most of all. At least, she told herself, the horses heading east toward the Front had a chance.

The newspapers were full of calls for patriotic French people to donate their horses and mules to the cause, and Elodie fretted about Brûlée. If her father had escaped the German onslaught at Reims, her horse was with the French army. If he had not, Brûlée had forcibly joined the Germans. Either way, her beloved horse was gone.

One morning in early October, Elodie walked toward the vet hospital. While the building was never quiet, it now almost burst with noise that spilled out onto the street in a volley of English accents that hurt her ears. Captain Harris' troops had arrived. She opened the door to find men milling around, feeding horses, sorting out new arrivals, carrying bundles, and shoveling manure.

"Here, Miss, you don't belong here. Ally. Ally." A gruff man in a dull green uniform spun toward her and approached, flicking his hand toward the door she had just come through. She assumed that 'ally' was his best pronunciation of *allez*.

"Sergeant, this is Miss Fabien. She has been invaluable here." Captain Harris emerged out of the crowd. "Miss Fabien, my men have arrived." He hesitated. "Thank you for all you have done." He held out his hand for her to take. "I shall miss your help and our lunches together. If I can be of assistance, you know where to find me. And best of luck. I hope you get your horse back." His voice trailed off and he looked uncomfortable. Elodie stood nonplussed for a moment, then gathered her wits.

"Thank you, Captain." She shook his hand gently. Tears prickled in her eyes as she turned away and the door closed behind her. She stood outside the former factory for a few moments in the dreary sunlight. She did not want to go back to her grandmother's house. It would be too easy to lose these few concessions that had allowed her to work with the horses. Perhaps, she would walk for a while, and something would come to her. Otherwise, it would be more needlework and listening to her mother and grandmother gossip.

Weeks later, Elodie hunched over a pillow top, carefully sewing it closed with tiny, uniform stitches. It seemed endless. She sighed, stabbing the needle into the fabric to keep it safe. This project mimicked the war that stretched on in a monotony of reports from Belgium. The French and British had stopped the German invasion and turned it back, hoping that the Germans would retreat. But that hope had been dashed. The Battle of Ypres had devolved into two static lines of trenches that were starting to snake across Belgium and France. The war was now at a stalemate in these trenches, stretching on and on into the foreseeable future.

Elodie picked up some papers from the French Red Cross, rereading the requirements. She would have to go to one of the training hospitals in Paris to complete a nursing course, and she would need her father's permission. The Red Cross worker had told her there were other options – soup kitchens and canteens had been suggested. Elodie laughed to herself. She could suggest to her mother that she join a soldier's club where she would entertain the *poilus*, the 'hairy' enlisted French men. That would bring her mother around to the idea of nursing.

She decided to go down to the wharves and use the walk to marshal her arguments. Sitting around was getting her nowhere, encouraging her mother to think that she had forgotten about her need to serve. Theo had been roaming the docks the day before and reported that the wharves were as busy as ever.

Elodie tucked her hair into her blue mushroom hat, a soft velvet crush cap cheerfully adorned with a red, white, and blue ribbon. She made her way to the Quay Colbert and walked along it, breathing in the sea air strong with the smells of oil, smoke, and horses. Two ships were unloading at the wharf.

Elodie sat down on a bollard to watch. A car was lowered over the side of one ship, and she realized with amazement that the person overseeing the unloading was a woman only a few years older than herself. The woman was dressed in a dark green skirt and tightly belted jacket with collar emblems and a red cross patch on one arm. The ensemble was completed by a floppy beret with the same emblem. As the car reached the dock, Elodie could see it was packed with bags and boxes. Another young woman in the same outfit stepped forward to drive the car away.

"Not that one. It wasn't to come," the woman yelled up at the men on the ship. "Put it back."

"Sorry, ducks. It's got to go," the loading officer yelled back. The car continued its slow descent to the wharf where the stevedores on the dock released the cables. The winch and the dangling cables moved back up toward the ship. This car, Elodie noted, was empty. No one stepped forward to claim it.

"Push this one over there. Push...." The young woman made shoving gestures, but the stevedores only looked at her, deliberately baffled. They made a few less-than-complimentary comments in French that the young woman did not understand. Elodie frowned.

"I shall help, yes?" Elodie called out, hopping up and crossing to where the woman stood. "She wants you to push the auto over there," she said in French.

"Not our job. We only unload. Tell the English

she can move her own auto," one of the burly men replied, and his companions laughed.

"They do not wish to move your vehicle." Elodie turned to the young woman. "Can I help? I can drive." The men watched in curiosity. Someone on the ship yelled down at them and they roundly cursed him, telling him to wait.

"That's Jezebel," the woman said with a laughing shrug. She was taller than Elodie, her face plain but filled with enthusiasm. She smiled tentatively. "She only starts if the stars are aligned. She wasn't to be loaded, but someone in Old Blighty made a mistake. You are welcome to try but shoving her over the edge of the dock would be kindest." Elodie hurried to the maligned car as yet another vehicle appeared over the edge of the ship, the stevedores yelling at the crane operator to wait.

Elodie glanced into the car, relieved to see that her boast could be met. She shifted the spark lever until it reached dead center. It moved reluctantly, but as she wriggled it a bit, it slid into position. She pulled on the hood latches, twisting them slightly, and folded back the hood. She then switched on the gas lever to flood the carburetor, pulling on the pin.

When the pin became hard to move, she went to the front of the car, acutely aware that the young woman was watching her. As Guillaume had taught her, she slid her thumb under the crank and pushed it into the engine. It turned readily once, twice, thrice.

The engine gave a surprised splutter and then caught. The noise of the engine drowned out all the other sounds until she reset the spark and it dropped to a slightly quieter purr.

"Well, she likes you." The British woman appeared at her shoulder. "Move her over there and then come find me." She moved away, yelling at one of the workmen. Elodie slid into the seat and shifted the car into gear. It puttered tamely to its assigned parking space. Elodie turned it off and then walked back to the young woman.

"Are you French?" The woman asked.

"Yes."

"Can you speak Flemish?"

"It's actually Dutch, but yes, I can be understood."

"Hmmm. I don't suppose you can ride horses?"

Elodie's face lit up. "Even better than I drive. I had to leave my horse in Reims. He's a Norman Cob..." The woman held up her hand with a laugh.

"I'm Charlotte Mullins with the First Aid Nursing Yeomanry, the FANYs. Everyone calls me Lottie."

"Elodie Fabien."

"How old are you? No, never mind. Don't tell me." The young woman grinned at her. "How would you feel about helping with the war effort?"

"I was working at the BEF veterinary hospital

on Usine Bundy while they were short of men. But now my mother has me embroidering." Elodie made a face. "I wish to join the French Red Cross, but I must have my father's permission." Lottie sized her up.

"Wait here." She hurried off to talk with the other waiting women. Five minutes later, a slightly older woman dressed in a green skirt and jacket walked over to them.

"Elodie Fabien, Captain Wollert. The captain is in charge of the FANYs," Lottie introduced them. The captain - tall, spare, and weather-beaten - looked at her as Elodie would examine a horse she was interested in buying. Elodie looked back patiently, thinking that this woman could have been an artist's model for an English Country Lady.

"Mullins tells me you can drive, ride horses, understand Flemish, and are interested in nursing."

"Yes. To all. And it's Dutch, not Flemish."

"We are on our way to be ambulance drivers and orderlies for the Belgian army. One of my girls fell sick before we sailed and we need another driver, just to get us to Calais. Would you be available?" Captain Wollert said briskly. "I can get you a train ticket back." Elodie's face lit up and then fell.

"I will have to ask my mother."

"How old are you? Never mind. If anyone asks, you are twenty-three." Captain Wollert looked at her closely to make certain she understood. Elodie nodded. "We leave at dawn tomorrow. If you want to come with us, bring warm, sensible clothing, money, and toiletries. We are a volunteer organization and there is no pay."

"I shall do my best to be here." Elodie felt her heart lift.

"Captain," the older woman prompted. Elodie looked puzzled for a moment and then understanding dawned.

"Yes, Captain. Excuse me. Shall I be driving Jezebel?" Elodie asked eagerly. The captain looked at Lottie in surprise.

"She got that old scrap heap started and drove her over there," Lottie answered with a grin, waving her hand in the direction of the car.

"My goodness," Captain Wollert said faintly. "In that case we certainly need you. If nothing more than to move Jezebel."

"Yes, Captain." Elodie waved goodbye to Lottie and then walked as quickly as she could back down the quay. She felt as if she had wings under her feet and excitement thrilled in her chest. As she neared her grandmother's home, her steps began to drag. Working in Le Havre was one thing, leaving for the Front would be another entirely, possibly even worse than working in a soldiers' club.

The house was silent when she arrived and Elodie took it as an omen. She sorted through her clothing, picking out the most serviceable of her skirts and jackets, adding shirtwaists that were ready to be retired and a heavy woolen coat. The local *marché* had equipped her with several pairs of jodhpurs and two pairs of riding boots for her work at the veterinary hospital. She added these and then filled the bag with anything she thought might be useful. Packing finished; she sat down to write a letter to her mother.

October 29, 1914

Dearest Maman,

I have been offered the opportunity to drive vehicles to Calais for an organization of Englishwomen. I have been promised a train ticket home for my efforts. They need someone who is good with horses and speaks Dutch, as they are going to Le Front Occidental.

Since my work with the veterinary hospital ended, I have not found a place for myself, although I am considering joining the French Red Cross when I return. I will leave information about them with this letter. I am very sorry to cause you distress, but I must help when and wherever I can.

Please don't be angry. I will be home soon.
Your loving daughter,
Elodie

She folded up the note and put it in an envelope, setting it down with the Red Cross paperwork. With a good conscience, she went back to her embroidery. Perhaps she would put it in her bag, finish it later, and send it to her grandmother, she thought charitably.

Before dawn, Elodie slipped out of bed, dressing quickly in the warmest of her clothing. In stockinged feet, she moved as silently as possible through the house to the front door. There she paused, looking down at a pile of blankets. As she went to move them, she uncovered Theo's head. He snuffled awake and looked up at his big sister.

"Be careful, Elodie. I'll miss you," he said softly.

"How did you know?"

"They were talking about you on the wharf. I knew you would go." He rubbed his face on the blanket. Elodie knelt beside him.

"You take good care of Maman and Grand-mère. There is a note in my bedroom. Tell Maman I'll write as soon as I can." She hugged her little brother and tousled his hair.

"I will." He stood up and pulled his blankets away from the door. Elodie opened it and slipped out. Behind her, Theo pushed the door closed and she heard the snick of a lock shooting home. Just for a moment, she questioned her impetuous actions and rested her hand on the doorknob. Then she turned away and pulled on her low riding boots, her most sensible shoes, and laced them tight. That task accomplished, she stood, bag in hand, and turned away from her grandmother's home and toward the war.

Chapter 4:
October to November 1914

"It seems paradoxical to unite these two words: woman and war..." *Francois de Witt-Guizot, author, 1912*

The FANY cars were lined up at the wharf, each one filled to the roof with supplies and luggage. Women in dark green skirts and jackets milled around, obviously waiting for someone. Elodie stood awkwardly, wondering what she should do next. For a moment, she wanted to turn around and run back to the comfort of her grandmother's house. Deliberately heading into the heart of the war seemed foolhardy. Before she could change her mind, the young woman from the day before slid off the fender of a car and rushed over, her face bright with fresh air and enthusiasm.

"Hello! We were hoping you'd come, otherwise I was assigned to drive Jezebel." Lottie made a face. "Throw your kit behind the seat, I left space for it. I'm to ride with you. Right-o, Captain's here so you better get this scrap heap started." All around them, car engines were sputtering to life, coughing out fumes and smoke. Elodie put her bag in the car and then began the start procedure. Jezebel stayed stubbornly silent. Elodie's heart clenched. All this sneaking about to get away and now this miserable hunk of tin was about to make it all pointless.

"As God is my witness, I will push you off this wharf and you can rot at the bottom of the ocean," Elodie hissed at the car's engine. This time it grumbled to life. Perhaps it was possessed.

"I think the owner is hoping this car dies over here. They'll get her back at the end of the war. See the nameplate?" Lottie tapped on a brass plate mounted on the dashboard. "Car owners all over Britain are contributing vehicles to the war effort. Captain Wollert will lead out. We are to follow," Lottie continued cheerfully as Elodie climbed into the car beside her. "If any cars go off the road, we are all to stop and help but not block the way. There are more troop transports following."

Lottie bundled herself in a blanket and the two women's breath rose as they waited for what seemed an interminable time. When the car in front of them moved out, Elodie let out the clutch and followed with a sigh of relief. She had been imagining her grandmother coming to the wharf and ordering her home.

The line of cars moved slowly through Le Havre and out into the open countryside. It had been a wet fall, and the roads were slick and sticky with mud. It took concentration to keep the car from sliding off the *pavé* made of cobblestones and packed dirt and into the ditches. Despite that, as the town fell behind, Elodie relaxed, feeling her shoulders loosen.

"Run away from home, did you?" Lottie commented, noticing Elodie ease a bit.

"I left a letter, but my mother and grandmother will be most furious. They have rather strict views on women. Were your parents supportive?"

"They both passed away years ago. I lived with the local gentry, and they support my efforts. I say, you do know this is volunteer work? We provide our own kits."

"I took all the money I had with me. I hope my parents will be able to help me later."

"If they don't, maybe I can."

"That is very kind of you. Tell me more about these women and your," Elodie waved one hand at Lottie. "Army?"

"First Aid Nursing Yeomanry, but everyone calls us FANYs. The organization was set up in 1907. You should have seen our uniforms back then - scarlet jackets with gold buttons, long blue skirts, and fancy hats. Thank goodness someone realized we needed to be able to work, and not look as if we were on parade. Our job is to provide support for wounded men after battle. We go out on horseback to fetch the injured and they can either ride pillion or on a stretcher. Our horses are trained to carry stretchers," Lottie said all this practically in one breath. Elodie was impressed if somewhat lost in the English.

"Pillion?" she asked, hanging on to one word she definitely did not know.

"Carry two riders. Then once we have the wounded to a clearing station, we provide nursing care under the supervision of a nursing sister. It's more like being an orderly. Running, fetching, that sort of thing. It's bloody brilliant. But here's the rub. The British Expeditionary Forces don't want us, but the Belgians do. I rather think they are desperate. They've a hospital in Calais for us and we'll provide support at their clearing station and in the trenches at the sorting station. I'm not so sure I like that part." They continued in silence for a time.

"What is a clearing station?"

"It's a field hospital where the men are sorted."

"But what happens in the trenches if they are sorted twice?" Elodie wondered if her English was letting her down. Lottie grimaced.

"It's a bit complicated. At the back of the trench line is a sorting station. A doctor and some orderlies provide immediate medical care. The men who can, go back to their posts. The ones who can't are brought out at night. Once they get to the clearing stations, they are sorted again and sent to the barges or trains or ambulances."

"Is the hospital we are going to a clearing station?"

"No. The clearing stations are pretty primitive, sometimes just a tent. They are supposed to be out of shelling range, but the artillery can reach about five miles into France. I say, do you know Madame Curie is putting together radiological cars? Those will provide X-rays for the men at the clearing stations."

"The *poilus* call them Petit Curies, according to the newspapers."

"Brilliant. Anyway, once the men are sorted at the clearing station, they come to a field hospital like ours."

"It seems a bit complex." Elodie thought about the number of hands each man had to pass through to get help.

"I say, can I call you Elly?" Lottie asked suddenly.

"Please, no. I hate that name."

"I feel that way about Charlotte. Captain says we may need extra help once we get to Calais, Elodie. Especially from someone who can speak French. We are short of housekeepers and chauffeurs, and we can quickly get you up to speed on any nursing. I promise you won't be bored."

"I told my mother I'd be home after this."

"Well, think about it. Now, enough about the FANYs. Tell me about you."

"My father is a judge in Reims. We had a small farm and winery north of the city. When the Germans invaded, he sent us to live with my grandmother in Le Havre."

"Us?"

"My mother and brother, Theo. He's only ten," Elodie added before Lottie could ask if Theo was in the army. "We haven't heard from my father since Reims was invaded." Tears sprang to her eyes, and she wiped them with her mitten. Lottie reached over and squeezed her hand.

"I'm sure he is all right." That comforting lie fell flat. After a moment of awkward silence, she went on. "Do you speak German?"

"Only a few words, most of them rather naughty. I know more Luxembourgish, which is part German and part French."

Lottie laughed. "Those naughty words may come in handy; you'll have to teach me them! Why do you know Dutch? Isn't Reims rather far from northern Belgium?"

"It's about one hundred miles. My father had a Flemish man to train some of his horses. I played with his daughter." The car ahead of them slipped off the *pavé* and Elodie stepped on the brake, sliding to a stop. The two women stepped out of the car to help push the other vehicle back onto the road.

When that task was finished, Elodie stomped thick mud off her boots in displeasure and restarted the car. It was going to be a long drive to Calais.

"What did you do for those two months between the invasion and now?" Lottie asked.

"I worked in a vet hospital with a Captain Harris. He was short of men and needed a hand for a month. He's the reason my English is decent."

"Where was the hospital?"

"The Usine Bundy on Sadi Carnot. And for the rest of the time, I crocheted," Elodie said glumly.

"No crocheting here. There goes another car. Damn." Lottie groaned.

After three long days struggling over roads sided by verges knee-deep in mud, the convoy of women arrived at Calais. They had stopped at inns along the way, crowding into rooms to save money and eating what they could find in local shops. Because it was a volunteer organization, the women came from wealthier families who could afford to financially support their daughters, but money was always in short supply.

Elodie had heard crude humor claiming that women could not work together but watching the FANYs pitch in to dig out vehicles, change tires, and cook over smoky fires, she thought the men saying those things were foolish. Every woman did her duty, sometimes with a few sharp complaints, but always willingly.

During the long drive, Elodie discovered the reason she was to tell everyone she was twenty-three; that was the minimum age to enlist in the FANYs. Most of the women, with the exception of Captain Wollert and Sergeant Mason, were under thirty.

Calais was barely habitable. For two months, the city had been filled with troops and refugees. The streets were ragged, and the buildings looked tired and unkempt. Everyone stopped to stare as the convoy of cars went past them on the Rue Cambronne, turning as they reached the Notre Dame Cathedral and entering a wide gate into a courtyard. The sergeant motioned to switch the engines off. The women clambered out, clapping hands or holding them under their armpits for warmth and chattering to each other. As they looked around, silence descended. The courtyard was filthy, filled with trash and remnants of people's lives.

Their new hospital had started out as a school. On either side of the courtyard were two long buildings, each two stories tall. They were constructed of gray brick and windows, some boarded up, were regularly placed to provide maximum light inside. Each building had wide steps leading down from a central doorway. Across the back was a line of latrines, partially blocked from view by a low wall. Behind the latrines, the cathedral rose above the high wall separating the church from the school. The steeple reached toward the sky while the unlit stained-glass window provided the only hint of beauty.

"Thank God you've arrived!" A woman in uniform burst out of the building to the right. She hurried over to the captain, followed by five exhausted-looking FANYs. "It's not a moment too soon. We've held the fort, but that's all."

"That's Lieutenant Richards. She came out in the early days to get things running," Lottie whispered to Elodie.

"Sergeant, have the girls stow the medical supplies in the left-hand building. The room on the far right of that building is the typhoid ward. We've set aside a room on the far left as the storage room. We'll sort the supplies later. Hustle back and I'll introduce you. Things are rather… terse here."

"Terse?" Elodie whispered to Lottie.

"Means things are awful. It's FANY slang, not real English."

"You heard the Lieutenant, girls. Get unloaded," the sergeant called, and the women fell to with a will.

Entering the left-hand building was almost excruciating. It stank of vomit and worse. Elodie gagged the first time and then managed to breathe into her sleeve on the next few trips. As a group, they went over to the main building and up the stairs. It opened into a cloakroom and on either side were two long rooms.

The captain met them, her face suddenly looking older than her thirty years. Inside was a scene that made even the strongest FANY blanch. The smell was intense. Row after row of men - wounded, bandaged, and dirty - lay on straw pallets, some on makeshift beds. They looked dully at the women who passed them. The Belgian doctor, nurses, and orderlies were as worn as the men. At the end of the room was a short hall that led to a kitchen with barely any furnishings.

When the women gathered in the kitchen, Captain Wollert held up her hand for silence.

"As Lieutenant Richards said, this is terse. The Belgians have been overwhelmed with wounded and a severe lack of supplies. Plus, typhoid has been going through the trenches and it's a bad lot. Here's the plan. Half of you, volunteers only, are to go to the typhoid wards and start cleaning there. The other half, you'll stay in this building and clean. Get to work." She glanced around the room and her eye fell on Elodie. "Miss Fabien, please wait."

As the room cleared out, Elodie looked around. Unwashed dishes overflowed the sink and a pile of dirty linen and bandages filled one corner. There was no stove, only a drainpipe that had been fashioned into a fire pot. A pan was balanced precariously on top, and several exhausted Belgian nurses were huddled around it.

"Miss Fabien, I promised you a train ticket home and I will make good on that. But will you do one last service for me?" Captain Wollert asked.

"Of course, Madame, excuse me, Captain."

"Good. Go to the Belgian headquarters and talk to the commandant. The quartermaster is supposed to provision the hospital, but things are sorely lacking and there is a language barrier. Go out the gates and turn left. Command is three buildings down."

"Yes, Captain. What do we need?" Elodie asked and then felt foolish. The captain waved her hand in the air.

"Everything. Just everything." She left the kitchen as Lottie returned.

"I'm to boil gallons of water on this… this… stove. That should be a task. And I'll try for tea. Mother was a great believer in tea. Go on, Elodie, and get us a laundress and a cook. And anything else you can scare up."

In the main part of the schoolhouse *cum* hospital, the FANYs spread out under the dubious eyes of the Belgian staff. The Belgians had been fighting and surviving at this outpost since September, and they were careworn and overwhelmed with the sheer numbers of their countrymen passing through the hospital. With occupied Belgium sealed off behind the trenches and free Belgium surrounded by an electrified fence patrolled by German forces, nothing from their homeland was available to their beleaguered countrymen in France.

Elodie held her breath as she hurried past the latrines and across the courtyard. Distantly, she could hear the pounding of artillery, and the occasional faint smell of gunpowder drifted in on the breeze. If the defenses failed, Calais would be overrun. She shivered at the thought.

After the Battle of the Marne, each army tried to make a run around the other's flank. For the French and British, it was to prevent passage into France by the Germans. For the Germans, the race was to gain entry into France. By late October 1914, the Race to the Sea was almost finished, resulting in a tie as each side reached the ocean near Nieuwpoort at roughly the same time. The armies dug in, constructing lines of trenches from Belfort near the Swiss border across France to Nieuwpoort.

The Belgian command was located in an old hotel, the black, yellow, and red flag flying defiantly above the door. A soldier in the bright blue tunic and gray trousers of the Belgian army stood guard. Elodie approached him.

"Good afternoon… *Goedenmiddag,* I wish to speak with the quartermaster, the *intendant,*" she said in French. The young man looked at her suspiciously. "I need the man of supplies to speak with me, please, *alstublieft*." She tried Dutch, suddenly realizing that talk between little girls had not given her the words needed in an adult world. After some sign language, English, French, and Dutch, she was ushered in to see the *kwartiermeester*.

At first, the quartermaster was almost surly but had better French than Elodie had Dutch. He seemed very doubtful as to the wisdom of giving equipment to the English, particularly English women.

"I will see the commandant, please. He is expecting us."

"He is busy with the war," the quartermaster said dismissively.

"And we are trying to save the lives of your wounded," Elodie snapped back. She turned, leaving the room with a bang of the door. In minutes, she located the correct room, leaving behind her a trail of opened doors and men staring after her.

At first, the commandant glared at her, but Elodie had not come this far to be deterred. When her objective was finally made clear, he leaped up from behind his desk and approached her eagerly, engulfing her in a bear hug. She squeaked and the man let her go, pressing kisses on each cheek.

"Ah, Mademoiselle, the lieutenant of the FANYs said you would be arriving at the hospital.

Whatever I have at my disposal, I shall give to you. The *kwartiermeester* will see to this. And the hands of the English are welcome. Our medical people have had no support to deal with all the details."

She left the building with the promise of a washerwoman, a cook and anything else the commandant could quickly lay his hands on to help the English with their work. The quartermaster had given in with reluctance, but under his superior's enthusiasm, made promises to help.

Elodie stared in amazement as she entered the old school building. The patients had been crowded in one room and the other was being scrubbed by FANYs and Belgian orderlies on their hands and knees. Already the ward smelled and looked like a proper hospital, and the clean windows let in the fading afternoon light.

"Captain, the supplies will start arriving soon. The commandant had to speak sharply to the quartermaster, but we are to have a real stove, a washerwoman, and a cook once he can find them."

"Quartermasters must be the same in every army. Well done."

"Thank you. Is there anything else I can do?"

The captain waved the lieutenant over.

"This is Lieutenant Richards; Ricky, this is Elodie Fabien. She is a French girl who speaks Dutch. Mullins found her in Le Havre. As it turns out, Miss Fabien drove a car that no one else can start and she knows horses."

Elodie found herself under the direct gaze of very bright blue eyes. She looked back steadily.

"Perhaps Miss Fabien would be willing to stay here? We need a housekeeper and someone who can speak French more fluently than you, Ricky."

"Would that interest you, Miss Fabien?" the lieutenant asked.

"Oh yes, Madame. I mean, Lieutenant."

"It will be long, hard hours for no pay."

"I understand. But like the FANYs, the British and the French do not want me, but the Belgians do, so this is a good fit." The two older women looked at each other and laughed.

"Welcome to the FANYs, then. Your first task will be to scare up some food for the patients."

Elodie skirted past two women who were carrying supplies from the storeroom to a room upstairs that had been turned into a dispensary. Another FANY was setting up shelving made of old boxes to stow away the precious medical supplies they had brought. The Belgian doctor and nurses were beaming with joy as they collected clean dressings for the evening bandaging, as the new supplies improved the odds that their charges would survive. Elodie suddenly realized that come what may, she had made the correct decision to come to Calais and to stay.

She went down the stairs and into the kitchen.

Lottie had sorted tea and figured out a way to make barley stew. She was peering into the first pot with a puzzled expression, poking at the contents with a long spoon.

"I do believe this may be horse," she told Elodie, who glanced into the pot at the dark red, dense slivers of meat floating in the broth. Both women looked at each other for a long moment.

"*Eh bien*. They are Belgians and eat as much horse as we French do." Elodie shrugged. "But perhaps we will not tell the English."

"That is probably for the best," Lottie agreed faintly.

"I shall start on the dishes, so we have enough to serve the *blessés*." She used the French word for the wounded men in their care.

When the men were fed and tended to, the exhausted FANYs gathered in the second-floor room designated their break room. Normally they would purchase their own food, however just this once, the women shared the same meal as the wounded men.

"Those of you not assigned to chauffeur duties, hands up," Lieutenant Richards said briskly. "You'll divide up into twos and head for these addresses." She handed out slips of paper to the women with their hands raised. "These are homes that will keep you for three days. Then you'll switch to a new house. I'll get a schedule drafted up tomorrow."

"Why do we have to change homes every three days?" One of the women asked.

"Because that's how the bloody Frogs - I beg your pardon, Miss Fabien - the French want it. I've been looking for a building for us."

"Why not the typhoid building?" There was a rush of agreement from the women. Lieutenant Richards fixed them with icy blue eyes.

"You go to the addresses and change every three days. Understood? Now, I need three girls on each ward at night and the rest of you during the day." Richards surveyed the tired faces and softened. "You've done well. Go on now and get a good night's sleep."

Elodie found her belongings in Jezebel and carried them up to her tiny room. It was above the kitchen and smelled of stale food, but it was warm and all hers. She fell into bed, more tired than she had ever been.

And so, the first day in the Lamarq Hospital in Calais passed.

November 3, 1914

Dearest Maman,

I hope you have forgiven me for my rapid exodus. I have arrived in Calais and accepted the position of housekeeper for the Belgian hospital. I know I said I would return, but the conditions here are frightful and we are making a huge difference.

I want to reassure you that my colleagues are fine young women. They provide medical aid between the front lines and the hospitals. Since it is all voluntary, the women are well-educated and from wealthy families. I assure you I will not be exposed to women of low character here.

My new friend, Charlotte (Lottie) Mullins, is the daughter of a vicar and in true English fashion, her father died impoverished. Lottie was taken in by the local gentry and there she learned to ride horses and drive a car. She is a great girl and has taken me under her wing, so I am quite safe and well cared for.

The Belgians have been so glad to see us. There is nothing that the commander will not do for us, including the promise of weekly horse rides as conditions permit.

As the housekeeper, I must oversee food acquisition – the Belgians provide the hospital with food stores, but they sometimes run low. I am to have a cook and I hope she will be better at charming food out of the locals than I am. There is a washerwoman to do the laundry. As you may imagine, this task never ends. I am also kept busy translating between the English, the French, and the Belgians. My English and Dutch have both improved markedly.

The FANYs drive ambulances and act as orderlies to keep the patients clean and fed. It is not glamorous work, but it is very important to the war effort. We are a long way from the front lines, so please do not worry about me. Because the FANY is all volunteer, I must pay for all my equipment and food, so I beseech you to send money if you can.

I must post this soon and get some sleep. I will write more later.

With love and respect to you, Grand-mère and Theo. If you hear from Papa, please tell him I love him.
Elodie

In the first few months of the war, thousands of Belgian soldiers had been wounded. The Battle of Yser had just ended, and the hospital staff had been inundated by eighteen thousand soldiers who passed through clearing stations and the hospital. Within two days, the eager extra hands of the FANYs had wrought huge improvements. The doctor and nurses were still overwhelmed by the sheer number of wounded coming through their doors, but now their faces held hope and their hands made ready use of the badly needed medical supplies. The FANYs had arrived just in time.

From somewhere, the quartermaster located a temperamental wood stove for the French cook. Elodie looked at it askance, suspecting from its perfect fit that it had been stolen from this very kitchen. He had also found a huge vat for heating water and Elodie scrubbed it clean with goodwill and aching arms. It sat on the back of the stove, continually heating water for the wards, while the multitude of burners on the front were always cooking something.

In a flash of genius, Elodie offered the cook a

tiny percentage of any money she saved on purchases. Eventually, word got back to the hospital that the woman was feared for her haggling skills. With more plentiful food, the wounded began to rally.

The quartermaster showed up one day with men and mattresses, meaning the patients no longer had to lie on piles of straw covered with sheets. Beds on legs would come eventually. Elodie looked over her domain with pleasure.

The washerwoman, Madame Vincent, had arrived with a horde of youngsters, all blonde-headed and full of enthusiasm. Elodie never quite determined exactly how many there were, but the children did odd jobs around the hospital and ran errands for the FANYs. Their father was German and had vanished just before the war broke out. Madame claimed not to miss him.

With the help of Madame's oldest daughters, the kitchen now held clean plates, pans and utensils, obtained from who knew where. Nothing matched, but no one minded.

The laundry facilities had been thrown together outside, as far from the latrines as Elodie could manage. The quartermaster promised to provide a tent eventually, but for now, at least, the bedding would be clean. Madame Vincent and her horde of children had brought huge vats with them the previous day and balanced them on top of stone rings they had built. The children had then run back and forth filling the containers using wooden buckets. The older boys proceeded to chop wood to heat the water. Eventually, the vats were full and boiling in the cool air. The strong smell of bleach rose from clouds of steam, while piles of sheets stained with blood and worse waited on the ground. The trenches were the perfect breeding ground for diseases like typhoid and dysentery, and the bleach was an important part of sanitation.

Madame Vincent leaned over the cauldron, looking for all the world like a witch as she stirred the boiling sheets. Elodie stifled a giggle. When Madame Vincent determined the contents of the first vat were well boiled, the sheets were moved into the second for a scrub, and then the third for a rinse. Elodie and one of the older boys had figured out how to install clotheslines across the rear of the courtyard and these waited for the first of the clean sheets.

"Madame, I have come to help you with the laundry. What would you have me do?" Elodie offered. The older woman looked at her skirt and shirtwaist and snorted.

"You will ruin your clothing."

"It is what I have. The *blessés* are more important and they require clean sheets. Where shall I start?"

"*Bien*, Mademoiselle," the washerwoman said with a shrug. "I have sheets ready for the mangle." Madame Vincent pointed at the set of rollers braced over a washtub. "You will run them through and then hang them on the lines. Whether they dry or freeze is in God's hands."

"*Oui,* Madame." Elodie went to the mangle, examining it closely. She had seen their laundress use one but the actual mechanics of it were going to take some getting used to.

"Surely your Maman taught you the use of a mangle?" The laundress' tone held derision. Elodie tossed her head.

"Madame, my father is the *procureur de la République* in Reims. My Maman did no laundry. And neither did I. If you will tell me how to run this contraption, I will then be able to assist you."

"*Fille gatée,*" the older woman muttered under her breath – spoiled child. "Turn the wheel at the top and the presses come apart. Place the sheet between the presses and use the wheel to lower the top press. Then turn the big crank at the side. Keep your hands out of the mangle. When the sheet comes out, hang it up. May I presume you can operate the clothes pins?"

Elodie looked down at the basket of pins and back at the older woman. Good manners warred with the desire to put this woman in her place.

"I am certain that you will assist me, should I need help." The two women glared at each other for a moment. From far in the distance, both could hear the thunder of artillery and any petty disagreement faded into nothing against that noise. Each turned to their work, a *détente* reached for the moment.

Cautiously, at first, and then with growing confidence, Elodie fed sheets through the mangle. It was easy, but eventually she turned the crank first with one arm and then the other, feeling her muscles screaming in protest. Water splashed and ran down a tiny ditch toward a mucky expanse that might have been a vegetable plot in better weather. Soon, the clothesline was heavy with clean sheets that flapped first stiffly and then more gracefully as they dried in the breeze from the ocean.

"Gather up what is dry to give yourself room to hang more. Put the dry ones in the linen closet and we will fold them later. I'll take over the mangle." Madame Vincent dried her hands, chapped red from hot water and bleach. "You may be *société*, but your servants would be proud of your work today."

"Thank you, Madame," Elodie said, and went to bring in the dry sheets. Lifting her arms high enough to unpin each sheet was a trial and she knew that in the morning she would be miserable.

The threatening rain from lowering skies held off for a week until the laundry backlog had been washed, then it began in earnest, making the already muddy ground and roads almost unpassable. Elodie sent a stiffly worded note to the quartermaster, and eventually it resulted in a tent that he had placed over Madame Vincent's cauldrons. It was almost unbearably humid inside, but at least it was warm. The sheets had to be dried in the second school building, which seemed to take forever.

Early one morning in November, Elodie pulled on her coat and woolen beret as Lottie clattered in for her shift.

"It's raining," Elodie observed her friend's wet coat.

"Does it always rain this much in France? It is as bad as England."

"It could be snowing."

"Perish the thought. Are you off? You'll need a mackintosh and some galoshes today. The roads are running with water."

"I am on a search for bread. Shall I bring anything?"

"Tea, if you find it. And something for ten o'clocks." She referred to the morning meeting where mail was distributed, and cases discussed. Elodie pushed out into the rainy early morning. It was still dark; the stars were hidden behind heavy clouds. Mud sucked at her feet, and she occasionally slid on ice pockets that edged streams flowing down the roads.

On the way around different bakeries and houses where she knew women would sell bread, she passed the coffin cart, an old truck covered in black canvas that whipped in the wind like a ghostly galleon under sail. The coffin man traveled the roads and byways between the clearing stations and the hospitals. He made the rounds every day, filling his cart with the broken bodies of young men sacrificed to vanity and arrogance. As he traveled between these places of death, he retrieved corpses dumped from ambulances as casualties died on their way to the hospitals. He carried them to the churchyards and cemeteries, where priests oversaw their consecration. His job was a bitter one.

The driver nodded to her as he passed. Elodie nodded back and crossed herself covertly, not wanting to hurt the man's feelings. She knew he was only doing his job, but the tattered sides of the truck and his rusty black clothing were the stuff of nightmares.

Elodie's rounds of the city bakers yielded fresh bread with a beautiful yeasty smell that brought memories of home. One baker had small rolls that would do well for the morning meeting. Elodie smiled to herself. Yesterday's mail had brought one FANY several carefully wrapped jars filled with marmalade, and she had put them in the hospital kitchen for safe storage. When sunlight touched the jars, a warm golden-orange color filled that section of the room. Tea, marmalade, and fresh bread would make the FANYs very happy.

When Elodie returned to the hospital, the cook immediately pounced on the bread, adding slices to the breakfast trays that the orderlies and FANYs were carrying to the *blessés*. Elodie stowed away the buns and crossed to the typhoid ward to make certain everything was in order.

She had quickly learned not to become attached to typhoid patients. They died in far greater numbers than the physically wounded soldiers did. Their faces became almost translucent with fever and seemed to glow. Pneumonia accompanied this typhoid, and the gasping was painful to hear. FANYs were helping typhoid patients to eat their thin porridge – all their bodies could handle. Elodie admired those who volunteered in the typhoid wards for their cheerful faces and comforting words. She had seen them outside, however, crying when a favorite patient died.

Madame Vincent was doing the typhoid linen wash and she nodded grimly to Elodie as she peeked into the tent to check on her progress. Elodie greeted her respectfully, a lasting truce having been declared.

By ten o'clock, the FANYs had gathered in the comfortable break room, an old classroom on the second floor. One enterprising woman found crates to turn into seats and the small fire pot, once in the kitchen, now sat in a corner, pouring out heat and hot water in equal measure.

Lieutenant Richards came in with a bag of mail that she handed to Sergeant Mason to distribute. She allowed the first few minutes for the women to read letters from home and talk about the news. Elodie handed out buns with oily butter and marmalade.

"Girls… girls." Richards began the briefing. "The doctor has finished the charts on patients who are to leave on the mercy ships. The ships should be in harbor by eleven and taking on *blessés* by noon. You are to put charts with each patient as you load them into the ambulances. Double-check the destination. In addition, there are a number to go to convalescent homes in Le Havre and Paris. Take those to the *gare* for train transport. We've a few from the typhoid ward that will join this group.

"Miss Fabien, there has been an influx of Belgian refugees, and the nursing sister there has asked that you attend the holding center to translate. It's in the warehouse directly across the boulevard from the train station.

"Now, we are expecting casualties shortly. Belgian command reported that there has been heavy action near Ypres. Let's be smart and get the transfers done in good fashion." She paused as a voice cried out in French from below them.

"Where are the English?"

"Upstairs." Heavy feet raced up the worn treads and a man in a muddy Belgian uniform burst into the room.

"Barges," he gasped in French. "Barges coming down the Canal du Calais. They've been sighted at Coulogne. They will be here in less than an hour,"

"Thank you," Richards said and translated for the FANYs who did not speak French. "Girls, the barges are carrying the wounded who cannot be jostled. You will take them directly to the mercy ships and they will be loaded immediately. I want two groups, one to move patients from here to the ships and one to transport from the barges. Let's see. Five to move patients from here and the remainder to the barges. Whichever group finishes first, you'll fill in with the other. The commandant will let us know if we need to run to the Belgian lines. Elodie, get Jezebel started and then walk over to the warehouse."

As she finished speaking, the women scattered, pulling on warm clothing as they ran to start the vehicles. Nurses and the single Belgian doctor were readying the operating theater and preparing for the wounded who would be following the barges in trucks and ambulances. Orderlies waited to load the first batch of injured for their voyage to Britain or Le Havre. As each bed was vacated, the sheets were stripped off and the bed newly made for the next inhabitant. Cars rattled to life out in the courtyard. It was chaos, but chaos with a purpose.

Elodie felt slightly left out. Surely moving the wounded or helping to get the hospital ready was more important than talking to the refugees?

However, even in this quasi-military organization, orders were orders. She started Jezebel, whispering threats if the car failed to run or offered even a moment of trouble for the FANY driver.

Once the car was purring, Elodie walked toward the train station and the warehouse where the Belgian refugees hoped for a safe haven. They were still trickling into France, mostly from the Netherlands, somehow crossing trenches and avoiding German patrols who shot anyone trying to escape.

Elodie let herself into the warehouse and glanced around. There were not many, just a small group huddled against one wall, close to a wood stove giving out heat that quickly dissipated in the vast building. Each one held a tin cup filled with soup. One young woman cuddled a small child on her lap, feeding it small sips. In the opposite corner, a nursing sister was seated with a young woman. Elodie crossed toward the pair. The women she passed looked at her with no emotion. It had been wrung out of most of them in the months since the German army had rolled over the border.

One woman had a piece of chalk and was writing names on the warehouse wall, finding a space not covered with the names of previous groups. Another in a black Belgian lace cap searched the names and notes, turning away in tears as she failed to find what she was looking for.

"Good morning, Sister. I am Elodie Fabien with the FANYs. I've come to translate for you."

"Ah, Miss Fabien, good." The nursing sister glanced up at Elodie. "This group just came in on a fishing boat. I need names, home addresses, that sort of thing."

"Of course." Elodie sat down, looking at the old face of the young woman sitting in front of the nursing sister. Her grasp of Dutch had increased greatly in the week she had been in Calais. She gathered the necessary information.

"The sister wants to know if anyone has a fever," Elodie translated a request from the nursing sister.

"No. The baby is teething, so she is fretful."

The young woman stopped Elodie as she started to get up.

"We went to Holland at first, but there was no work for us. We had heard that there was work in England or in France, if we could get there," she told her. "We gave the last of our money to the fishermen who brought us here. Where will we go?"

"We are sending people to Le Havre to work in the factories," Elodie told her. "Is there anything else you need?" The young woman looked away, her face aging even more. Elodie waited for her to speak, knowing she was about to hear tragedy.

"We are from Leuven. I was there at the market when the Germans attacked. My husband was killed in the fighting. And I... please, *mevrouw*." The young woman buried her face in her delicate lace handkerchief, crying quietly. After a few moments, she looked up. "It was awful. The smoke from the buildings. My father had a heart attack, and we could not even bury him properly. They caught me as I tried to go home and.... Then we walked to Antwerp. We were supposed to be safe there. But the Germans came again and again I was... So we went to Holland. And now here. My courses are two months late. Please, *mevrouw*, I can't... I can't."

Elodie closed her eyes to the pain and then opened them, looking at the nursing sister who watched them with a flat expression. The nurse could guess what had just been said. This was not a new story. Elodie took a deep breath and let it out slowly. She began to translate.

"I think she is saying she was raped twice. Her husband died in Leuven and now she is two months late. She wants to know if we can help her." The sister rubbed her face, fingers pressing the edges of her eyes. The Belgian woman watched her stolidly.

"Tell her if she bears a child, it is God's will, and the child is the innocent in this."

"But Sister..."

"Tell her," Sister said harshly. "Tell her perhaps the child is her husband's, and she will love it because of that chance." The nurse turned abruptly; fists clenched by her side. Elodie bit her lip.

"There is nothing we can do to help. I'm sorry. Sister prays that it is your husband's." The young woman shook her head.

"It's not. It can't be. Please." The cry for help tore at Elodie's heart and she looked around desperately. The older woman who had been writing on the wall came over, wrapping her arms around the distraught young woman.

"We cannot help. A train leaves from the station at noon. Tickets for you will be at the counter. Tell them you are refugees, and they will write your names in a log. Perhaps someone can help you when you arrive in Paris or Le Havre."

"Thank you, *mevrouw*," the older woman muttered. Elodie went to join the nursing sister.

"Will she be all right?" Elodie asked quietly.

"Probably not. None of us will ever be all right," the sister said bitterly.

"Do you need me for anything? I should go back to the hospital."

"They are all from the same family, you can go."

Elodie left the warehouse, stepping out into the weak sunlight. Mud sucked at her shoes, threatening to pull them off with each step. She slogged her way back to the hospital, wondering how the men in the trenches handled this muck. Vehicles streamed past her in both directions. The ones bound for the harbor practically crept along, trying to avoid the worst of the potholes, while the outbound ones raced back toward the barge wharves, unconcerned about anything but speed.

In the hospital, the wards were filled with new soldiers, familiar faces having been transferred to the waiting ships. FANYs were hard at work cleaning the men and helping them into nightshirts. Upstairs Elodie could hear the noise from the operating theater.

She went to the kitchen to see how the cook and the laundress were faring under the onslaught. A cauldron of soup roiled cheerfully as the cook cut bread into thin slices and placed them on plates. Two of Madame Vincent's brood were preparing tubs to wash the dishes that would be returning as the soldiers were fed.

On her way out to the courtyard, Elodie passed by piles of filthy uniforms gathered by orderlies and left outside. She looked at the discarded uniforms. This surely fell within her responsibility as the housekeeper.

Madame had finished the typhoid wash and was starting the regular wash. Sheets flapped in the wind.

"Good afternoon, Madame. Is all well with you?" Elodie asked. The woman grunted, engaged in carrying heavy piles of wet sheets to the rinse. The older daughter began adding dirty linen to the first cauldron. "What happens with the uniforms from the *blessés*?"

"They rot. And sometimes I burn them."

"Could we perhaps wash and mend the ones in decent condition?"

"'We,' Mademoiselle? Who is this we?" Madame Vincent asked sourly. Elodie flushed.

"I can mend, and we could find some other women to do the same. What do the healthy men wear to leave the hospital?"

"I don't know. I have not seen one walk out of here."

"Oh." Elodie was silenced. It was a startling observation. "I shall speak with the Belgians and Captain Wollert and see what they wish to do," Elodie said thoughtfully. Madame shrugged. Elodie began to gather in the dry sheets, making room for the wet piles that sat in baskets next to the wash vats. Eventually, they would fold and store away the dry sheets against the next influx of patients.

The rush ended and Elodie made certain that there was tea and soup for the FANYs. They came in carrying their personal metal mugs and poured whichever they wanted, some wandering off to rest. Lottie sat down at the kitchen table. Her face was strained, and she hunched over the tea mug, breathing in the steam.

"You would not believe just how… how awful that was," Lottie said softly, and Elodie heard her voice quiver. She sat down beside her friend. "We couldn't go fast; those men were so badly wounded. If I hit the smallest bump someone would moan, and the others would apologize. They kept begging to know how long. I had to creep to the ships. And the smell. Mud and blood. Vomit. And it went on and on. Oh, Elodie, when they said this would be over by Christmas, it seemed a lark, but this... This will not end by Christmas." Lottie put her head in her arms and sobbed. Elodie rubbed her back comfortingly.

When Lottie recovered, the two women sat in silence in the warmth of the kitchen and sipped at their tea. There was nothing else to say.

Chapter 5:
November to December 1914

"We have lost the war. It will go on for a long time, but it is already lost." *German Crown Prince Wilhelm after the Battle of the Marne, September 1914*

The sun poked a finger of light into Elodie's room and across her face. As the rainy, gloomy winter took over northern France, sun had become a rarity. Elodie squirmed out of the light and blinked her eyes. Now that the FANYs had the hospital under control, Sergeant Mason had begun scheduling the women more efficiently and assigning days off. Elodie lay for a moment, looking up at the ceiling and wondering what she could do with the first of hers.

There might be some musical entertainment in the evening. Occasionally, the FANYs put on their own concerts and sometimes the Belgian, French, and English commands allowed their officers to attend parties hosted by the other allies. There was no shopping, even if she had the money to spend. The

Belgian command did lend horses to the FANYs, but only as a group. The day stretched long before her.

Elodie rolled over and covered her head with a pillow as the morning shift began their rounds and noise drifted up the stairs. She sniffed at the stale odor under the pillow. Suddenly, she remembered that Lottie had mentioned the French had set up a bathing house and the FANYs were welcome to use it. A bath would be just the ticket. She was stale and her clothing was worse.

Climbing out of bed and gathering up the clothes she had brought from Le Havre, she wrinkled her nose at the somewhat rank odor. The FANYs had done their best with buckets and washcloths, but a real bath! Elodie shivered at the thought. And since it was also Lottie's day off, perhaps she would be up for the adventure. Elodie bundled the clothing into her valise, dressed, and walked quickly to Lottie's boarding house, finding her in the kitchen. Lottie offered her a roll and a cup of coffee.

"Fancy a bath?" Elodie asked.

"More than you can imagine."

"My goodness, I can imagine quite a lot," Elodie laughed. "If that bathing house is a reality, we should investigate."

"Maybe Madame Vincent will take pity on us and wash our uniforms," Lottie wondered.

"That I sincerely doubt. She is convinced we are all very spoiled. I have mine in my valise and I can bathe with them. It might be a bit *grossière*, but they will be as clean as I am."

"Brilliant. Shall we?"

The two women ate quickly. Dressed in an odd assortment of their cleanest clothing from the ankles up and filthy boots from the ankles down, they made their way through the sticky mud to the train station, the *Gare Centrale*, where the bathhouse was rumored to be located.

They passed by the train shed used as a *Hôpital de Passage* for less injured French and English soldiers. Here they received treatment from nurses and orderlies while they waited for ambulances or trains to transfer them to their own hospitals. The FANYs had been informed that they might need to provide these transfers while the Red Cross was getting on its feet.

Elodie and Lottie looked at each other and skirted around the building. Both knew that if they went in, their day off would be over. There would be no leaving the patients inside without trying to make something better. And there were just so many flooding in from the battlefields every day…

"I've heard one gets bath passes from the commandant of the railway," Lottie said.

"Of course. And train passes from washhouses," Elodie giggled, pleased that her command of English was increasing enough to make jokes. Lottie smiled at the attempt. She pulled open the door to *Gare Centrale* and the two peered around. An elegantly dressed man in a dark blue railway uniform looked down his nose at them.

"Is that him?" Lottie asked in a tiny voice.

"I'm not sure. It's the right uniform," Elodie whispered back.

"He's rather grand." They went a bit farther into the building and paused in consternation. It seemed rather indelicate to ask this man for a pass to the bath house, but his face lit up with a welcoming smile and a hint of laughter in his dark eyes as they approached hesitantly.

"Ah, the English mademoiselles are here for *un bain?*"

"Yes, please," the two managed.

"Very well. You are in good time. The water will be extra hot this morning" He handed them two pieces of blue pasteboard, cut from an old railroad schedule cover. *'Un bain'* was written in black ink across the front. "You proceed through those doors." He pointed towards the track. "The railroad car is outside on the far tracks. It is the one with a boiler car attached."

"For a bath?"

"*Oui,* mademoiselle. We have divided a train car into four bathing rooms. You will find it most comfortable," he assured them.

The women looked dubiously at each other and then went out the doors. Several tracks away was the promised bathing train. They stepped carefully across the rails until they reached it.

A steep stepladder led up to the main doors and Lottie clambered up first, reaching down to take the valises filled with their dirty clothing from Elodie, who climbed up next. A very old man looked at them from rheumy eyes. He held out his gnarled hand and the two women handed over their passes. He jerked his head toward two open doors.

"I bring hot. You add cold," he mumbled in French. Elodie translated quickly for Lottie. The old man shuffled off to where the engine of the bath train was heating water in its tank. Painfully slowly, he tottered back with buckets of boiling water that steamed in the cold air. Eventually, each basin had enough hot water to make a decent bath. The two women nodded to each other, going into their respective bathrooms, and closing the doors.

Elodie pulled the pins from her hair, delighting in the feel as she washed the dirt away. Eventually she and what passed as her uniforms were clean. Quickly, she bundled her hair up in a turban and pulled on the clothes she had worn to the bath train. She could hang the wet things to dry either on the clothesline or in her room if the rain started again. Hopefully, they would not get too musty.

Lottie was waiting for her, gamely trying to carry on a conversation with the old man in a mix of English and very bad French. Elodie pressed a fifty-centime piece into his hand. The man shook his head, mumbling something. Elodie took his hand, folding his fingers over the coin.

"*Alles voor Vlaanderen*," she said loudly, realizing he was hard of hearing. His eyes brightened for a moment with tears, and he slipped the coin into his pocket. The two women clambered down out of the bath train and walked toward their rooms.

"What was that about? Allies fur flounder in?"

"*Alles voor Vlaanderen*. All for Flanders. It's a part of their motto. All for Flanders, Flanders for Christ."

"Oh."

It was delightful to be clean again and to have fresh clothing to change into, but the process took hours. Going to the bath train became code for being unavailable all day.

A few days later, Lieutenant Richards found Elodie in the storeroom, sorting out a supply shipment from England and checking off the contents of two lorries against a list of what was supposed to have come. The FANYs always seemed to have been shorted desperately needed items and sent too many items they could not readily use. Once the list was prepared, Captain Wollert would send sternly worded letters to England to try and get the right supplies. Inevitably, the next shipment would be just as cock-eyed.

"Elodie, I have two tasks for you once this mess is sorted." The older woman smiled pleasantly at her. Elodie put down the sheaf of shipping papers and took out a small notebook, ready to write. "First, I think the French are finally going to let us turn a house in Saint-Inglevert into a convalescent home for our *blessés* who will return to the Front. To that end, the Belgians are providing us with a refugee who speaks a bit of French. She'll be the housekeeper there and you are to train her. Her name is Mila. She should be here within the week. I expect the wrinkles will be worked out in a few months and we can get the home opened up."

"Finally. You'd think as allies the Belgians and French could figure out how to work together," Elodie grimaced.

"I suppose it is generations of bad blood and all the invading each other. Next, we are on the list to receive an X-ray machine from Madame Curie." She dropped the name casually, but Elodie could see that the lieutenant was as impressed as she was. "There is a team of workmen coming to prepare the upstairs room next to the operating theater. I'm told that all we need to do is provide the space. Once it is completed, the machine will arrive along with a technician to install it and train the doctor."

"The hospital in Reims has one. Our neighbor broke his arm, and the doctor X-rayed it. He showed the pictures around for months. He said it was very loud and burned his skin."

"I haven't seen one myself. It should be very

interesting. I shall let you get back to your work." Lieutenant Richards nodded and left the room. Elodie turned back to the sorting, her mind racing with the logistics of the new tasks ahead of her.

Mila turned out to be a very friendly woman in her late twenties. Elodie found that she learned quickly and worked very hard, grateful for the opportunity to serve her countrymen. They divided their days between French and English, trying to get Mila comfortable working with both the English FANYs and the French villagers. Mila quickly found an unused room for herself in the typhoid hospital, much to the chagrin of the FANYs, who complained bitterly and ineffectively to the sergeant and lieutenant. Mila proved very adept at scrounging as she fixed up her room.

Elodie found herself almost envying the brightly painted walls and shabby second-hand furnishings. But her own room, although small and sometimes smelling of meals, was very comfortable and above all, warm in the bitter cold.

One December day brought a Christmas package for Elodie. She knew that this box would contain letters and small gifts, but most importantly, it carried the scent of pine trees and cinnamon – the smells of Christmas. She put it beside her chair, wanting to open it in private, not during morning break. Tomorrow, she would share the homemade cookies she was certain this parcel contained.

As soon as her day's work was done, Elodie hurried up to her room to open the gift. She removed the paper wrapping with as much care as she could – thinking of her mother and grandmother as she did so – and knowing that the paper would be useful. The smell of Christmas intensified. Inside the wooden box were carefully thought-out presents. A soft scarf, fur-lined mittens, heavier stockings, a tin of macarons, and another of lace cookies. A tiny wreath of pine twigs. A bar of her favorite soap, smelling of cloves and cinnamon. She held the soap to her nose, thinking of her family. At the very bottom were four letters, each one addressed in distinctive handwriting. Elodie closed her eyes and chose one at random, smiling at Theo's messy penmanship.

December 1914
Le Havre, France
Dear Elodie,
Papa has joined us from Reims and Maman says I must go back to school after Christmas. I wish you were here to tell her I don't need to go. After all, I will be joining the war as soon as I am able. I tried last week, but the men turned me away.

Grand-mère says I am too noisy and must go to the park at least once a day. I go to the wharves and watch the ships come in. I have learned the best curses. Grand-mère told me that Le Père Fouettard would come with his whips to punish me, but if Père Noël is not real, neither is old Fouettard.

Papa says that the house was still standing when he left. I wonder if we will have a place to live when we go home. Papa says the French came and got all the horses before the Boche could. I hope my cats are all right. I suppose they will be. Cats do land on their feet. I hope you are having many adventures, and you will write me and tell me about them. Maman reads your letters out loud, and I think she leaves some parts out.

Maman says I must close and say I love you, so I suppose I do.
Theo

Elodie folded up the letter and put it back in its envelope. Theo's letter had told her everything that she needed to know. She would open the others one at a time and savor each one, enjoying the bittersweet pain of reading and rereading them. She hoped that Brûlée was safe behind the lines in a kind officer's care, but she knew that the French army did not view horses with the same compassion that the British did, and they used their animals badly.

The first Christmas passed oddly joyfully. The FANYs gathered in the church for services, not minding that they were in French and Catholic for the mainly Anglican women. Outside, the guns had fallen silent, and no airplanes crossed the sky. In the parish hall, the townspeople gathered for a meal cobbled together from whatever the parishioners could spare.

Elodie looked around at the faces red with cold and pinched with exhaustion. Children sat gathered at the foot of the creche, waiting for *Père Noël* to arrive or at least for presents to be handed out. The FANYs had spent many off-hours knitting mittens and scarves for this day.

In the beginning, none of the women thought they would still be here at the muddy, cold Front at this time of year. As October had faded to November and then to December, the realization that the war was not going to end by Christmas had brought sadness to the FANYs. Elodie knew how many tears the mittens and scarves had soaked up. Despite the fear and poverty, the celebration was comforting and a bright reminder that someday, the war would end.

Lottie and Elodie walked back to the hospital through the cold night. The town was dark, hiding its lights from the enemy only a few miles away, while the stars overhead were brilliant. From somewhere very far off, she thought she heard singing - men's voices raised in a carol. She and Lottie looked at each other, each wondering if they were hearing something from the battlefield or merely ghosts in their heads. Then a sharp gust of wind cut down the street and the voices vanished.

On December twenty-sixth, the guns began again, shattering the brief calm that had settled over the Front.

Chapter 6: January 1915

"Trench War was a grubbing kind of business." *Major Sir Frank Fox (aka GSO) in G.H.Q., 1920*

The New Year was bitterly cold, and the ambulances refused to start. The cars had been outfitted with asbestos-lined bonnet covers, but in the unrelenting cold of the winter of 1915, these did not help. The only recourse was to assign two women to stay up all night and race out every thirty minutes to start all the cars and let them idle for a while. The vehicles were then tucked back into their bonnet covers and the women retreated to the kitchen for a hot drink.

Elodie took to staying up with Lottie when it was her turn, keeping the cups of tea coming and talking desultorily to pass the time.

"What do you plan to do when the war ends?" Lottie asked, warming her fingers around her tin mug.

"I'd like to go to the Sorbonne, but I don't know if that will happen. I expect there will be a good deal to do to rebuild France after this is over."

"No marriage?" Lottie asked, taking a sip of her tea. Elodie flushed.

"I haven't met anyone yet. I have too many things I want to do first, and I suppose with all the young men dying in the trenches, there might not be anyone to marry. What will you do?" Elodie moved her feet farther from the stove where her shoe leather was starting to get horrendously hot.

"I'd like to have a house in the country, a dozen horses, and maybe one or two babies. Too many babies interfere with riding."

"No husband in all that?"

"I suppose there will be one. They are rather necessary for the baby part. Oh, bother - it's time to start the ambulances. Wake up, Sally." Lottie shook the other FANY awake, and they trudged out into the cold. Elodie made another pot of tea as the engines choked and coughed to life.

The trenches were mostly quiet that winter as the armies strived to understand this new style of warfare. Belgian refugees trickled into France and men wounded in artillery bombardments came by ambulance. Typhoid raced through the muddy trenches, and the men arrived stinking of mud and filth and blood. Overhead there was a new threat, as airplanes and Zeppelins tested weaponry that sowed death on troops and civilians.

On the bright side, Captain Wollert had

begged, bullied, and argued with the French town council and the Belgian army until the FANYs had their own quarters in an old store building, ending the movement from house to house. Initially, the French had offered this building to the Belgians as a convalescent home. It was too small to be of use, so they had finally agreed on nearby Saint-Inglevert instead. Captain Wollert eventually acquired the storefront for FANYs.

Elodie had been asked to gather up any paper she could find and bring it to the new building. She complied, mystified by the request.

"It's an old shop," Lottie told her cheerfully, relieving Elodie of a stack of scavenged paper. "We need something to cover the windows, otherwise every French man and boy around here will be peering in." Other women were sticking the paper up by first painting the window and then plastering it to the glass. It made the interior dim. Mattresses filled the floor; most set on the floor instead of frames. Any frames went to the hospital.

"Are there more beds?" Elodie counted curiously.

"No. There isn't room for more. When one of us gets up, there is always a girl waiting to fall into bed. I don't think the sheets ever cool off."

Elodie shuddered, grateful for her private bedroom where only one person ever warmed the sheets.

"I've got to head back," she told Lottie, and went out into the cold, muddy winter's day to slip and slide back to the hospital.

"Ah, good, Elodie," Lieutenant Richards glanced up from a patient she was rebandaging as Elodie walked through the ward. "We are changing the women in the trenches tonight. Would you make certain ambulances one and three are packed with woolens and medical supplies?"

"Of course." Elodie smiled at the patient, who grimaced back as sticking plaster pulled off some arm hair. She went to the storeroom where socks, mittens, and mufflers arrived from volunteers in England and France. She carried burlap sacks filled with the woolens out to each ambulance, filling the spaces as full as she could.

The haggard faces of women who had been in the trenches and clearing stations only nominally out of artillery range played on her mind. They tried to describe the misery and filth, the terror and stench, but words could not do the experience justice. All they could say was that the men were desperate for socks. Elodie thought about how much she had begrudged knitting and felt guilty. She decided she would try the double knitting method that turned out two socks at once, and not feel sorry for herself.

"Time for a break?" The cheerful voice startled Elodie out of her thoughts. Lottie waved at Elodie as she stepped up onto the cobblestones that created the parking area for the ambulances and tried to scrape the mud off her shoes. Lottie peered into the back of the ambulance, reaching in for one of the pairs of hand-knit socks and turning over the note that was attached to it.

"What does this say?" she asked. Elodie took the bundle.

"'Bless you for fighting for us,'" she translated for Lottie. "I wonder if they really understand what it's like here."

"Oh, dear. Bad hour?"

"Yes. I feel so useless. I want to do more. It was great fun at the beginning when we had challenges all day long, but this has gotten quite tame."

"I know." Lottie looked at her sympathetically. "Talk to Sergeant. She'll pass the word up and maybe you can do more."

"We'll see. I do hope the commandant will let us take the horses out for a ride. I need some fresh air."

"If the bloody snow lets up. It's almost ten and I am parched." Lottie closed the ambulance doors and took Elodie's arm, pulling her toward the hospital and the break room. The morning meetings were a ritual that they needed to make it through each day.

The room was filled with women. The kettle boiled and the cook had brought up a small basket of hot muffins. Elodie took one and poured a cup of tea for herself. One of the women handed around letters. The sound of ripping envelopes and chatter died away as each woman opened her mail, some reading out segments they thought the others might like to hear.

"All right, settle down," Lieutenant Richards said briskly as she entered the room ten minutes later. "You can show that photo around later, Dora. Listen up. Tonight, Charlotte and Timmy are going to the trenches to deliver woolens and take over the first aid station. Dinky and Sarah are assigned to the typhoid ward for the night shift for the next week. I'll need two volunteers to go to the clearing station for two weeks so the girls there can wash off the mud. That's you, Thomas, and…." The lieutenant looked around the group. "Thank you, Alice."

At first, Elodie had found the names confusing. Some of the women went by their last names, some by their first, and some by nicknames.

"Frenchie, what was the word on Belgian refugees this morning?" She turned to Elodie who brushed a few crumbs off her fingers, sighing at the inevitable nickname.

"It's been quiet. Anyone who could get out of Belgium has done so, the nursing sister says. They are planning to turn operations over to the Red Cross in a few weeks."

"Excellent. All right, any other news? No? Then finish up and head back to the wards. Elodie, would you stay just a moment?"

"Of course." Elodie agreed immediately. As the women finished their tea and headed downstairs, gossiping about their letters from home, Elodie picked up the mugs and muffin basket, getting them ready to take to the kitchen.

"How is the new housekeeper doing?"

"Mila? She knows more than I did when I started. Her English is coming on a treat, too."

"Will she be ready when the convalescent home opens?"

"She should be."

"Good. Then I'd like you to start filling in on other jobs as they come up. Sergeant Mason says your first aid skills are improving, at least for your human patients. You've always done well with the horses." She smiled at Elodie's eager expression. "The more you know, the more useful you can be, and it will be good for Mila to practice running this place for a time."

"Thank you, Lieutenant. I'll take the dishes to the kitchen and tell Mila." Elodie hurried down the stairs, excited to start on this next phase, even if it was just for a little while.

There had been so much to learn. If Elodie had imagined herself as a lady with a lamp drifting through the hospital, the reality was that all the FANYs took turns to ensure the wards and aid stations functioned properly. On any given day, she could cross the motor yard to find at least one FANY with a wrench or a tire pump working away on the vehicles or chopping wood or doing what they could to spread the hospital's burden. There was even a rumor that someone had put a bath house on a truck bed and FANYs were to drive it to the clearing stations so that the men in the trenches could clean more regularly.

The workmen for the promised X-ray room arrived on the coldest day of the year. They were grizzled old men, too old for military service, whom Madame Curie had trained to her exacting specifications. Elodie found them gruff and unfriendly, but they set to work almost immediately, and, for a time, the wounded put up with feet stomping above them and the sounds of tools being vigorously wielded. They were surprisingly quick in altering the upstairs room.

Elodie crept up after the men had gone for the day. There was just enough daylight to see the changes they had wrought. The former classroom was now divided into two. The larger main room still had windows and a chalkboard hung on the wall, while the smaller room was completely dark. There was a long table and they had somehow run a water pipe up from the kitchen. Elodie touched the tap, happy to find that it was dry and not leaking on patients below. There was nothing else to see. The magic would come with the X-ray machine.

A week later, vehicles rattling into the courtyard brought every FANY on duty to the hospital's front door, expecting to see ambulances bringing a new batch of wounded. Instead, it was a truck with its load carefully tarpaulined against the weather and a small blue van with *Service Radiologique* painted on the sides.

"It's the X-ray machine," one of the FANYs breathed in excitement. They had heard that Marie Curie sometimes came to hospitals herself, and the women hoped for the first glimpse of this remarkable scientist. Instead, a young woman climbed down from the front seat and looked around. She was small and dressed in a dark brown duster which the wind blew back to reveal a long white dress, almost like a nun's habit. Her white veil extended to her shoulders and dark hair peeked out from beneath it, framing a small face undeniably younger than the FANYs. There was a sigh of disappointment from the waiting crowd. Instead of coming herself, the great woman had sent her daughter.

Briskly, the young woman crossed to the front door, followed by three men, two from her vehicle and the lorry driver. Elodie shooed the FANYs away and smiled down at the girl on her doorstep.

"Good morning. I am Irène Curie. I've brought your X-ray equipment." Her English was flawless.

"Welcome to Lamarcq. I'm Elodie Fabien, the housekeeper. Please come in. Captain Wollert should be down any minute." Elodie stepped back, letting in the arrivals. Any wounded men who could, sat up in their beds to see what excitement might brighten their dull days. Captain Wollert hurried down the stairs, greeting their visitor with only the faintest start of surprise at her youth.

"Welcome, Miss Curie. Your men have the facility ready for your inspection. Miss Fabien can help with whatever you need while you are here."

"Thank you, Captain. Miss Fabien, if you would be so kind as to show me the location?" Irène said, almost shyly.

"Up here." Elodie gestured and led Miss Curie to the remodeled room. She waited while Irène inspected it carefully, even going so far as to close herself in the darkroom while Elodie turned on the lights outside the door. Elodie felt a bit intimidated. This girl was only seventeen but carried herself with absolute confidence. She tried to remember what she had been doing at seventeen and made a face. It had been just over two years ago, but those days had faded into nothingness. She was very certain that seventeen had involved horses and not much else.

When Irène had pronounced the room good, the men wrestled crates and boxes up the stairs and she supervised the unpacking of all the bits and pieces that would become the X-ray machine and the darkroom. The Belgian doctor and his nurses stopped by several times, clearly excited by this new marvel. Elodie watched the assembly process curiously, finally excusing herself.

"I'll be downstairs in the kitchen. Serving lunch to the patients takes every hand," Elodie told

Irène, who waved her off, busy fine-tuning something on the X-ray apparatus.

Toward the end of the day, Irène, looking pleased, came down the stairs and pronounced the installation a success.

"My men will stay in town but do you have anywhere appropriate for me?" she asked.

"We can put you up in the FANY house. It's a short walk from here," Elodie offered.

"I need to be close to my machine, in case wounded come in while I am training your doctors," Irène said. Elodie smiled at her.

"We haven't much room here. I can have a bed set up in the other building. It is the typhoid wing but Mila, the other housekeeper, sleeps there. You won't catch typhoid if you stay away from the sick."

"Nothing closer?"

"I can move a bed into my room for you? It's the only private space we've got. It will be a bit tight, but you'll be just down the hall from here. And it is warm."

"That seems like the best choice, but I do hate to crowd you."

"I don't mind. You could sleep in the room with the male orderlies, but they snore. Sometimes quite loudly."

"Oh, dear. In that case, I will take you up on your offer." The two women grinned at each other.

"I'll move a bed in," Elodie said.

With two beds in Elodie's tiny room, the space was tight but neither minded for the short time Irène would be there.

"What is it like? Being your mother's daughter?" Elodie asked as they lay in their beds the first night. The room was dark, and no light shone from the nearby buildings. There was too much danger of an airplane or a Zeppelin targeting a stray light.

"It can be difficult, and she pushes me. Do you know I used to have a tutor all the time, even when we were on holiday? But I do love science. And I love working with my mother. I think my little sister Eve gets away with a lot. She's refused a tutor."

Elodie laughed. "My little brother Theo is the same. I would love to learn more. I want to go to the Sorbonne."

"When this is over, perhaps you will. I'll be there. We can meet over coffee." The conversation trailed off as the two women fell asleep, Elodie dreaming of university.

Within three weeks, Irène pronounced the training complete. She and Elodie kissed cheeks and promised to meet in Paris, then she was gone, on to the next hospital.

"Elodie? Elodie?" Mila's voice drifted down the hall where Elodie was folding freshly dried sheets for the typhoid ward.

"In here," she called back.

"Ah, *bien*, Captain Wollert is…" she started in French. Elodie frowned at her.

"English, please."

"*Mierenneuker*," Mila sighed. "Captain Wollert for you is looking. A message from the Belgian command she has."

"Thank you. And what does *mierenneuker* mean?" Elodie asked. Mila blushed.

"It means to pick at the things that live in hair. *La petite bête.*"

"Ugh. Can you finish folding these sheets? I'll go see what the captain wants."

Elodie crossed the courtyard and hurried up the steps to Wollert's office.

"Ah, Mila found you." Captain Wollert looked up from a report she was writing. "The Belgians are moving some German prisoners to Guines and have asked for a driver. We are expecting wounded, so I'd like you to do the transfer. The Belgians have a guard to go with you." Elodie did not even wonder at the request. The Belgians used FANYs for the oddest of tasks.

"Of course, Captain. I was going to hunt *moutons de poussière,* the slut's wool as Lottie calls them. I'd rather go for a drive."

"I prefer the term 'dust bunnies'," Captain Wollert laughed. "Thank you, Elodie. They will be waiting at the *Gare Centrale.*"

Elodie located one of the ambulances which had begun life as a delivery van and started it, puttering through the gate and toward the train station. Guines was not far away, only about ten miles, and it was a decent day for a drive.

She stopped in front of the station and guards herded out six men dressed in light blue trousers and off-green jackets. They shuffled awkwardly in their ankle chains and manacles, their shoes much the worse for wear. Their heads had been shaved and were now covered with wool caps. Elodie put the van out of gear and picked up the wheel chocks before stepping out. She shoved the chocks onto one wheel either side before moving around to open the rear doors. As the men climbed in, they looked at her curiously. As the last one approached, Elodie drew a sharp breath.

"Lothar," she whispered. The man turned toward her, his blue eyes almost too large in his pale face. The last time she had seen Grete Rohr's oldest child had been three years ago. He had been starting his first year at the *Kriegsakademie* and he had kissed her behind the barn. Inwardly, she shuddered. She had never really liked Lothar, but now he seemed pitiable. Then he was aboard the van. One guard clambered up and she closed the doors on her unhappy passengers. The other guard followed her to the front where he would ride with her, eyeing her suspiciously.

"You are known to that one?" he asked.

"Oldest son of my mother's dearest friend."

"You have feelings for him?"

"No. And if you mean 'will I help him escape,' then no. I am French." Elodie tossed her head. "He is my enemy."

"Good."

The drive to Guines was uneventful and silent. The prisoner-of-war camp held thousands of men behind barbed wire fences. Guards in the towers watched the van as it drove up. The Belgian soldier spoke with the French prison guard, who cleared them through the first set of fences. Here they unloaded their cargo, Lothar stepping out first and blinking in the bright sunlight.

"Tell my mother where I am," he pleaded softly.

"If I can, I will," Elodie answered as he was led away, vanishing into the crowd of shaven-headed men. Elodie and the guards made the short drive back to Calais in silence.

Elodie dropped the men off at the Belgian headquarters, wondering if she should write her mother about Lothar. But her mother could not write Grete. Espionage was rampant in France and sending a letter to Germany could create more trouble for her family than it was worth. Perhaps the prison would let the prisoners send letters.

The wheel of her ambulance jerked hard as she

turned into the courtyard, almost sending her into the gate post. Elodie groaned. A flat. Tires tended to blow at the worst possible moments and today's cold weather was no exception. The only difference was that they were not on the side of the road, collecting comments from passing soldiers as the FANYs struggled in mud changing a tire. The car limped to its parking place and Elodie went to find the mechanic who helped keep the ambulances on the road. Guillaume had refused to teach her to change a tire and she had only watched FANYs complete the task.

The red-headed mechanic was taking tea in the kitchen, practicing very bad French on the cook. He grinned at Elodie's request and drank down his tin.

"You've not learned yet?" He spoke English, but his accent was heavy and Elodie had to listen hard to understand him.

"No."

"Ach then, I'll be teaching you. Come along." He led the way to the ambulance.

"First, Miss, you chock the wheels. Then take this jack and put it here." Elodie followed his directions, occasionally stopping to blow on her cold fingers. Eventually, the wooden-spoked tire lay at her feet. The mechanic pulled out what had caused the flat.

"Horseshoe nail." He dropped it into her hand. Elodie turned it over and put it in her pocket. At the mechanic's direction, she worked the rubber tire off the wheel.

"Excuse me, young man," a very British voice behind her made Elodie start. She looked up and the newcomer huffed a laugh. "I beg your pardon, Miss. I'm looking for the FANY in charge."

"That would be Captain Wollert. Ask the first FANY you see in the hospital; she'll tell you where the captain is." Elodie pointed toward the building. "She's usually around the wards at this time of day." The man looked curiously at her.

"A French FANY?"

"I am not an official FANY. I joined them in Le Havre."

"An ally is always welcome. Good day, Miss." He nodded to Elodie and the mechanic and walked toward the building.

"Yon man is a doctor. Wonder what he is doing here." The mechanic wiped his hands on a rag. "Now, put the disc over the hole with the cap here and screw it all together." Elodie complied and then wrestled with the air pump. When the ambulance sat on four full tires again, the mechanic sent Elodie to clean up and have something warm to drink. She went inside to hang up her overcoat and then headed to the kitchen.

"Elodie, up here. I've news for you." Lottie leaned over the second-floor banister to hiss at her friend. Elodie dutifully went up the stairs to the break room. She could find something warm to drink there as easily as she could in the kitchen. Lottie grinned at her. "You've grease all over your face."

"Just wait until it's your turn," Elodie said with a smile, scrubbing at the offending spot. "What news?"

"The nursing sisters at the BEF hospital at Béthune outside Neuve Chappelle want some FANYs to help with the nursing. The Brass Hats have finally agreed to try us out. I'm to pick six girls to go. Are you interested?"

"Of course. If Captain Wollert agrees." Elodie poured hot water into a tea pot.

"I've already asked. We are to pack up and drive over tomorrow morning."

Elodie gripped the pot in excitement, making the china rattle. "Thank you for asking me."

"Of course. Plus, you can terrorize the washing women in Béthune as easily as you can here," Lottie winked at her, and Elodie laughed.

In the morning, Lottie looked over her new charges. Elodie, Timmy, Charlie, Sally, Lizzie and Dora sat on Jezebel's running board or fenders, their eyes bright and eager. FANYs were known for being independent, but this group was exceptionally creative and keen.

"Mount up, girls. We've a way to go." Lottie called out, and the women rushed to their respective cars. Each vehicle grumbled to life, coughing in the cold air, and soon the convoy headed west toward Béthune, a small town not far from the Ypres Salient.

Along the way, they stopped at a café for lunch. It was rough-looking, but some enterprising person had created cold-frame greenhouses out of old windows. The leafy greens growing within drew the women's attention immediately. Even though the offerings were slim, hot-house lettuce over tinned meat brought all the women, except Elodie and Sally, to ecstatic rapture. Elodie wrinkled her nose. Lettuce was not her favorite food, and she thought wistfully that hot-house tomatoes would have been perfect.

After lunch, they drove on, occasionally feeling more than hearing the thud of artillery through the ground. The Battle of Neuve Chappelle was winding down, but casualties had been high. A harried nursing sister met them at the hospital.

"I am glad to see you, we've need of girls with your skills. There is an old house for you not far from here. The Frenchies were supposed to patch up all the holes and we cobbled together some furniture. We've also had a huge shipment of woolens and need to get those out. Two of you are to go to the first aid station tonight. The replacement doctor for the clearing station will guide you in. The rest of you I leave you to your leader's discretion for today." She gave them directions to the house and hurried off. Elodie turned to Lottie, who was looking rather green and sweating heavily. A quick glance around showed that four others were looking ill. Only Sally was not looking as if her stomach wished to be somewhere else.

"What's wrong?" Elodie asked.

"I feel awful," Lottie groaned. "I don't think I can go..." She turned suddenly and rushed into an alley, where she was gloriously and violently sick. The other four rushed after her.

"Oh dear. I think we may be in a bit of a sticky situation," Sally said, her voice grim. Eventually, the five returned, leaning heavily on any stationary object that would support them.

"Sally, you'll have to go to the trenches. And Elodie. I'm sorry, you'll have to go too," Lottie managed and then vanished into the alley again. When she reappeared, Sally and Elodie helped the women down the street to their house.

They stopped outside in consternation. It was a plastered stone building that had stood second from the end of a row of connected structures. The endmost building was gone, a pile of rubble all that remained. Its neighbor, their appointed home, might have withstood the shelling but it sagged drunkenly. Shutters had been secured but hung at an angle. It still had two stories, but the second floor had lost all its windows, the empty spaces now boarded up. The roof was no longer shingled and looked as if someone had spread sail cloth over it, tacking it down with spare lumber. Elodie and Sally stared at each other in dismay until someone groaned.

Two steps led up from the street and Sally went first, pushing at the door. It swung open at the slightest touch and then refused to close. They helped the sick women in and settled them in rickety chairs near the entrance.

Elodie and Sally explored the dimly lit interior. To their right was a kitchen, the wood oven and stovetop liberally coated with dust. A table, one leg replaced with a wooden plank, held a selection of cookware, obviously scavenged from other homes.

Across from the kitchen was a sitting room filled with wooden shipping boxes and some worn cushions. A short hallway led to two bedrooms where seven mattresses were piled against one wall. At the end of the hallway, the stairs to the second floor were gone and the ceiling above was full of holes. Sally dusted off her hands.

"Home sweet home. I'll wrestle mattresses into place and get the sickies into bed if you want to find some supper. And maybe some cleaning supplies." Sally gingerly opened one shutter to let in the light. It creaked and sagged ominously. Elodie sighed, thinking of her comfortable if slightly claustrophobic room in Calais, and made her way back out into the street.

By dusk, they had the house almost set to rights. Lottie and the other women were tucked into beds and left to fight off whatever was making them sick. Elodie had found easy-to-prepare food and then transferred their belongings out of Jezebel.

"Are you awake, Lottie?" Elodie went into the

bedroom to check on their leader.

"Over here," the weak voice directed her to the left of the door. Elodie held up a lantern, shaded to its dimmest light.

"Sally and I are ready to go. There is tea and bread in the kitchen and our next-door neighbor will check on you in the morning," Elodie whispered. Lottie raised herself up, peering around.

"Buckingham Palace this isn't. Ready for the trenches?"

"I think so," Elodie answered. Sally came into the room, pulling on her great coat.

"I'll take care of you," Sally assured Elodie. To Lottie, she said, "Elodie found provisions."

"Well done. I am sorry."

"Not to worry. Let's go, Elodie," Sally said softly. The two left, walking to the hospital where an orderly was stuffing woolens into a lorry. Eventually, a nurse came to find them, accompanied by a tall man in the British Expeditionary Force uniform. His appearance seemed to be a signal, as the lorry chugged to life.

"Sister, the other five FANYs seem to have food poisoning. We've left them at our lodgings, but can you check in on them?" Sally said briskly. The nurse looked annoyed.

"Very well, although the last thing I need is more patients. This is Doctor Delacourt. He'll be escorting you."

"I'm Sally Baker and this is Elodie Fabien. I'm a FANY and Elodie is a French volunteer we couldn't do without. This is her first time in the trenches, but we've done our best to bring her up to speed," Sally said. Elodie smiled shyly at the doctor who had mistaken her for a man back in Calais.

"A pleasure," he said shortly. "We need to go. Hop in." The two women clambered into the back of the lorry, finding places to sit. Elodie pulled off her gloves to feel rough wooden boxes under her fingers: medical supplies for the first aid station.

"Over here, Elodie. The woolens are a softer seat," Sally whispered and Elodie eased down beside her.

The lorry rattled over the rough roads, halting occasionally for an exchange of passwords with sentries along the way. Eventually, it stopped for good, and men came around to open the back. The women stepped into the cold, seeing soldiers in rough uniforms huddled around. Each one came forward to take some of the supplies, leaving the bags containing woolen goods for Elodie and Sally to carry.

"The casualty station is two streets back that way," Dr. Delacourt whispered to them. "It's still in range of the Huns, but it is a decent building. Now, we'll head to the trenches as soon as it is fully dark. I'll go first, followed by one of you and then the other. Keep twenty paces apart. It's hard to tell how close you are but it keeps down the deaths if we get shelled." Elodie gulped. Delacourt looked at her sharply but went on.

"Keep low and don't say a word. Not even a squeak. If you see a flare or the Germans set haystacks on fire, fall flat and stay down until I tell you to move. Be absolutely still. The bloody Jerries shell anything that twitches. Once we are in the trenches, I will take you to the first aid station. Do you have everything?" Dr. Delacourt peered through the dim light at Elodie and Sally.

"We do." Sally patted the bags draped around her. Elodie shifted hers into a more comfortable position. The donated socks, scarves, and mittens might not seem as important as the medical supplies, but these small comforts meant the world to the men. Slowly, full dark settled in, and the doctor squeezed Sally's hand. He started into the inky blackness. Sally followed.

Elodie looked back at the town, lights flickering in one or two windows, and then turned after Sally. Every few minutes, artillery fired off rounds that exploded in brilliant light over the German lines. Elodie kept her eyes down, trying to keep what night vision she could. During one of the quiet moments between shelling, there was a delicate pop high in the sky and brilliant light poured over them. Elodie dropped flat, the bags of woolen goods cushioning her fall. As the light from the Very Light flare faded, there was a volley of rifle fire and the rattle of a machine gun. The artillery resumed its deep barking. Under her, the ground trembled at each explosion.

Delacourt rose to his feet and started on, glancing back once to check on his charges who followed silently. A shadow materialized out of the dark and Elodie caught her breath. The shadow and the doctor stood for a second and then the doctor moved on. The shadow resolved itself into a man in a very muddy British uniform. He nodded to Elodie as she passed, his eyes catching the light from the artillery.

Elodie walked on and on, feeling the strain in her legs and stiffness in her back and neck from moving partially crouched over. The smell of the trenches met her long before they could see the great black lines that snaked off toward the sea to the west and the Swiss Alps to the south.

"Kneel down and wait," the doctor whispered. She and Sally complied as he vanished into the trench that led down to the main trench line. Moments later, someone touched Elodie's shoulder, and the two women followed their guide. This first trench ran from the main line to the rear, providing a marginally safe exit and entrance to the system.

The trenches were not straight lines, rather they zigzagged every few yards to prevent bullets from traveling the entire length. The outpost trench faced the enemy directly, and here the men served a week of front-line duty. From this line, lonely trenches reached into No-Man's-Land, acting as listening posts or access for sappers who crept out to plant mines. The support trench was second, home to the reserve troops, and the trench furthest back held the first aid station, ammo dumps, and places for additional troops, and sometimes a kitchen. Between each main trench were communication trenches. It seemed like a simple layout on paper, but over time it became a bewildering maze.

As Elodie followed Sally into the system, they walked on wooden planks called duckboards, keeping them somewhat above the mud. The doctor turned down the first alley where tiny flickers of light glowed from the walls.

Sally bent down in front of a cloth-covered dug-out and said very quietly, "Would you gents like new socks or gloves?" She pushed aside the cloth and three very surprised soldiers looked up from piled straw. As Elodie pulled out woolen items, dirty hands shot forward, taking them with pleasure.

"Thank you, Miss. God bless."

"It's been months since I've had new socks. Thank you, Miss."

Elodie backed away from the dug-out, eyes stinging from more than the smell. She heartily wished she had more to give these men. Word of their coming seemed to filter through the ground, and as they turned into one of the zigzags, men waited outside their dug-outs. At the end of the trench was the first aid station.

"Dr. Elliott, this is Miss Baker and Miss Fabien." Dr. Delacourt introduced the women to the doctor who was collapsed on a rough table. "They are the FANYs who are here to help with first aid per the Brass Hats."

The exhausted man sat up with a curse. "Damn it, Del, I told you. Send me nurses if you have to. I'd rather have shirkers than these… women."

"They won't send the nurses down here. The girls are fully trained as orderlies, and they've been running a Belgian hospital in Calais. They've done trench duty already. At least give them a try," Delacourt said in a reasonable tone, but Elodie could hear stress and anger underneath his words. The other man glared at him. "They are here for two weeks. After that, you can refuse, and I'll send the whole lot back to the Belgians."

"Oh God. Do they speak English?"

"Elliott, these are volunteers from England. Of course they speak English."

"Fine. Two weeks."

"We'll take the wounded out with us. How many do you have?"

"Six."

"I'll find some stretcher-bearers. Girls, it has been a pleasure." Delacourt ducked out of the first aid station, leaving his charges to the mercies of Dr. Elliott.

Elodie took in the wooden sidings and canvas roof that was braced up with wired-together boards. Lanterns were strung across trusses that held up the roof, shedding a fitful light. Boxes of medical supplies were haphazardly piled in one corner, while wooden crates set up like shelves held other equipment. Big cans filled with water stood near a wood-burning stove and along the farthest wall, Elodie made out six blanket-covered forms – the men awaiting transport to the casualty station.

"We've woolens to hand out to the men. If you will allow, Dr. Elliott, we'll take care of that and then be back to help here," Sally said. The doctor waved his hand at her, gesturing them out of the dug-out. They ducked down and stepped back outside.

"Well, that was certainly rather terse," Sally whispered. "Set back the bags of socks. We'll need those for the trench foot later."

They started down the trench away from the first aid station. "Keep your head down. Don't peek over or hold a hand up above the trench wall. The Heinies mount snipers and they'll shoot anything they see."

The two women balanced carefully on the boards that lined the communication trench and then turned right into the next alley. This one was lined with sandbags and holes dug into the walls. Sally peered carefully into each hole, taking the woolen scarves and mittens that Elodie handed to her. As they inched along the boards, Elodie peered down at a black object in the filthy water, horrified to see it swimming through the mud. She squeaked and then bit down on the sound. It climbed onto pieces of a wood box and glared at her. Elodie backed up a step.

"It's all right, Miss." A deep voice in her ear made her jump. She turned around on the plank and almost lost her balance, flailing and unable to decide whether to drop the precious woolens or save herself. The man's hand shot out, catching and steadying her. The tall officer smiled, his green eyes almost laughing. His dark mustache drooped down to his chin and bristled cheerfully.

"Is that… is that a rat?" Her voice shook.

"I'm afraid so. We've got rather a lot of them here. Some of the men even have them as pets. Can't stand the things myself."

"Oh."

"You aren't English, are you?"

"No, I'm French. I work with the FANYs."

Behind them, the British artillery opened fire and the two stood in silence as the cacophony screamed overhead. Elodie ducked reflexively.

"That won't help. You don't hear the ones that hit you." He leaned over to yell in her ear.

"*Mon Dieu.*"

"What are you doing here?"

"Working at the first aid station."

"That should improve morale. Here, your

friend is waiting for you." He let go of her arm and stepped back. "Thank you for this." He gestured at her bags, now less than half full. Elodie smiled and nodded.

"Goodbye." She turned away and walked carefully to where Sally was waiting. At the zig, she looked back to see the British officer watching her. By the time they had walked less than halfway down the furthest trench, they were out of woolens. The disappointment in the faces beyond made Elodie want to cry.

The two women walked carefully back to the first aid station and entered it to find the wounded men gone and the doctor asleep on a cot.

"Let's get the boxes emptied and make some sense of the shelves," Sally whispered, and Elodie nodded. It was a testament to how tired the doctor was that the sound of them moving about failed to wake him.

Eventually, Doctor Elliott sat bolt upright with a muffled curse. He glanced around the first aid station. The two women watched him warily until he grunted with approval.

"Have you eaten?" he growled.

"No, sir," Sally answered. He grunted again.

"There are two Tommy cookers and some tins of Maconochie's stew on the shelf behind me. Make yourselves some breakfast. We'll be having patients as soon as roll call is over."

Sally scrabbled for the items, handing a cooker and a yellow tin embellished with "Maconochie Military Rations" to Elodie. After a few more moments, she had a cast-iron can opener and a box of matches. Elodie set to opening the tin, stabbing the tip of the can opener into it and sawing until the lid peeled back. Both the lid and can were now jagged-edged, and she handled them carefully. Sally lit the Tommy cooker and guarded the sluggish white flame. Elodie poked in dismay at the tin's contents, where broth had set into a gooey gelatin. Random root vegetables and white beans studded the gel beside the dark brown lumps of what she assumed was beef.

"If you can get it at least warm, it is tolerable. My brother, he's a Tommy, said to never eat it cold," Sally said. Elodie grimaced at her. Eventually, the inefficient white flame heated the gelatin enough that it melted.

As Doctor Elliott promised, there was a steady stream of men coming through the first aid station. Medical care in the trenches was rudimentary. Each man carried a first aid kit filled with bandages, a tourniquet, iodine, fainting salts, and gauze soaked with mercurous chloride to clean wounds. They tended their own injuries and those of their comrades. Men needing more treatment came to the first aid station.

Most of the men reporting were in some stage of trench foot and the women quickly had each man seated with his feet in warm water from the stove, while the men waterproofed boots with whale oil that smelled of fish.

"Dry your feet," Sally ordered briskly. "Make sure you get a good coating of whale oil between the toes. Now, Elodie, hand out two sets of socks to each man. And you lot," Sally glared fiercely at the men, "change your socks three times a day and make sure you always have a dry pair." The soldiers laughed and chattered among themselves as Elodie handed out socks and tins of oil. Staying dry was an ongoing challenge. As they worked, Doctor Elliott handled the cases of typhoid and trench fever as well as wounds on the verge of going septic.

When the day was over and the line of men trickled to nothing, Doctor Elliott sent Elodie and Sally to get some rest, promising to alert them if he needed help.

The two found a nearby unoccupied dug-out and moved in, setting up their few belongings. Someone had draped a ragged French uniform coat over the entrance, the bright red faded to a bloody gray. Elodie knelt on straw that would serve as a bed for the next two weeks. Their new home was dark and dank.

"My room at home overlooks the horse pasture," she said softly.

"Mine has a sitting room attached." Sally stretched out both arms to touch the sides of the hole.

"Maybe we can borrow a spoon and dig out a sitting room?" Elodie suggested. The two women rolled up in their individual blankets and slowly fell asleep to the barely muffled boom of artillery and rattle of machine guns.

Without a formal battle going on, the days fell into a routine. The Germans shelled the British trenches at semi-regular hours; the British artillery answered back. Then there would be a period of calm, broken by gunfire as each side sniped at the other. Both sides would take a short break, then the booming would begin again.

In between times, men arrived at the first aid station to seek out treatment. As word got around that there were two women in the first aid station, the men came to look, their eyes diffident or hungry or lonely. Most just stayed long enough to be checked over, but some had to be ordered off by their superiors.

When Elodie or Sally had to go to the latrines, they went together. Latrines were merely a hole dug into the ground with a cover of cloth. Often, there was lime to sprinkle over their waste, but the stench was terrible, and it drifted downwind, adding to the miasma of the trenches. When it threatened to overflow, that dug-out was collapsed and another was built. The occasional unlucky artillery shell might land on a latrine, blowing the contents over a wide area. It was no wonder that typhoid and dysentery stalked the confined soldiers as effectively as the German bullets.

Elodie and Sally had brought one change of clothing and, after a week, both sets were filthy, bloody, and stiff with mud. Like the men in the trenches, they eventually stopped trying to stay clean and only their hands got regular washings as they assisted in the first aid tent.

The soldiers generally spent two weeks at a time in the trenches. Most nights, there was a constant flow of men creeping across the fields towards supply stations and villages behind the lines, as the wounded were evacuated and returning soldiers brought food, water, medical supplies, and woolens from the hospital stores. These woolens resulted in the one bright spot of the entire day for Elodie and Sally - handing out socks, mittens, and scarves to the mud-encased, hollow-eyed men deep in the trenches.

As they ventured into the outpost trench for the first time, Elodie was appalled to discover that conditions for the soldiers were even worse than in the rear trenches. The men stood watch, peering out over the trench walls through barbed wire barriers. The duckboards that were supposed to keep them out of the mud barely functioned and sludge and filth slopped over. Used ammo cases and makeshift wooden benches were all they had to try to keep their feet out of the quagmire, but there were not enough to go around.

Periodically, there were dug-outs reinforced with sandbags, serving as quarters and places to get warm. The officers' dug-outs were larger and better fortified, as they served as both communication centers and bed space.

Elodie glanced into one to see men clustered over maps spread on tables, tin cups filled with tea and several blanketed shapes on cots who slept on despite the noise inside and outside the dug-out. One of the officers looked up to see who had pulled aside the door covering. His eyes lit up above his mustache.

"If it isn't our French FANY. Welcome to the neighborhood," he said, and the other men looked around. Elodie smiled at the officer who had greeted her the first night in the trench.

"We have scarves and mittens. Would any of you like some?" Elodie asked shyly.

"No. Save those for the enlisted," he answered and glanced around. "Gentlemen, if you would excuse me for a moment." There was a mutter of agreement as the officer walked over to the two women. "Where have you come from?"

"We entered at Piccadilly and are walking north toward the end. Then I suppose we'll go back along the second trench to London Lane and head for the first aid station." Sally told him, using the soldiers' names for the communications trenches.

"Beyond here are only the sapper trenches," the officer told them. "Have you seen No-Man's-Land yet? No? I'll take you to the nearest hyposcope and you can get a look at our enemies." He led the way down the outpost trench, waiting as the two women handed out woolens. Finally, they turned east, down a narrow alley that led directly toward the German trenches only four hundred yards away. At the end, three men stood watch, one soldier at a machine gun emplacement that looked out over No-Man's-Land.

"Keep your voices down," the officer whispered. Elodie and Sally nodded, their eyes wide with apprehension. The man in the machine gun post gratefully accepted the woolens without glancing at the women; his eyes scanned the enemy lines continually.

"Put up the 'scope if you would," the officer whispered. One of the men lifted a metal tube painted a drab green over the edge of the trench. It was about three feet long with openings on opposite sides of each end. Elodie bent to put her eyes to the lowest opening and gasped as she saw the wide expanse of churned mud and blast pits left from exploding artillery. Barbed wire created a hazy series of lines across her vision. Someone on the German side fired and she saw the flash from the muzzle. There was a volley of shots from both sides and then the firing stopped. She stepped back, letting Sally peer into the hyposcope. Elodie looked up at the officer, who smiled.

"I'll take you back now. Don't want to be out here too long. Jerry gets trigger-happy." There were *sotto voce* thanks for the woolens as the women followed the officer out. At his dug-out, he looked down at them.

"Thank you. This might sound as if I'm mad, but seeing you makes me remember what I am fighting for. Can you find your way back?"

"Yes. Thank you for showing us No-Man's-Land." Elodie said softly. The man waved and then went into his muddy home. The women made their tortuous return to the first aid station.

At the end of their second week, Sally and Elodie, clutching their filthy belongings, crouched at the end of the access trench where it exited into France. Doctor Elliott was with them as he was rotating out of the trenches. Behind them, wounded men and stretcher-bearers waited silently for darkness to fall.

"I almost don't want to leave," Elodie whispered to Sally.

"I know. It's so awful here but we did such good," the other woman whispered back.

"I badly want a wash."

"And clean clothes. I hope they get that bath wagon going soon."

Before long there were soft calls of challenge and recognition and then a man with the caduceus of a doctor on his collars slipped into the trench. Elliott greeted him gratefully. Lottie and Dora climbed down behind him. Elodie and Sally gave them quick hugs.

"How is it?" Lottie asked.

"It's horrid. We've left you a dug-out. It's twenty feet from the first aid station and has a French uniform coat as a door," Sally whispered back.

"Let's go, girls," Elliott hissed, and led the way out in front of the stretcher-bearers. The reverse trip was almost as nerve-racking as the walk in, but the promise of a bath and clean clothing made it bearable.

A Very Light exploded overhead, illuminating the ground. Elodie dropped, holding very still. In the harsh glare, she made out the forms of cavalry horses tied a distance away. As the light died, the image of the horses was burned on her retinas. An artillery shell screamed overhead and exploded, deafening the terrified people on the ground. Another Very Light lit the scene. Where the horses had been was a crater, one dead animal lying just outside the edges. Elodie felt hot tears spring to her eyes and stifled a moan.

As the light faded, the group was on their feet, moving rapidly toward areas at least nominally out of shelling range. Elodie wiped away tears and could hear Sally sniffling softly. Neither dared to let out a sound because any noise could call in artillery.

An hour later, they reached waiting ambulances and were ushered into the front seat as the wounded were loaded into the back. Doctor Elliott leaned into the cab.

"You've been absolute ducks to work with. I'll put in a good word for you, and I hope I get you with me in the trenches. Or in the hospital," he said softly. Then the driver climbed in beside them and they pulled away, heading for Béthune.

Bathed and with a good day of sleep under their belts, Elodie and Sally were ready to take up their duties. Timmy and Charlie were working the day shifts at the hospital with Lizzie working nights. Sally immediately volunteered to join her. Elodie sighed. Life in the trenches had given her a feeling of usefulness, but now she was back to making certain that sheets were washed, and food was gathered.

"Lottie left this for you." Timmy, on her way to her shift, handed Elodie a note scrawled on the back of parcel paper. Elodie looked at it. She could read printed English from books, but handwriting was far more difficult for her, especially the copperplate that Lottie used.

"Can you read this for me? I don't read handwritten English very well," she asked Timmy, who looked at her in surprise but took the note.

"'Elodie, there is a convalescent hospital in Drouvin-le-Marais. Head there to get some ideas for our convalescent home. I've cleared it with Matron at the hospital and she'll put you on one of the ambulances. Be back in two weeks – I need you to go into the trenches again. Lottie.'"

"Oh, my, thank you. Shall I find some provender before I go?"

"Lottie scared some up and we've been able to draw a bit on the hospital stores. You'll find Matron in her office for elevenses," Timmy told her.

Elodie folded up her change of clothing and

shoved it in a small bag before walking to the hospital.

Very quickly, she found herself in the front seat of an ambulance heading for the small town of Drouvin-le-Marais, a mere three miles away. Those three miles made all the difference between Béthune on the edge of the war and the peaceful village where cattle grazed on winter sere grass. The buildings here stood without gaping holes in the roofs or blown-out windows.

The convalescent home was a former inn leased by the BEF. Elodie knocked on the front door and was met by a very young orderly.

"The matron at the Béthune Hospital sent me. I am to help out your housekeeper," she said, and the young man stepped back, letting her into a building crammed full of beds. Each bed had a man resting on it, and further back she could see and hear a raucous card game. The men were in varying stages of recovery, but all were returning to the front lines for more service. Those who would never serve again were shipped directly to England, where they might stay in a convalescent home for the foreseeable future or be discharged to a world embarrassed by their injuries.

Every eye turned to look at her and Elodie blushed as she hurried after the orderly. In short order, she had been turned over to the housekeeper and followed the woman around, wondering at the very strange accent she used. Elodie could barely understand her, although it was English that she was speaking.

That night she wrote to her family.

March 1915

Somewhere in France

Dearest Maman, Papa, Grand-mère, and Theo.

I hope this letter finds you well. I am presently working at a convalescent home. I can't tell you where for security reasons, but it is British. I have been sent here to learn how a convalescent home operates so that when I return to Calais, we can start our own.

It's very interesting. The biggest difference is in what the men do. First, they get much heartier food so that they are ready to return to the trenches. As they eat, I can only think of pigs being fattened before they're sent to slaughter. Sometimes I just want to cry because of it. The British serve gallons of tea. Possibly the only way to end the British Empire is to take away their tea! I think they would all perish.

The men who are ready to be discharged are taken on long walks every day while the newcomers go on shorter ones. This allows time for the orderlies to clean the wards. Since the men are mostly healthy, there is far less laundry.

I watched patients do exercises designed to make the men stronger. Sometimes, the men have limbs straightened or bent or have to pick up small objects. Do you remember when Old Jacques broke his arm, and his fingers wouldn't straighten? I wonder if these exercises might have helped him. It is fascinating. I have a notebook that is full of ideas, and I am eager to return to Calais to share them.

I'm not certain when I will be in Calais again, but your letters will be brought to me here, so please write. I miss you all so much.

With much love,

Elodie

"Have you been to a meningitis ward?" the housekeeper asked. Elodie shook her head. "These are all exercises developed by Sister Kenny. We've adapted them for our wounded."

"Who is Sister Kenny?" Elodie asked to the housekeeper's shock.

"My word, Miss Fabien. She's practically as famous as Edith Cavell. Sister Kenny is an Australian nurse from my home state of New South Wales. She discovered how to get meningitis victims back on their feet. I served with her on a troop ship. You'll see some real miracles if you are around convalescent homes long enough," the housekeeper said proudly. Elodie looked with new interest at the men having limbs manipulated or lifting weights or moving small objects.

By the end of her two weeks at the convalescent home, Elodie left with plenty of inspiration. The nurses had generously shared their knowledge and the housekeeper invited her back any time she wished, to work with people who spoke 'bloody good English' and not the Frogs, apparently not cluing into Elodie's own accent.

Elodie walked the three miles to Béthune, finding herself thrust back into the immediacy of war with each step. She felt the weight of the conflict grow on her shoulders and her ears rang again with the sound of artillery.

Their little house was quiet, the two nightshift FANYs collapsed into exhausted heaps of bedclothes. Elodie made a quick luncheon and then got ready to go to the trenches. There were woolens to load and notes to write about the convalescent home.

"You're back," Sally's voice startled Elodie, who was deep into recording the final rounds of Kenny exercises. The pen blotted and Elodie cursed. "Good. Lottie says you are going with me to the trenches tonight?" She half stated and half asked. Elodie nodded. "You are a peach to work with. I'll get the woolens loaded."

"Already finished. Sit down and have some tea. It won't be dark for a few hours," Elodie offered. Sally pulled out a rickety chair and poured a tin of tea. Elodie detailed her stay at the convalescent home and explained some of the exercises to Sally's intense interest.

By early evening it was time to go, and the two women made their way to the ambulances, repeating the same nightmare journey of two weeks ago. As they slipped into the access trench, Lottie and Dora were waiting, their faces pale in the moonlight. Elodie embraced her friend, feeling it had been a lifetime since they had first come to Béthune and the trenches.

All around them, wounded men were being carried up and out of the trenches, and soon it was Lottie and Dora's turn to crawl up the ladder, always careful not to show themselves above the skyline. Elodie resolutely went to the first aid station where Doctor Elliott greeted them with pleasure.

As the week went on, the two women again grew used to the sound of shells screaming overhead and the continual gunfire. The noise barely woke them now, so it was a surprise when Elodie sat up in the dark dug-out, listening intently. There was screaming somewhere nearby. Too near.

"Wake up, Sally! Something's wrong." Elodie shook her companion awake. The sound of screaming intensified and was interspersed with explosions. Dirt sifted down from the roof. The sound of the gunfire was different, louder perhaps, and more rapid. Elodie thought it was one of the trench brooms, the rapid-fire shotguns used from the lip of the trenches to kill soldiers trapped like rats .

"Girls! Get up and run. Run for the rear." Dr. Elliott ripped the covering from their dug-out. His voice was harsh with fear. Both women scrambled out.

"Trench raid. Run! You can't be found here."

Terror lent wings to their feet as the two scrambled for the exit trench. Men streamed past them, heading toward the commotion. Elodie pressed herself against the wall as they went by and then ran a broken pattern between groups. At one point, she saw the grim face of the officer who had befriended her. He was driving his troops before him, yelling encouragement. She watched him vanish around a zig-zag as his men raced toward the melee.

As the women fled west, the noise began to die down. They were just at the head of the trench as the sound of machine guns ripped through the dawn.

"Wait," Sally gasped, and they stopped, listening. Trench raids never took very long. Maximum fear, confusion, and casualties were the main goals. "I think it's over." The chaos faded into the normal sounds of gunfire but, over that noise, both could hear the screaming of wounded men.

"We should go back. Dr. Elliott will need us." Elodie forced out the words.

"I am so tired of being afraid," Sally whimpered into her hands, scrubbing away tears. Elodie wrapped her arms around her friend.

"I know. And so tired of being dirty," she whispered. After a few moments, they turned, walking back down into the trenches as if going into the mouth of hell.

Chaos hid organization as the men began to sort themselves out after the brief but bloody skirmish. Bodies were stacked in one trench to wait for an officer to identify them. Eventually, they would be transported toward the rear where they would be buried in a mass grave.

Fit men brought grievously wounded ones to the first aid station while the less injured treated themselves. Someone pushed past Elodie, a blond soldier dragging a man who had been gutted. Elodie felt her stomach turn and swayed on her feet. The man dropped the body and then ducked past her; his face averted. Elodie frowned, looking at the retreating back in puzzlement. There was something familiar about him.

"Sister... Sister, help me." A quivering voice broke her thoughts and a hand tugged at her skirt. Elodie forgot about the soldier as she turned to help the man on the ground at her feet.

Unjacketed bullets, bombs, and machine guns made bloody messes of men. The melee weapons created wounds that Elodie thought were far worse. The men had to be face-to-face to bludgeon each other with sharp-edged shovels, bayonets, and spiked maces, their bodies ripped and torn in gruesome fashion. Dr. Elliott worked tirelessly, bandaging what he could not repair quickly. Both women learned to sew up gaping wounds under Elliott's harsh direction, although Elodie thought she would never get used to the feel of a needle going through flesh.

Slowly, the number of wounded thinned and the ones who needed more medical care lay waiting for darkness to fall so they could be transported to the hospital. Elodie checked on each man, giving sips of water and thin gruel to those who could eat.

Occasionally, she signaled to two men detailed to help and they would carry off the body of a comrade who had died waiting for medical attention. At one end of the trench were the men whose minds had broken from shell shock. The misery emanating from them was so strong that Elodie could barely make herself walk among the crying, shaking figures.

Finally, the longest day in a string of long days came to a close. The men who were leaving for a rest crouched next to the wounded they would carry out. Elodie moved among them, offering what aid she could.

When night came, the men moved out. Elodie stumbled back to the dug-out, crawling inside. She curled up into a ball, crying silently as the day's events whirled in her brain. Two more days of this and then she could escape. But then she would return, voluntarily, knowing what she was walking in to. She began to understand how soldiers felt about returning to the trenches after their brief sojourns behind the front lines.

When the two-week shift came to an end, Elodie, Sally, and Dr. Elliott waited at the exit trench, along with a small group of men who were being relieved. Since there were no wounded, they would carry out dead comrades.

When the replacements flooded in, however, there were no FANYs with them. Elodie and Sally looked for them in vain.

"Do we have to stay?" Sally whispered. Elodie shrugged, feeling tears burn in her eyes. Elliott and his replacement were arguing at the far end of the trench and then the doctor came toward them, his face flushed with anger.

"Come on, girls. We need to make the most of the night."

"But the FANYs?" Sally asked. Elliott shook his head.

"They won't be coming. The Brass Hats think it is too dangerous for women."

"But this is what we train for, to provide care on the battlefield," Sally protested.

"And you've done a fine job. I'll take up the fight for you. But now, we need to go." He stalked off into the darkness and they heard him getting the stretcher-bearers organized. Tears poured down Sally's face.

"I can't believe they are taking this away from us. It's our job. I hate it here. I hate brutality, but this is our calling," Sally choked. Elodie put her arm around her friend and hugged her before leading her out of the trenches. In front of them, the blond soldier glanced covertly back at the two women as he carried a body over his shoulder.

At the hospital, the five other FANYs waited, faces set. Sally and Elodie went to them, and they fell back at the stench coming off their clothing.

"Dr. Elliott said no FANYs are replacing us," Sally said.

"It's too dangerous, or so the Brass Hats say," Lottie answered grimly. "They've been fighting back and forth since the trench raid. But the Belgians want us back. They don't care if we wear skirts, they just need us." Her voice was harsh with anger and disappointment. "I've packed your kit. We are to head back to Calais as soon as you get cleaned up." Silently, Sally and Elodie went to do as they were bid, and eventually the seven women started their ambulances and puttered off through the brightening dawn.

Chapter 7: February 1915

"What harm did he do thee, O Lord?" *Grave marker for an Anzac soldier, Gallipoli, 1916*

Their arrival in Calais was met with mixed reactions. The other women greeted them as long-lost comrades, while Captain Wollert and Lieutenant Richards took the returnees into a room the two used as an office and questioned them closely.

"I've had glowing reviews of you from the doctors and the matrons. In fact," Wollert sorted through the letters on her desk and pulled one out. "Here's what Doctor Elliott said: 'I was loathe to have your FANYs in the trenches, but their knowledge, abilities, and courage were second to none. They might be neither fish nor fowl, but I will serve with them at any time.'" The women passed glances of pleasure to each other. "Well, you've proven our worth to the people at the Front. Maybe they will realize it farther up the chain of command."

"Barges. Barges. Barges!" A male voice rang

out as heavy footsteps raced up the stairs toward the second floor. There was an instance of silence.

"Will this never end?" the captain muttered to herself. As one, the FANYs dropped what they were doing and hurried for the door. Lottie paused to grab Elodie's hand.

"Come on."

"You don't need Jezebel."

"No but come see how this goes. The laundry can wait, or whatever you were going to do," Lottie encouraged her.

Out in the courtyard, women pulled bonnet covers from the ambulances, throwing them into a corner of the yard while others cranked the engines. Immediately, the drivers leaped into their seats and the ambulances pulled out of the yard, heading for the docks. Elodie started the engine on Lottie's ambulance and slid into the passenger seat as Lottie let out the clutch. The vehicle jolted forward. Any traffic on the road yielded to the oncoming line of cars. Outside her window, Elodie caught sight of faces watching the procession with either fear or exhaustion.

"Maybe I should be getting the hospital ready. Whatever has happened, this looks bad." Elodie said at the sight of a line of barges making their way down the canal.

"It'll be good for Mila. You've a few hours before the ambulances with wounded get there," Lottie said as they pulled in line at the docks. "Just think, if you didn't have the vile Jezebel, you could have an ambulance and be part of this."

"Without Jezebel, I'd still be embroidering pillowcases in Le Havre."

At the moorings, one barge was already tied up and others waited in the slow current. On board, nurses in white uniforms directed orderlies to carry stretchers off with as much care as possible. They loaded four stretchers into each ambulance and closed the doors with a hard slap to let the driver know they were finished. The woman at the wheel then eased the ambulance into gear and very gingerly drove down to the harbor, where a hospital ship would be waiting. As soon as one ambulance was filled, another took its place.

Finally, it was Lottie's turn. She backed the ambulance in, and the back end jostled as the stretchers were loaded. The women gagged as the stench of blood and feces drifted up through the cab. Then the doors were shut, and Lottie maneuvered the ambulance past the line of waiting cars. Elodie looked out at the river where dozens of barges waited to unload their occupants. Someone in the back whimpered.

"Tell them we will be at the hospital ship in two tics," Lottie muttered, her eyes focused on the road ahead. Her main goal was to miss potholes and ruts while avoiding sliding off the *pavé*. Her concentration was almost superhuman. Elodie relayed her words to the wounded in the back.

"Thank you, Miss," a very English voice answered weakly.

They crept through town, listening to the men groan and then apologize. Elodie had to bite her lip to keep from crying. Finally, the wharf came into sight, mercy ships moored alongside it with others waiting their turn. Lottie reversed the ambulance, backing down the narrow passage to the hospital ship. It had not been built for automobiles and one slip of attention meant the ambulance and all its occupants would be over the edge into the sea. Elodie's fingers dug into the seat in terror, but Lottie never flinched. The van stopped and the rear doors were opened by orderlies. Fresh air flooded in.

Elodie watched them carry the first patient toward the gangway while the others were unloaded and set gently on the wharf. The men paused, allowing two more orderlies with a stretcher to make their slow way off the ship. As soon as the gangway cleared, the waiting orderlies hurried up it with their cargo. The ship orderlies carried the stretcher farther from the gangway before setting it down. Elodie craned her neck to watch as Lottie started the car toward the waiting barges.

"Hold up, Lottie. Let me out," she said suddenly. "That man is still alive."

"Go on. I'll pick you up on the next round or you can walk back to the hospital," Lottie said, and

Elodie slipped out, running to where the stretcher and its occupant rested. Behind her, Lottie sped up the ramp, past the waiting ambulances.

Elodie looked down at the man on the stretcher. He was very young, with fair hair glued back from his forehead by sweat despite the cold weather. The man's skin was almost translucent, seeming to glow in the sunlight like fine china. His lips were almost white except where a tiny trickle of blood leaked from one corner. Elodie had seen that look on too many patients. His eyes fluttered open and he looked up at her, unfocused. He reached feebly out with a finger. An orderly coming down the ship's gangway looked over at them and beckoned for Elodie.

"I'll be right back," she told the soldier and went to the orderly. "I'm with the Belgian hospital here, should I have him moved?"

"No, Miss." The orderly shook his head. "The doctors say he will die, and we may as well have the bed space for someone who might live. They said maybe an hour or two." Elodie looked down to hide the sudden rush of tears.

"Thank you," she managed to whisper, and turned away to go back to the soldier, alone on his stretcher. She knelt down, taking his hand, her heart aching at how very young he was. His fingers moved slightly against her palm.

"Why did they take me off the ship, Sister? Will

they put me on one soon?" His voice was barely a whisper.

"You'll be going home very soon," Elodie soothed him and wiped away the blood with the edge of his blanket. She sat down cross-legged on the wooden planks. He lay silently for a time. Footsteps sounded behind her on the wharf and a blanket dropped over her shoulders. Elodie huddled into the warmth gratefully. It was still winter and the breeze off the ocean was stiff. She wiped away blood again and brushed his forehead. His fingers twitched.

"Sister, when are they coming for me?"

"It won't be long."

"Will you sing me a song? My mother always sang to me when I was sick," he mumbled. Elodie closed her eyes, her jaw clenching in pain.

"Of course." She tried to sing but her throat was closed. She swallowed hard, then started the *Berceuse de Brahms*, the beautiful lullaby that had sung so many children to sleep. She only knew the French version, but the melody was what mattered.

At the end of the song, the man was silent for a long time, so long that Elodie thought he had died. She pulled up the blanket covering him. His fingers twitched. Elodie took his hand again, pressing the fingers of her other hand into her eyes.

"I don't want to die, Sister, but I am, aren't I?" he murmured.

"Yes."

"I don't want to die."

"I know."

"Will you help me pray? Our Father, who art…" he began in a faint whisper. Elodie joined in in French, matching her cadence to his. She doubted he realized. The whisper faded away as they recited, 'Deliver us from evil.'

Elodie looked down into the silent white face and finished the prayer. She passed a hand over his eyes and leaned forward to kiss the pale forehead. Once again, she smoothed back the hair before drawing the sheet up over the man's face. Reflexively, she started to cross herself and then let her hand fall. There was no God here, only humans who claimed to know what God wanted. And if He wanted this pain and suffering, Elodie was unable to genuflect.

Instead, Elodie covered her face, wailing into her hands, rocking back and forth. She cried for the young man in front of her. For her loss of innocence. For this young man's mother who waited in vain. For all the men who were dying so far from all they loved. For the pain that came from caring.

Gentle hands patted her shoulders. Elodie started, looking around wildly. It was the coffin cart man, his face sagging with sadness. She quickly wiped her face dry on the borrowed blanket and allowed him to help her to her feet. He steadied her for a moment.

"He is with God now. I will take over from here," he said in French. "Go back to the hospital.

There are those who still need you."

Elodie nodded blindly. She folded the blanket and set it beside the silent figure. Then she walked slowly up the ramp and toward the hospital, unaware of the vehicles carrying load after load of grief and pain toward the mercy ships.

Chapter 8: March to April 1915

"The gaseous vapor which the Germans used against the French divisions near Ypres…. introduces a new element into warfare. The attack… was preceded by the rising of a cloud of vapor, greenish gray and iridescent. That vapor settled to the ground like a swamp mist and drifted toward the French trenches on a brisk wind. Its effect on the French was a violent nausea and faintness, followed by an utter collapse…"
In the New York Tribune *of April 27, 1915*

Lottie and Elodie had just finished another all-day bath and were walking home in the chilly afternoon. In the brisk sea wind, their clothing would dry quickly on the clothesline, and each looked forward to an evening of writing letters and reading news from home. The two stood chatting for a few moments at the gate to the Belgian hospital before Lottie headed back to the FANY house.

"Lottie, Elodie!" A voice called out from the hospital door. They turned to see Lieutenant Richards slogging towards them. "Brilliant. You've had a bath. The Belgian command has set up a concert for tonight. They want some girls and you two look perfect for the role."

"Do we have to sing?" Lottie looked appalled at the thought.

"No, just dance with the officers and clap enthusiastically if someone bellows out a song. I know this is rather short notice, but the Belgians..." She shrugged. "It's at the church hall this evening. Eight or so. If we aren't too busy, I'll send more girls, but at least Britain will be represented in the crowd. Britain and France, I mean - I think of you as British, Elodie." Deciding to leave before she tasted more shoe leather, the lieutenant hurried off with a wave. Elodie was torn between pleasure and annoyance.

"Cheers," Lottie grumbled. "I've a stack of newspapers I've been meaning to read."

"All in the name of troop morale or showing the flag or something. Let's get these clothes hung up to dry and find something cheerful to wear," Elodie suddenly found herself excited by the prospect.

The Brass Hats organized these concerts semi-regularly to welcome visiting dignitaries or to give line officers a brief respite from the trenches. Being women of good character and breeding, the FANYs were regulars at these official gatherings. Sally and Timmy had come from one such event bubbling over with tales of meeting the Prince of Wales as he served with the Grenadier Guards. He had been gallant and so handsome, they reported giddily. Calais was as close as they would allow him to the Front, and he was occasionally seen on the streets.

Elodie and Lottie hung up their wet clothing and walked to the FANY house. The FANYs had come to France with only practical attire, not expecting to attend parties. Women who could sew, those who visited Paris on their week off, and packages from home added to their wardrobes somewhat, and all were happy to share. Before long, Elodie and Lottie had a modest pile of contributions to sort through.

Lottie immediately dug out a black dress trimmed with sparkling buttons. She held it up and turned for Elodie to see. The dress set off her blonde hair and Elodie nodded in approval. Lottie stripped down and pulled it on, turning her back for Elodie to button her up. The skirt hung to her ankles, allowing her boots to show.

"See if there are any shoes to match." Lottie smoothed down the skirt with pleasure. "This is fine. I was between stairs in the big house, so I had good clothing but nothing very fancy," she said, twirling. She let her hair down from its chignon and began to fashion a pompadour. Elodie sorted through the offerings and found black shoes.

"Will these fit?"

"I think so. What have you found?"

"This shirtwaist. I do like the color." She held it

up and Lottie nodded approvingly at the rich blue. "There is a skirt that matches it. It's a bit plain." She pulled on the shirtwaist, discovering that it was fancier than she had thought. A fine lace placket with three buttons set off the shirred front. The Panama skirt was in three tiers, the first two trimmed with three bands of ribbon each and the third fell to the tops of her ankles.

"I say, Elodie, you look fine," Lottie said cheerfully. "Turn around and I'll pin up the back of your blouse. It's a bit loose and taking it in will show off your figure. There. You look so graceful."

Pleased with their appearances, the two bundled into their overcoats and boots, carrying their dancing shoes.

"It seems sacrilegious for us to go to a party when men are dying out there." Lottie slid her arm into Elodie's so they could navigate the mud.

"Perhaps they need a reminder of why they are fighting," Elodie said softly. It did not seem like a good reason and neither felt their meager presence would make a difference.

The church hall windows were covered with thick curtains and the building loomed dark in front of them, but the two women could hear laughter. They were ushered in quickly, the man at the door trying to let as little light as possible leak out.

A slightly tinny piano played sedate songs in respect for their surroundings. Coming in from the cold spring weather to the stuffy, overheated interior made Elodie feel a bit faint. They changed into their dancing shoes and their muddy boots were put away with their heavy coats.

Elodie glanced around. Belgian officers, resplendent in dark blue tunics and gray pants, chatted with their French counterparts in red pants. Several priests provided a black counterpart to the brightly dressed soldiers and townswomen who had been asked to attend.

"Where are the Brits?" Lottie whispered. Elodie peered around.

"Over there."

Five men were dressed in dull khaki uniforms that faded into obscurity amid the colors around them. Elodie suddenly realized just how practical the British uniform was. Khaki would make them far harder to see in the trenches or on the sere battlegrounds.

There were not many women in the hall. The men immediately surrounded Lottie and Elodie. A fiddler and a trumpet player joined the pianist, and they began to play a ragged foxtrot. Elodie had a drink pressed into her hand, but it was lost as one after another of the officers swirled her away to waltz around the hall. She spun past Lottie, her face flushed and laughing at the French and Belgian men who made gallant comments in broken English.

As the musicians paused to catch their breath, Elodie fanned herself, thinking she was warm for the first time since winter had come to the Western Front. She would have liked to mop her face but had nothing suitable.

"May I?" One of the British officers stood in front of her, a glass in one hand and a handkerchief in the other. Elodie accepted both eagerly, delicately dabbing at her face with the rough handkerchief. She handed it back with thanks. "Our allies have quite put you through your paces tonight," the officer commented idly.

"Yes, they have, but I am one of the allies." Elodie looked up at the tall officer, taking in her breath at the brilliant green eyes. His hair was black shot through with red that shone in the lamplight, and his regulation mustache had been carefully trimmed. Recognition dawned on both their faces. He looked her up and down and then laughed.

"I must say, that outfit is far more becoming than what you wore in the trenches." The musicians started a waltz and he bowed quickly. "May I have the pleasure of this dance?" At her nod, he swung her out onto the dance floor. "I haven't seen you or your friends around Béthune. Let me see - FANYs, and you are the unofficial FANY."

Elodie nodded. "We were there during a trench raid and the FANYs were pulled out and sent packing."

"Can't say I blame them."

"I saw you during the raid, running with your

men toward the outpost trench. We - my partner and I - were making for the exit."

"That was a wise decision. I'm sorry I won't be seeing you in the trenches, but they are no place for a woman." He spun her gracefully, making her skirt swirl. "I suppose I shall have to be bold and introduce myself. Lieutenant Giles Ellery, British Expeditionary Forces."

"Elodie Fabien."

"It is a pleasure to meet you, Miss Fabien." The waltz ended and a Belgian officer stepped up, bowed elegantly, and swept Elodie away. When the dance ended, Giles was right there to claim her for the next one. She searched her brain for something interesting to say but nothing occurred to her.

"Is it true that there was an impromptu truce on Christmas Eve?" Elodie asked, remembering the distant sounds of singing on that night. The rumors had circulated around the hospital that men from both sides had met in No-Man's-Land for a soccer game and drinks. Giles looked over her shoulder, weighing his words.

"I can't really say. If there was one, the Brass Hats would have to quash anyone involved and that would be bad for morale. Can't be having enemy soldiers declaring impromptu peace. There'd be no work for the politicians."

Lottie swirled by in the arms of an enlisted man in a BEF uniform. He glanced at Giles and flushed. Lottie's dress sparkled and she was laughing at something the man was saying. Elodie smiled after her, thinking her friend looked uncommonly pretty.

"I didn't know enlisted men came to these dances. That's rather egalitarian for Britain," Elodie said curiously. Giles looked around.

"I don't see your *poilus* filling the floor here, my republican friend. The lance corporal is part of the evening's entertainment, and he happens to be my most excellent Soldier-Servant, my batman. I think you call them *ordonnance.*" Giles checked his watch and caught his batman's eye. He gestured toward the stage with his chin. The black-haired man responded immediately, ending his waltz with a graceful turn that delivered Lottie back to Elodie. Giles escorted both women off the dance floor and found drinks. Giles' man vanished into the crowd before reappearing on the stage. He and the pianist spoke to each other for a moment, Gallic shrugs of incomprehension meeting British gesticulating.

"What is he doing?" Lottie asked, leaning around to speak to Giles.

"Starting the singing. His voice is famous in my unit," Giles said. "That's why my lowly self was asked to this dance, to bring him. Do either of you girls sing?" Elodie shook her head while Lottie grimaced.

"I love singing, but the choirmaster refused to let me," Lottie laughed. The piano player and British soldier seemed to come to some sort of agreement and the pianist played an arpeggio. The soldier began to sing.

It's a long way to Tipperary
It's a long way to go.

He gestured to Giles and Lottie, who were grinning. They immediately joined in, followed by the rest of the crowd who might not have known the exact words, but knew the meaning. The voice that rolled out of the slight lance corporal was rich and deep. Elodie looked over at Lottie to see her eyes locked onto the man.

It's a long way to Tipperary
To the sweetest girl I know!
Goodbye Piccadilly
Farewell Leicester Square!
It's a long, long way to Tipperary
But my heart's right there.

The singers all laughed, congratulating themselves on a good finish. One of the French officers was pushed onto the stage by his friends and bowed deeply, flushing as his eyes crossed Elodie and Lottie's figures. He began to sing a slightly less risqué version of *Madelon*, the lilting French drinking song about a barmaid true to the entire regiment. Elodie giggled, whispering a translation into Lottie's ear.

We dream of her at night, we think of her in day,
It is only Madelon whom we love.

One of the priests came up to the stage and the music stumbled, changing instantly to *La Marseillaise*. When it was finished, Giles looked at his watch and then tapped it. His batman nodded at this cue.

"I would like to sing a song from my country, Wales, about a battle that took place in 1461. It was a seven-year siege and I hope that this war will not last as long."

One of the French officers quickly translated his words to the applause of the partygoers. The lance corporal took a deep breath and began to sing.

> *Men of Harlech, march to glory,*
> *Victory is hov'ring o'er ye,*
> *Bright-eyed freedom stands before ye,*
> *Hear ye not her call?*
> *At your sloth she seems to wonder;*
> *Rend the sluggish bonds asunder,*
> *Let the war-cry's deaf'ning thunder*
> *Every foe appall.*

His baritone rolled across the crowd and his passion for this song fairly rang in the listeners' bones. Elodie looked at Lottie. She was no longer just watching the man, her heart shone in eyes that memorized his every move. As he finished and stepped off the stage, close to tears, he had to fend off many drinks and back slaps from men who may not have understood the song but felt the sentiment.

"Well done, Evans. Miss Fabien, may I present my batman, Lance Corporal Siôn Evans. Evans, Miss Elodie Fabien. And I'm afraid I have not made your friend's acquaintance."

"Lieutenant Ellery, my friend Charlotte Mullins." Elodie introduced them. Lottie was polite but with eyes for only Evans.

"Thank you for singing tonight," Elodie smiled at the man. "I am confused. Is Wales a separate country to England?" The three looked uncomfortable for a moment. Whatever might have been said next vanished in the throbbing of an engine far louder than any airplane Elodie had heard. Silence fell as all the merrymakers looked up at the ceiling.

"The lights! Put out the lights," someone called, and in an instant, the hall was plunged into darkness. The engine sound grew louder. Elodie felt Giles' arm around her, drawing her close to him. For a moment, she was shocked at the liberty, but realized this was protective, not suggestive.

"What is it?" Lottie asked.

"Bloody Zepp. Begging your pardon, Miss." Lance Corporal Evans answered. They had heard about these airships, but Elodie had not seen any over Calais. Lottie opened the entry door, boldly stepping out into the darkness, Elodie following, drawing Giles perforce beside her. They scanned the sky for the source of the noise.

"Up there," he whispered, pointing toward an

inky black shape blotting out the stars. Below the huge ship was a shimmering light. It was low on the horizon, traveling down the coast.

"Why are the French not shooting?" Evans asked as he joined them, looking up at the dark object that was fading away. The town lay silent, seeming to hold its breath.

"It's making another pass." The sound of the engine turned back over land and began an arc toward the harbor. In those few minutes, the French army had found their weapons and lit the sky with searchlights. Someone started launching star shells that burst high above them, sparkling blue, green, and pink. Elodie caught her breath and shivered. Giles wrapped both arms around her just as the spotlights bracketed the Zeppelin. Rifle and machine gun fire ripped through the stillness.

"He's too high. It'd be sheer luck if they drop him," Evans said. The Zeppelin glowed in the searchlights. Something far above them hissed and the two men swore, driving the women back toward the building, shielding them with their bodies. Elodie was smashed between the stone wall of the church and Giles' chest, his arms over their heads. The explosion sent out a wave of air, followed by fire. Every window in the church hall shattered inward, the shards catching in the blackout curtains.

"What was that?" Elodie said into Giles' ear.

"Incendiary. Bastards."

Roofing tiles rained down off buildings, creating a sharp cracking sound under the gunfire. Someone screamed shrilly. Fire licked at one of the buildings near the harbor. The Zeppelin continued back toward the German lines, bombs falling every few seconds.

"The hospital," Lottie gasped. "They'll need us. Come on, Elodie. Your singing was beautiful," Lottie called over her shoulder as the two women started running.

"Good night, Lieutenant." Elodie turned and waved.

"Miss Fabien, wait," Giles cried and ran toward Elodie. "Can I see you later?"

"Of course." Elodie's smile seemed to brighten the night. Then she turned, picking up her skirts and racing after her friend.

In the morning, Elodie was helping Madame Vincent with the washing. Since her coat and boots were still in the church hall, she was wearing four sweaters, each one more disreputable than the last. The top one had been borrowed from their mechanic and was grimy with oil and dirt. Her boots were Belgian military issue, run down at the heels and slightly too big, so she shuffled as she walked. She and Lottie had promised each other that one of them would retrieve their missing clothing as soon as the day's chores were finished. Her hair was tied up with a kerchief. Despite the cold, she was sweating.

"Mademoiselle, there is an English officer for you," Cook called from the kitchen doorway and Elodie stopped mangling the sheets in horror. Not today. Not looking like a washerwoman from an old fairy tale. The officer, dressed as if he were posing for a recruiting poster, stepped from behind the cook. The grin that spread over Giles' face made Elodie want to run and hide. He was carrying her coat draped over his arm and her boots in his hand.

"Yes?" Her words were colder than she might have intended. His grin faded and he blushed.

"I say, I am sorry, Miss Fabien. You look so, so, ah, oh hell. Miss Fabien, I wanted to see you again before I return to the trenches." He looked anywhere but at her. "I am taking the liberty of returning your coat and boots." He held them out in proof of his good intentions. "Evans is delivering Miss Mullins' to her as we speak."

Elodie looked at the interested and amused faces of Madame Vincent and the cook. Since the conversation was in English, she doubted either woman could understand a great deal of it.

"Madame, with your permission, I shall return in a few moments," she told the older woman, who nodded and turned back to her work, peeking every few seconds at Elodie and Giles. Elodie gestured to Giles, and he followed her out into the courtyard. Privacy was only an illusion as the windows of both buildings looked out over the space, but at least they could speak without being overheard.

"If I may be bold, Miss Fabien," Giles began. "I enjoyed our short meetings in the trenches and, of course, at the party last night. Particularly at the party last night. I was hoping to talk with you and maybe see you again when I get my leave? Or if you will be in Béthune, we could meet, when I'm not in the trenches." His words came out in a rush. He was handsome and kind, and so obviously embarrassed that Elodie took pity on him. She took her clothing back, pulling the coat over the oil-stained sweater.

"I would like that, Lieutenant. But I'm not certain I will be in Béthune since your superiors don't want us."

"We all know that you lot were amazing," Giles said stoutly. "And it made the trenches so much more bearable." His voice trailed off to a whisper and his eyes clouded. Elodie took his hand in sympathy. The cloudiness faded and he beamed at her. "If I may, I'll write you here. May I? And if you have the chance, I certainly would enjoy a letter from you. If things go well, I'll be back in two weeks. You'll be here?"

"I should be. Can you read French? I don't write English very well, but I can write you in French."

"Use small words." They smiled at one another for a long moment. "I have to go, Miss Fabien. I'll be back." Giles' voice was very soft. "Now," he said in a louder tone, "I must find my batman. I assume by his continued absence that your friend did not throw him out on his ear."

"Is that him coming out of the hospital?" Elodie pointed toward the front door where a small, dark-haired man was turning to speak to Lottie, who followed him.

"Yes. Good. Over here, Evans," Giles called out. The batman joined him, greeting Elodie shyly. As the soldiers headed for the gate, Elodie joined Lottie in the doorway. The two men paused to wave at them. When the drab green of their uniforms had blended into the town, Elodie and Lottie closed the door to the hospital and exchanged highly amused looks before going back to their duties.

Days later, during their morning meeting, Dora opened a thick letter from home and unfolded several clipped-out articles. She read them through and then laughed.

"Oh my, girls. Listen to this. It's from the *London Daily Chronicle.* 'One bomb fell on Notre Dame Cathedral in Calais... This same bomb, which must have been of considerable size, sent debris flying into the courtyard of the Lamarcq Hospital, full of Belgian wounded being tended by English Nurses.'" The room erupted in jeers and laughter at that phrase. "'Altogether these Yeomanry nurses behaved admirably, for all the menfolk, with the exception of the doorkeeper, fled for refuge to the cellars and the women were left. In the neighbourhood, one hears nothing but praise of these courageous

Englishwomen.'" There were cheers and clinking of tea mugs from the listening FANYs.

"Maybe this will stop my mother from sending clippings about the un-womanliness of driving cars," Sally put in cheerily. The laughter went with them as they tromped down to their waiting patients.

Elodie went up the stairs of the Belgium High Command, passing the guard who now knew her on sight. He nodded politely and opened the door. The commandant wanted a report on Mila, the housekeeper destined for the convalescent home.

"I'd say she is ready to go. Her English is a bit shaky but the FANYs who are to go to the convalescent home were chosen for their French, which is also shaky, but they'll all try," Elodie told him honestly. He gazed at her over his mustache.

"That's good. King Albert wishes for us to continue to fight and so many are trapped behind the German lines or in Free Belgium that we cannot afford to lose men to England."

"The home is a start. Perhaps the English will begin sending back your Belgians."

"One hopes."

"When will the convalescent home open?" Elodie asked. The man gave a disgusted gesture of dismissal.

"The French are dragging their feet. As usual. I beg your pardon, Mademoiselle. Your countrymen fear that we shall declare an enclave here. Bah, we just want to go back home."

"As do we all. My home in Reims is under occupation."

"But that has brought you to us," he said with great panache. "So perhaps it is not all bad. Are the FANYs wishing to ride? My horses grow bored with nothing to do."

"I do. And I'm sure the others will want to, as well." Elodie looked at him eagerly.

"Commandant, I beg your pardon." An aide opened the door. He looked troubled, so Elodie immediately stood up, excusing herself. Whatever was worrying the young man, she would soon see the after-effects at the hospital.

Elodie went back out to the street, narrowly missing running into a soldier in a British uniform. He mumbled an apology and turned away. Elodie stared after him in puzzlement. His profile reminded her of someone, but the only Englishman she knew by sight was Giles.

March 2, 1915

Béthune

My dear Miss Fabien,

I hope this letter finds you well. I am in the trenches, so I apologize for both the pencil and the stains. As you know, it is very hard to keep things clean here. I shan't write much about the conditions - I don't want to create extra work for

*the censors and their black pens - and you are familiar with
everything I could say.*

> *One of my men found a rat terrier in an abandoned
house. We've named him Chip and he lives with us. You can
imagine how busy he is. His first night he took out seventeen
rats.*

Yours,

Giles Ellery

Elodie imagined someone bending over the letters with a thick black pen, ready to draw lines through offending material. She also imagined this person reading the painful French and developing a headache.

March 10, 1915

Calais

Dear Lieutenant Ellery,

*I received your letter and hope all is well. Your note about
Chip came with the number of rats blotted out. I suppose the
censor did not want anyone to realize that one side has more
rats than the other. We were able to go for a short horseback
ride with the commandant. I do so love riding in spring.*

> *We had a concert last night, put on by the most
talented of the FANYS. They sing an anthem all about being
a FANY. If it is just the girls, we sing tavern songs. I'm told
these have been made tame, but they still make us laugh.*

Yours,

Elodie Fabien

Elodie read over the letter, thinking it was dull,

but no mail meant low morale. She thought of these missives about laundry and gossip to be important war work and faithfully wrote at least a note each evening.

March 15, 1915
Béthune
Dear Miss Fabien,
What fun it must be to ride horses. I have never learned, so perhaps you can teach me. I am, as you can tell from the cleanliness of this letter, not in the trenches. I will not be able to visit you as we are having additional training.

There is a Canadian and a Scots division not far from us and the two have quite the rivalry when it comes to football. Our officers have set up a cricket pitch and we play in the evenings. Have you seen a cricket match? At the risk of having my school tie taken from me, I will say that cricket is a dull game when compared to the Scots and Canucks giving each other a good thumping. We've been promised a game by the Australian Rules footballers, eventually.

I've news hot off the press. I shall be able to visit in two days. I'll only have a few hours.
Yours,
Giles Ellery

Elodie read the letter with excitement, looking forward to seeing Giles again. Letter writing was all very well, but it was not as enjoyable as seeing his face and hearing his voice.

March 19, 1915
Calais
Dear Giles,
I so enjoyed your visit. I hope you were able to return in time to your station. Lottie and I have asked one of the girls to bring back decent wool from Paris. We are planning to knit socks for both you and Evans, so your feet will stay warm and dry! If we make too many or they are uncomfortable (I am not very good at turning heels), you can hand them out.

When I think of how much I hated knitting when I was in Le Havre, I am embarrassed. I do like to crochet but I cannot imagine that crocheted socks would be very comfortable. Would you like house slippers? Do junior officers wear house slippers? That seems rather below your dignity.

I had stern words with Cook, and she promises not to feed you stale rolls and watered-down coffee again. She did say some very rude things about the English and their tasteless bread and overly strong tea. We may be allies, but national snobbery prevails.
Affectionately,
Elodie

One blustery afternoon in March, when Giles was free of the trenches and Elodie could take time off, they walked together in the weak sunlight. Her hand was tucked into his elbow and her feet were light in her muddy boots.

"Will Evans' visits cause any issues for Miss Mullins?" Giles asked.

"Not that I have heard. I have no doubt our captain has heard that you and he are visiting us. As long as we do not neglect our duties, I think we'll be fine."

"Good. He's rather important to me and I'd hate to have him moping about."

"Assuming that you don't cause issues for me, and you are the one moping," Elodie teased. Giles looked surprised, then laughed.

"I suppose I think that being an officer gives one special privilege. Do let me know if your captain gets stuffy about it."

"What does Evans do, I mean, before he was your batman?"

"He was a schoolteacher in Wales. He's got to be the most organized man I've ever met. I don't know what I should do without him."

Elodie wondered to herself how a schoolteacher would be able to afford the country home with horses that Lottie wanted. Perhaps that was putting the cart before the horse. First, they all had to survive the war.

"I should return to the hospital," Elodie said, reluctantly, and they turned their footsteps toward it. "Mila is leaving tomorrow for the convalescent home."

"Shall you still have time for me?" Giles asked,

covering her hands with his.

"I'll make time." Elodie said with a smile.

At the hospital, they found that Lottie had not had time to walk out with Evans, so Evans had taken it upon himself to entertain the *blessés*. His voice rang through the hospital wing, followed by applause and cries for more. The disappointment at his departure was palpable, and the men shook his hand as he followed Giles out.

Lottie and Elodie grinned at each other. Evans had just found the key to keeping the patients happy and, with that, Captain Wollert.

"You seem rather smitten with the handsome lieutenant," Lottie observed. Elodie felt a smile grow inside her.

"I do believe I am," she said.

In April, little buds peeked out along the twigs of the hedgerows, promising that spring was coming. It had been a bitterly cold and wet winter. Elodie sighed as she walked down the road toward the hospital. The Kaiser had promised the war would be over by Christmas 1914. The French magistrate had said the same thing, but here they were, long past Christmas and with no end in sight. The work went on at the hospital; washing bed linen, washing patients encrusted with mud, scrubbing, cooking, and cleaning until hands were red and raw.

The Belgian commander had promised the use

of horses for Saturday. A good gallop on the beach would be a salve. Somewhere to Elodie's left, a church bell chimed the hour. Five o'clock. If she hurried, she might be able to heat some soup in the break room and it was always possible that the cook had found sufficient flour to make bread to give to the FANYs. She quickened her step. By the time she reached the hospital, her throat was scratchy, and her eyes burned. The air felt odd, and no birds twittered in the trees.

"What is that awful smell?" Captain Wollert stepped out of the doorway, looking around.

"Good evening, Captain," Elodie said politely. "I'm not certain. It's rather unpleasant." The older woman sniffed and then coughed.

"Come in then, and would you please see that all the windows are closed?"

"Yes, Captain." Elodie went from window to window, pulling each one shut. The wards were not full, and she was able to take a few moments to speak to each man who was awake.

"Elodie! El, where are you?" Sergeant Mason ran into the ward where Elodie looked up from the patient she was talking to.

"Here, Sergeant."

"Thank God. Come on. There's a Belgian officer in the courtyard. He's screaming about something." The two women raced down the stairs to where an officer in a filthy uniform held onto the stair railing. He was choking and gasping for breath, his eyes streaming with tears.

"*Onderluitenant*, what is the issue?" Elodie gasped. The odd smell was stronger now and her throat closed; she had to force words out.

"Gas. Germans… sent gas. We need help. There are thousands dead and dying," the man choked. Elodie frowned. His words were not making sense.

"What did he say?" Mason asked.

"He says the Germans have sent gas. I'm not sure… It is the same in Dutch and English, so that must be correct. And he says there are thousands of men dying and dead," Elodie translated. The FANYs who had followed the noise exchanged looks of confusion. Sergeant Mason coughed.

"I've heard the French tried gas at the beginning of the war, but it did not work. Perhaps someone tried again," Mason said slowly. The women looked in horror at the man, who had grown worse. He was grasping at his throat and choking, fluid streaming from his open mouth. Then he collapsed to his knees and two FANYs rushed forward, dragging him up the stairs and into the hospital.

"All right. This makes no sense. Girls, fire up the ambulances and head to the clearing station. Elodie, run to the Belgian headquarters and see what they know. Alice, you get - I don't know - hot water. We always need hot water. And see what the girls have to say about the Belgian officer. Come tell me when you find out."

The FANYs scattered at the sergeant's directions. Elodie ran for the Belgian headquarters, her throat hurting.

"We've had an *Onderluitenant* come to us. Says there is gas at the Front and thousands are dead and dying," Elodie gasped to the first Belgian soldier she saw.

"We've just had word. Chlorine gas. The French and Algerian lines have broken."

"How do we treat it?"

"How should I know?" The man was panicked, his face white. "Go on. You are in the way."

Elodie ran back to the hospital, finding Lieutenant Richards and Lottie loading first aid supplies into the back of Jezebel.

"Lieutenant. The Belgians say it was a chlorine gas attack and the French and Algerian lines have broken."

"Go tell Alice and then come back here. Take Jezebel to the *Hôpital de Passage* and help there. I will send ambulances to transport any Belgians here."

"Yes, ma'am." Elodie ran to start the car. She drove through the panicked crowds to the train station where she unloaded the supplies, telling the orderlies what little she knew. By that time, the first ambulances from the Front raced up. Orderlies went to unload them, coughing as they opened the doors. The sharp, pungent smell of pepper and something sweet rolled out. Elodie hurried forward and recoiled in horror. The first stretcher held a body so swollen that his blue uniform strained at the seams and buttons. His face was a terrifying shade of purple and his tongue protruded from his mouth.

"Is… is he alive?" she gasped, just as the man went into a paroxysm of coughing. The stretcher-bearers hung onto the stretcher as it shook and twisted under the man's spasms. "Take him into the hospital." Elodie recovered herself and sent them in the direction of the train station. Two more orderlies stepped up to take the second one out, but it was clearly too late. Elodie pointed wordlessly to the side of the station. The men carried the body and set him down gently, covering him with a blanket.

"It's bad, Elodie." Lottie had driven up. "Any Belgians?" Her face was ashen and her eyes wide. She had a scarf tied around her mouth and she lowered it to speak.

"Not yet. It's mostly French."

"I'm to go on to the Front then. Watch yourself."

"You, too."

As evening wore into night, the pile of bodies outside the station grew and the care the orderlies took in laying them down lessened. By full dark, ambulances were bringing in men who had been blinded, seated six to an ambulance. Men who could barely see led lines of men with gauze bandages wrapped over their eyes, their hands gripping the uniform of the man in front. The constant parade of ambulances finally slowed to a trickle by morning.

Elodie stood wearily in the entrance to the *Hôpital de Passage*, looking down the long lines of men on the floor. She was shaking with exhaustion, but there were still wounded to treat. Piles of clothing sat at one end, pulled or cut off bodies that swelled grotesquely. There had been very few Belgians in the mix, so the floor was covered in blue French uniforms and the dark green of the Algerians.

"What should I do now?" Elodie asked one of the exhausted doctors who hurried past her.

"Wash the eyes. Cold water and lots of it. We've been putting on petroleum jelly. Don't know if it does anything, but it makes us feel we are doing something. When you find a dead one, get him moved out right away."

Elodie found a basin, clean rags and several tins of petroleum jelly that she shoved into her skirt pockets. She picked her way over bodies that shook and gasped for air, and around puddles of green vomit, to a group of men who looked untreated.

Gently, she unwrapped each face, murmuring in French. She dribbled water into reddened and swollen eyes, sometimes having to pry apart the lids as the man whimpered. She finished by dabbing the slick jelly on reddened skin and rewrapping the eyes. These men seemed to just be blinded, not gasping for air. In a few weeks, Elodie guessed, if they recovered, they would go back to the trenches with this new terror waiting for them. As the ones who had not been fully blinded watched her, they started working on their fellow soldiers, not wanting their comrades to wait for thinly-stretched medical staff.

As she worked, trains entered the *Hôpital de Passage* and orderlies worked together to load up injured men. They were bound for Paris hospitals where doctors and nurses struggled to treat injuries wrought by this new weapon. There was not much they could do but provide support and hope the men recovered.

Elodie knelt beside the final man and peeled away the bandages. Unlike most French soldiers, his face was bare of a mustache. It took time for her tired brain to process the peach fuzz on his cheeks.

"How old are you?" she said softly.

"Eighteen," the dark-haired soldier whispered through a raw throat. Elodie looked at him more closely.

"*Les inepties*. You can't be over fourteen. You look like my brother." Elodie sat back, scanning around for someone with authority.

"Please, Mademoiselle. Don't. Please. I want to be here." He grasped her hand, his voice rough from both gas and emotion.

"You want this?" She waved a hand in the general direction of the chaos. "This is no place for a chi… a person of your age."

"My parents are dead. *Les poilus*, they take good care of me. I eat more regularly than I did, and I have something to do," the boy whispered. The war had worn away any traces of baby fat, but she could still see the faintest outline of a child's face. His eyes, reddened from the gas, leaked tears as his body tried to wash away the poison.

Elodie began to bathe his eyes, considering her choices. He did not belong here. None of them did but, for this very young man, what was the best option? Betraying him to the French command would put him back on the streets of Paris or Le Havre with even fewer possibilities for survival. Elodie shook her head at that thought but it was true, the trenches were probably a better place for him than thieving on the streets.

"I am at Lamarq, the Belgian hospital in town." Elodie gave up on the chance to take this boy from the fighting. "When you come to town, find me there. Ask for Elodie Fabien. Ask in English. Most of them have no French."

"Georges," he said softly.

"What?"

"Georges Laurent. My name."

"Miss? Is this one ready to go? We have space on the last train leaving." One of the orderlies came over, interrupting the quiet conversation.

"Yes. He's ready," Elodie said firmly.

"Goodbye, Georges. Don't forget what I told you."

"Goodbye, Mademoiselle," Georges said as the man helped him to his feet and led him toward the waiting train.

Elodie looked up at the skylights. Morning sun streamed through them, the light picking out leftover detritus and filth from the night before. The room was mostly emptied of the men who had been gassed; a few still shapes under blankets had yet to be removed for the coffin man to pick up. Elodie wiped her eyes and then looked at her sleeve in disgust. She found a cleaner spot and dabbed away a few tears.

"Elodie?" Lottie's gentle hand touched her shoulder. Elodie looked up. "This has been terse."

"What a night," Elodie sighed.

"And still the day to follow. Come on. The blasted Germans tried to break through last night and we've got wounded coming in." She pulled Elodie to her feet and exhaustedly, the two women went back to their hospital.

When the French and Algerian lines collapsed, the Belgians rushed into their trenches, repelling a German attack. The assault had been less than effective because the Germans had been so stunned by the after-effects of the gas that they had missed the advantage. The Entente forces had been very lucky.

This last attack was effectively the end of the Belgian Army. They had fought bravely since the invasion of their country, but the sad truth was that most Belgian men available to fight had been killed or injured and there were no more to put in. The Belgians would continue to fight, but no longer went over the top to die by the thousands with their British and French comrades. The King of Belgium knew that, eventually, the war would end, and he would need men to rebuild his country.

To fill the trenches, men from far-flung French colonies flooded in, filling the streets and the hospitals with their black faces and outlandish uniforms. Elodie learned very quickly that these foreigners died in exactly the same way as their white comrades.

Chapter 9: May to June 1915

"The infernal shriek and roar of high explosive shells and earsplitting whiz bangs accompanied by the almost incessant rocking of the Earth … continued for over two hours, during which period casualties came rapidly." *Description of the Battle of Festubert in the* Vancouver Province, *July, 1915*

"Mademoiselle, there is a *poilu* asking for you in the kitchen," the cook said grumpily to Elodie. The younger woman sat back on her heels where she had been chasing dust bunnies under the storage shelves. The cook's hands were white with flour, and she looked irritated at having had to track Elodie down.

"Thank you, Madame." Elodie stood up, wondering at this odd visitor as she went to the kitchen.

A very young French soldier, freshly washed with a neatly patched uniform stood on the kitchen step, his kepi held tightly in his hands.

"May I help you?" Elodie asked. The boy flushed.

"I am Georges. Georges Laurent. You helped me when we were gassed."

"Oh!" Elodie exclaimed. "I never thought to see you again. Come in. Cook, could I make a coffee and have a bun for this *poilu*?" The cook allowed Elodie to pour a tin of coffee and directed her to where that day's bread was stored. Elodie served the boy and sat down across the kitchen table from him.

"Are you well, Georges?"

"Yes, Mademoiselle. I am on my way to the Front, but my sergeant gave me a moment to see you."

"Your eyes? And lungs?"

"All fine. We have these masks to carry with us now." He held up a canvas bag that was attached to his uniform belt. "And all the soldiers of the Entente must now be clean-shaven. We are no longer *poilu*!" He polished off the simple snack quickly. "I must go. Sergeants do not like to wait." Georges thanked the cook and went back down the stairs to the courtyard.

Elodie watched him walk out of the gates, part glad to see someone survive and part grieving that he was going back to the trenches. She wondered if she was right in not reporting him to the French command for being under-aged.

On the third of May 1915, the Belgian commander came to see the men in the hospital and speak with the

FANY captain. When he had left, heading for the convalescent home, Captain Wollert met the FANYs in the break room. Her face was somber, and her eyes rested on Elodie and Lottie for longer than normal.

"As you may have seen, the commander dropped by to tell me that the French and British armies are planning a major offensive. He does not believe that Belgian losses will amount to much," Wollert said. Lottie reached out to take Elodie's hand. "However, we will be called to carry wounded to the mercy ships." She excused herself, leaving the women to their usual morning activities of reading the mail and discussing cases.

Elodie smiled tensely at the others and left the room as well. She busied herself with counting supplies in the typhoid hospital, but she had to go over them several times because her focus had evaporated with the morning's news. The British army would include Giles' unit, and Georges' French brigade could be involved. Elodie re-counted the same box of bandage rolls.

On the ninth of May, the Second Battle of Artois was in full swing. The British were driven back, and barges began their slow journey to Calais and then back to the battlefield.

On the fourteenth of May, word of shelling around Festubert was carried through the gossip chains and on the wind to the women at the small hospital in Calais. That night, Elodie went to bed only to stare at the ceiling for hours, thinking about Giles.

On the fifteenth of May, British, Indian, and Canadian troops went over the top into land that had been bombarded by more than one hundred thousand shells. It was a disaster for the BEF and their colonial forces.

Two smartly dressed women in green uniforms, accompanied by a British officer, pulled into the hospital courtyard and climbed out of the neat black vehicle. Elodie met them at the front door. They dubiously took in her unofficial uniform of a dark blue skirt and white shirtwaist.

"Good morning. We are looking for Captain Wollert of the FANYs," the officer said in French.

"Captain Wollert is in her office," Elodie answered in English. "If you will follow me." She stepped back to let them enter and led the way to the second floor. There were not many occupied beds and the two women's faces brightened as they passed through the quiet ward.

"Captain Wollert, visitors," Elodie tapped on the door frame and moved aside to let the strangers into the office. She closed the door at the captain's request and walked down to the kitchen.

Thirty minutes later, the meeting was over, and the trio left.

"Elodie, Wollie wants us all in the break room. Run over to the typhoid ward and get anybody you can," Dora called, leaning through the kitchen door.

Elodie waved acknowledgment and went to bring the others from across the courtyard. All the FANYs who were awake crowded into the break room, where Captain Wollert waited for them.

"Girls, we've just had a visit from two women from the Red Cross. They need volunteers to aid them and the Béthune Hospital because the wounded are coming in faster than they can handle," Wollert said abruptly. "Let's see. I'll keep the girls in the Belgian trenches, the ones at the sorting station and the six who are sleeping right now. That gives me ten to run this place. The rest of you are to go to Béthune Hospital. Elodie, they will need a touring car to run supplies. You may take Jezebel. Girls, you leave in ten minutes."

Elodie left the room at a trot to throw a change of clothing into her valise. The others ran for their rooming house to collect a few belongings. Elodie spent the wait prepping the cars to start. In five minutes, the women had returned. Lottie threw herself breathlessly into Jezebel, and a minute later the convoy streamed out of the courtyard bound westward to Béthune. The drivers pushed the vehicles as hard as they dared, other road users melting away from their obvious hurry. For Elodie, the fifty-mile journey seemed endless. Lottie said nothing but stared impatiently out the windshield.

When the convoy arrived in Béthune, the ambulances were pulled up as close to the hospital as possible. Around them was a scene of sheer horror and they exited the cars as if in a nightmare. Ambulances were coming from the Front, unloading their cargo and immediately turning around. Orderlies bent over each stretcher, starting to sort the living from the newly-dead. Bandaged patients waited outside as doctors and nurses worked their way through the masses.

The FANYs had all worked in trenches and in the hospital where the badly wounded were taken, but nothing had prepared them for the sheer chaos of men brought untriaged. There was simply no time to run the men through a sorting station. They had to be transported as quickly as possible in whatever condition they were in. The air was filled with cries and whimpers of pain, with the shouting of orderlies over it all. The women stood frozen.

"Those of you with ambulances, you'll come with me," a woman in the blue and red cape of the Red Cross called loudly, and the FANYs turned to go. Lottie glanced at Elodie; her eyes wide. Elodie put her hand to her heart and the other woman nodded and ran after the others.

"Miss Fabien. Thank God the FANYs have arrived," a man in a blood-soaked uniform stopped, swaying in exhaustion. Elodie immediately recognized him.

"Dr. Elliott! Yes. What can I do?"

"Take these chits of paper and come with me.

Wilson, hand them over." Elliott gestured to the soldier following him and Elodie found her hands suddenly full of slips of paper. Each was marked with a black, red, blue, or green blot of ink. "We've a triage system going. The men are graded into trivial, treatable, and terrible. And, of course, dead. Green is trivial, then blue for treatable, red for terrible, and black for the poor blighters who didn't make it. Wilson, you go help the stretcher-bearers."

Elodie followed the doctor for hours, tucking a piece of paper into the top of a bandage, or a pocket, or anywhere it would not be lost as the men waited their turn. The stretcher-bearers carried each man to the designated place for their wounds. Nurses cared for the greens, the trivials, and some of those men were pressed into helping. The blues waited outside the hospital for an operating table to open up as the doctors inside worked feverishly. The reds were taken into the hospital as space permitted, loaded onto waiting trains or put on barges to be taken to the mercy ships. The blacks were left with morphine to ease them out. Elodie found herself trying to not look for Giles' face on every wounded man. Then, as she did not see him, terror began to take hold in her chest.

Along the edge of the masses of men, a team struggled to erect tents. "Bloody Germans dropped gas. We'll put those under cover, but in the fresh air," Elliott snapped. "Does it help - God damn, how the hell should I know?" Elodie said nothing, just waiting until the doctor moved on to the next man.

As they worked their way through the waiting soldiers, more arrived on the ambulances that pulled in and dropped their charges off. Behind the hospital was a growing pile of bodies, waiting until there was time to record the death and dig a mass grave. Wilson returned slips of paper to her. Before long, there was a trail of paper behind her as the slips became too bloody to read and she discarded them. An orderly brought more.

Sixteen thousand men passed through the hospital that day.

Late in the night, Elodie walked through the gas victims who rested uncomfortably under the tent. These were survivors of an abortive attempt by the Germans to hold back the British. There were not many, a testament to the gas masks' effectiveness. Elodie held a shielded lantern in one hand, checking on the faces of the men. In the other, she carried a bag holding a canteen of water and petroleum jelly. If the men asked, she gave them a sip of water or smeared jelly on burns. There was nothing else to be done.

"Miss," a voice croaked softly from a row over. Elodie carefully made her way through the men to the one calling her. She knelt down.

"What can I get you?"

"The Lieutenant. How is he?" the man managed, his voice harsh.

"Which Lieutenant are you asking about?"

"Ellery. Giles Ellery. Have you seen him?"

Elodie saw the lights suddenly dim around her and she pitched forward at the waist, her head touching the edge of the man's blankets. Her breath came in short gasps. As the light returned, she straightened up, holding up the lantern to see the face under the glistening jelly and swollen skin.

"Lance Corporal Evans," Elodie whispered. "No, I haven't seen him." She let go of the bag and took his hand. "What happened?"

"Knocked unconscious just before the bastards dropped gas on us. Got his mask on before… before the gas. He was alive. I got mine on and passed out," he spoke only a few words at a time, gasping for breath. Elodie felt her heart freeze. It hurt more than anything she could imagine. She roughly wiped away a tear and then another. Evans' hand squeezed hers. "Mad about you."

"I haven't seen him," Elodie repeated numbly. They sat in silence for a few moments until someone moaned for water. Elodie glared around in frustration. She wanted to find Giles, to run through the hospital and search the bodies cooling behind the building. But duty lay here, with these men.

"Are you comfortable? As you can be? I'll be back." Elodie stood up shakily and picked up the bag and lantern. She returned to her tasks, tears cutting silent paths down her face.

When the canteen was empty, she hurried back

toward the main hospital to refill it and take a few moments to look for Lottie. Elodie eventually tracked her down, collapsed in a dim corner of one room, head against the wall, sleeping soundly.

"Lottie. Lottie, wake up," Elodie hissed. When her friend finally opened her eyes with a whimper, Elodie took her hand. "Evans is in the gas tent. Have you seen Giles?"

"What? Where?" Lottie came wide awake. She stood up, a blood-stained apron wrapped around her uniform gave mute evidence that Lottie had been in the operating room.

"Come with me." Elodie took her friend's hand and the two hurried out of the hospital. Elodie took Lottie to the lance corporal and then stood back in envy. She began to work her way through the gas victims again, offering comfort and looking more closely at each face.

During the next few days, Elodie found a reason to walk through every room in the hospital. When there were no faces to see because bandages covered grievous facial wounds, she would ask, hoping for a squeeze of her hand. The separate ward for shell-shocked men took special courage to enter. Some wept unstoppably. Others sat in silence, faces frozen and eyes fixed on a world no one else shared, or shook uncontrollably, their limbs contorted. Some screamed or started at apparitions only they could see. She cried as she left, but not one of the faces was Giles'.

Finally, she braved the Adjutant General's Branch of Staff Officer in charge of recording the dead. The men were supposed to wear identity discs, but these were frequently lost or separated from the body, leaving it unidentified for burial parties. He growled at her when she disturbed his work. She thought there was some sympathy behind his eyes as he told her 'No'. The chaos left from even this small battle would take months to sort out.

She went back to the gas tent to find Evans gone. Her lips trembled. She hadn't thought Evans had been that badly injured. Lottie would be distraught, but there was no time to mourn because there were still living men to care for.

"Elodie," Lottie came up to her friend, her face curiously alight. "Have you found the lieutenant?"

"No," Elodie whispered. Lottie hugged her.

"You will."

"I'm sorry about Evans. I thought he would make it," Elodie managed. Lottie looked at her in surprise, then almost laughed.

"Oh, dear. No. He is on his way back to England. The doctor said he will eventually recover. He won't sing again, but he is alive. And we are to be married when I get out of this bloody place. I told him I fell in love with his singing, but it is the man that I love now." Her words tumbled out. Elodie was filled with an unreasoning flash of jealousy. She stamped it down ruthlessly and embraced her friend.

"Good for you." She was proud that there was hardly a tremor in her voice. Lottie suddenly remembered and stepped back, eyes searching Elodie's face.

"Oh, Elodie. Giles is all right. Siôn said he was alive, and he got his gas mask on. You'll see," she said, as she smoothed back Elodie's hair with a gentle hand. Someone called for water and the two women returned to the duties that never seemed to end.

With the Battle of Festubert over, the wounded sorted, and the British army licking its wounds, there were no more actions planned. Elodie and the FANYs returned to Calais.

Elodie found herself forgetting what had to be done to keep the hospital running. Many years ago, she had fallen off her pony and hit her head. For months afterwards, she would find herself fading out, staring into space and barely able to keep up with her schoolwork. This felt very similar. She had not hit her head in Béthune, but the exhaustion and forgetfulness came anyway. She finally resorted to taking notes to make sure things ran efficiently, but she would still find herself motionless in a fog.

In the very darkest part of one night, she woke up with a clear thought. Somehow and some way, perhaps even on that very first day in the trenches, she had fallen in love with the English officer who haunted her dreams. It had been a *coup de foudre* - a lightning strike - but it had taken time to realize that she was irrevocably changed by that meeting, by swirling around the dance floor in his arms, walking through the streets together, talking of little nothings.

Elodie sighed, turning over in bed. The linens were rough from copious washings in harsh bleach. In the light of day, it did not seem possible that Giles had joined the thousands of unidentified dead. At night, all things were possible.

She had had so many plans, so many places that she wanted to see, so many things she wanted to do, but now, it seemed as if all she really wanted was to see Giles again. Fate was cruel. She could still do all those things she had once dreamed of, but with Giles missing, they no longer held any allure.

Every mail delivery, she hoped for something from or about Giles, and every mail delivery brought silence.

"The *poilu* is here to see you, Mademoiselle," one of Madame Vincent's urchins appeared at Elodie's side while she was writing a letter for a wounded man. Elodie sighed.

"Ask Cook to give him a coffee and tell him I will be right there." The boy nodded, turning back to the kitchen, and Elodie returned to writing the letter. She was struggling through some vagaries of Dutch spelling when the room seemed to darken. Elodie looked up to see Georges standing in the doorway. His face was gray and his uniform filthy. The wounded men seemed to shrink from this reminder of the trenches.

"I shall return," Elodie told the *blesse*. She stood, crossing to Georges who swayed slightly.

"Georges, are you wounded?" Elodie asked softly. He shook his head desperately. Elodie glanced around and then took his arm. "Come with me." It was a beautiful June day outside and they could sit on the low wall in relative privacy.

He seemed to slump into himself when he sat down. Elodie waited for him to speak. She did not want to touch the filthy uniform, but he seemed so much like her little brother that it was impossible that she would refuse. Elodie put an arm around him and that seemed to break the dam holding back Georges' raw emotion, an almost physical thing so painful that Elodie could barely breathe.

"What happened, *mon chou*?" she asked when he had slowed to painful gasps of air. He wiped his face off on his uniform sleeve.

"They told us we were to have a break. To go behind the lines. But then they gave us ammunition. And we were taken to the sapper's trench." His voice was so low that Elodie could barely hear him. "They said we were to go up the ladder and run to blast holes. They said they were deep. Like trenches. My sergeant refused. He said we would all die going up the ladder one at a time. The Boche would pick us off and we would not have a chance. The captain had men bring up a machine gun. Then he said he would shoot us if we didn't go over the top. My sergeant stood in front of us. But then, he said we had to go. We didn't have a choice. The officer was going to shoot us. We went over the top." There was another bout of uncontrollable crying. Elodie sat silently, her face contorted with grief and horror.

"We made it to the blast holes. But they were too shallow, just as Sergeant had said, and we were pinned down. My sergeant, he was shot in the face. He was in the blast hole with me but there was nothing I could do. I couldn't even crawl to him. The Boche kept shooting at us. He took… he took forever to die. We stayed there all day until dark when we crawled back to our trench." He was silent for a moment. "And then they pulled us out of the trenches. We are on relief in an old house outside of Calais. That coward of a captain did not even come to see what he had done." Elodie wiped her face. When Georges had stopped crying, she hugged him, cradling his head against her shoulder. It did not take an enemy to commit atrocities; it just took incompetence.

"Do they know where you are?" she asked. He shook his head.

"You've got to get back before they miss you. They'll shoot you as a deserter," she reminded him. Georges choked out what was either a sob or a laugh and Elodie felt stupid. "I can give you a ride part way. And then you can sneak back into your house." He gave a jerky nod and Elodie ran to tell Sergeant Mason where she was going. At the older woman's suggestion, she took first aid supplies to deliver to Georges' companions, creating a plausible reason for his leaving them.

Georges was silent on the drive. Elodie could think of nothing to say. At the rickety house where the men were staying, she stopped. Georges took the medical supplies and got out wordlessly. She watched him walk to the house. The boy moved like an old man. Someone called out a welcome and Georges held up the first aid supplies. The half-hung door closed behind him and Elodie drove back to the hospital.

Low tide, Saturday morning and Elodie's day off combined to mean that she could join other FANYs and the Belgian commander for a ride on the Calais beach. Seven FANYs walked down the street toward the Belgian cavalry stables, laughing over silly things. Their French neighbors had long since ceased to be scandalized by the sight of women in trousers and most smiled at them.

Eight horses stood tied outside the stables and after a quick look at the offerings, Elodie chose a fast-looking chestnut. The stableman carried saddles, bridles, and brushes out to the women, who chattered cheerfully as they saddled up the horses. The saddles were longer and flatter than the jumping saddles the FANYs were used to, and the cantle had a hard loop so that the saddle could be hung up. Elodie sorted out the double bridle's two bits and four reins, cradling the snaffle and curb bit in her left hand and sticking her thumb in the horse's mouth, pulling the crown over his ears. She adjusted it and the stableman nodded approval. Even though the FANYs were all accomplished riders, the stableman took the safety of his four-footed charges seriously. The odor of horse and leather was balm to her wounded soul and Elodie breathed in the smells gratefully.

"Mount up," the commander called from atop his horse. There was some good-natured griping about the hardness of the saddles and how they were made for larger men, but the FANYs adjusted quickly to the broader, flatter seats. The commander turned his horse, and they followed single-file down the streets and onto the beach.

The fresh breeze carrying a tang of salt air whipped around them. The commander raised his hand and dropped it, urging his horse into a canter that became a full gallop as the FANYs fell in behind. Elodie brushed her face clean from the sand that was thrown up by the horse in front of her and crouched over her horse's neck. A tree trunk, blown in by one of the winter storms, lay in front of them. In turn, each animal took the obstacle in stride. Elodie's heart soared along with her horse.

When they had galloped a fair way from Calais and were riding parallel to the open fields south of the town, the commandant turned inland. His horse climbed the dunes that separated the beach from the farmland. Elodie wrapped her hands in her horse's mane, allowing him to use his head and neck to heave himself up and over the tall dunes. Her feet were level with the animal's hip as he lunged up and out of the heavy sand. The women regrouped at the top, laughing and teasing each other about almost falling off the slick saddles.

Behind them, the unmistakable sound of rifle fire swelled from the garrisoned troops in Calais. As one, they turned to look, not certain what they would see.

"Up there," Lottie pointed skyward at two planes. One was a cream-colored mono-winged airplane with the black *Tatzenkreuz* painted on the underside of the wing. The other was taupe-colored with roundels of red, white, and blue designating it a French airplane. Planes were not a common sight, and single-winged planes were even more unusual. The riders sat transfixed, watching these new contraptions pass overhead.

Even to the novices on the ground, it was clear that the German plane was faster and more maneuverable than the French. The latter's engine was wound to a screaming pitch as it wove from side to side, attempting to shake the German pilot. Muzzle flashes from the German plane preceded the rat-a-tat of a machine gun. The horses began to move restlessly.

"In the newspapers, they are calling aerial combat a dog fight," Lieutenant Richards called out. "Although there doesn't seem to be a great deal of fighting. I rather think the French plane is getting the worst of it."

The French plane suddenly coughed out black smoke and the engine began to make gasping revolutions, revving and then dying away. Almost gracefully, it fell out of the sky, catching fire as it hit the ground a quarter of a mile from the watching riders. The cavalry horses shied away, and for a few moments, the riders were focused solely on controlling their mounts. The victorious airplane circled above them and then dived, making the horses scatter frantically, fighting their riders to race away from this awful thing above them. Elodie clamped down on one rein, spinning her horse in a tight circle. She risked a glance up, only to see the German plane race over their heads and out to sea.

The chestnut finally slowed, sides heaving. Elodie watched as the plane turned toward German territory. She sincerely hoped someone would shoot him down.

"Girls, with me!" Richards had her horse under control and was racing toward the flaming wreck. Elodie hauled the chestnut's head around and clapped heels to his sides, galloping with the others toward the burning aircraft. The horse gave up protesting, wanting only to stay with his herd.

The heat of the burning plane halted them, and the horses milled around nervously. That there was nothing to be done was very clear. The plane was crumpled on its nose and fully engulfed in fire. These fragile machines, made of lacquered wood and painted canvas, were filled with flammable gasoline that spelled death for pilots in a crash.

"There is nothing for you to do. Go on with your ride," the Belgian commander yelled to them. Richards nodded and waved to the FANYs who fell in behind her.

The silent women rode away from the burning heap, the morning's fun and excitement gone. As one, they turned toward Calais, heading back to the stables. The only sounds were the creak of leather, the clop of horse hooves on the *pavé* and the jingle of the curb chains.

Elodie rubbed the horse's neck. It seemed as if this war was bent on destroying more than men. It destroyed beauty, trees, animals, and even hope. And it seemed there was never an escape from it.

Chapter 10: June to August 1915

"Life is like a train station, people come and go all the time, but the ones that wait for the train with you are the ones that are worth keeping in it." *Unknown*

June drew to an end. It was as hot as the winter had been cold and the FANYs had taken to walking to the beach for dips in the ocean. Water was scarce and reserved for cooking and the wounded. The sea provided not only a way to cool down but to keep clean. Each woman carried a small container of fresh water to rinse off with, far less than a real bath would have taken.

Lottie, Elodie, and Sally had been to the beach to bathe and walked back refreshed but tired, and clean but sandy. Lottie and Sally left Elodie at the gates to the hospital where Elodie paused to brush at her clothing. She was a bit damp and her hair was wrapped in a turban. Once she was relatively certain that she would not track sand into the building, she went in the front door, greeting the patients cheerfully.

"Mademoiselle, a soldier is here to see you," one of the Belgian orderlies came through from the kitchen. Elodie sighed. Had it really been two weeks since Georges had last visited? She was beginning to lose track of time.

"Ask Cook to give him a coffee and tell him I will be right there," Elodie said to the old man. He nodded and Elodie set her foot on the first stair up to her room.

"I say, Elodie. It's not coffee I want." The deep voice held a note of laughter. Elodie whipped around, almost falling down the step in her haste. Giles stood in the doorway between the kitchen and the ward, leaning on a stick. His hair had been shaved off and was growing back in a stiff brush. He was thin and pallid, but he was there in front of her. Elodie ran straight to him with a shriek of joy. He took a quick step back to keep his balance, wrapping her tightly in his one free arm. His uniform was clean, and he smelled of citrus and cedar, a bright clean smell so far from the stench of the trenches. "That's better. Much better," he murmured against her turban.

"Where have you been? Are you all right? Are you injured? What happened to your hair?" Elodie gabbled, words falling over each other in her excitement. She stepped back slightly to make certain that he was real. Giles put a gentle finger on her lips, stopping the flow of questions. He leaned down, kissing her and drawing her to him. Elodie held him close to her, unable to believe that this was happening. The rough wool of his uniform tunic rubbed against her cheek, and she could hear the rapid beating of his heart beneath her ear.

The wounded men who could see through the doorway whistled and laughed, and the story began to make its way through the ward. The men were bored and restless, and this reunion was bringing a touch of excitement to their drab days. Elodie blushed, taking in Giles' face. Then she took his arm and together they edged past the interested orderlies, the smiling FANYs, and the cook. He limped badly, needing the stick to maneuver. She led him to the low wall outside and sat down, still holding tightly to his hands.

"I thought you were dead," she said softly, hugging him again.

"Just a run of rum luck. I've heard I owe my life to Evans."

"So he said. He's in England now, waiting for Lottie. What happened?"

"I got creased by a stray bullet that knocked me back into the trenches." He ran his hand through the stiff brush of hair and then reclaimed Elodie's hand. "Then the bast… Fritz dropped gas on us. Evans got my mask on. When I came to, I had wrenched my knee and had the mother of all headaches. It was pretty quiet since the boys had gone over the top. The orderlies found me and took me to the sorting station. I do see why old Edward Baker thought FANYs would be good morale boosters. Nothing would have made me happier than to see one of you lot. Especially you." His ears turned red, and he looked away. Elodie clung to his arm. She had not let go of him since he had appeared in the doorway.

"I somehow ended up on a wounded train bound straight for Le Havre," Giles went on. "I still don't know quite how, but I hear it was a hectic situation. I had double vision and the worst headache I've ever had for a few weeks."

"Why didn't you write to me? Oh, Giles, I thought you were dead." Elodie exclaimed. He looked at her in surprise.

"My darling. I did. A dozen letters. And I am sorry, I would never have worried you." He brushed away her tears and Elodie leaned her head into his hand.

"I received none of them. When do you have to go back to the trenches? Giles, I don't think I can bear it if you go," she whispered.

"That's the best thing, Elodie, the chap in the bed next to mine was with the Judge Advocate General, the British Expeditionary Force's legal arm. He got clipped in a shelling. But we started talking and he had me transferred to his command. I made captain and I am out of the trenches."

"*Dieu merci,*" Elodie whispered. Giles put his arm around her, pulling her in close. "What are you doing for them?"

"I read law before the war. I joined the infantry because I wanted to serve more actively." He laughed grimly. "I can't say I will miss the trenches, and I will get to see you more frequently." He kissed her again, much to the amusement of several of Madame Vincent's children.

Elodie shooed them away with a laugh and rested her head on his shoulder. They sat in the sun, at peace in a quiet corner away from the world.

The next day, seven of Giles' letters appeared in the mail for Elodie.

In early August, Lottie came into the break room for the morning meeting carrying the mail. She sorted through it, handing out letters to the women who were there and putting aside the rest for the night shift when they arrived. She glanced at one envelope with a smile and waved it teasingly in Elodie's direction.

"This came for you. Let's see, it's not your mother or your grandmother." She peered at the top left corner. "Captain. What captain could you possibly know?" Elodie rolled her eyes and laughed.

"You are a goose," she said. Lottie dropped the letter into her hand and Elodie caught the faintest scent of cedar and orange. Excitement leaped as she opened the envelope, pulling out a thin sheet of paper.

Elodie smoothed it out, her eyes running down it. Giles' handwriting had improved greatly since he was not writing hunched over in a candlelit dugout.

She could make out most of the message and her heart fluttered in excitement and hope, but some of the words… She leaned over to her friend.

"Lottie, can you read this for me and tell me what it says? I think I understand most of it, but I better make certain." She held out the letter. Lottie dropped her eyes to the note and scanned it.

"Oooo, it looks like the handsome captain wants a date with you. In Paris," she cried in excitement. The other women stopped to listen with squeals of delight.

"Lottie!" Elodie exclaimed in mock outrage.

"Very well…. 'My dear Elodie, I have leave on Monday week for six days, returning Saturday, and will be going to Paris to visit some dear family friends. If you would be able to arrange leave, we could travel together on the seven o'clock train. My friends have offered to put us up at their home. They are quite respectable and are also friends of my parents. I would greatly enjoy your company. Yours, Giles.'"

"What is Monday week?"

"A week from this coming Monday. Are you going?"

"Lieutenant Richards?" Elodie turned to the lieutenant. "May I have leave?"

"Of course," Richards replied immediately. "Elodie, I've been waiting for you to ask. With you not being an official FANY, I don't know how far my authority extends with you. But you have worked very hard, and all the other girls have had leave."

The chatter increased exponentially as each woman begged Elodie to purchase some needed item in Paris.

"Write it down and I shall do my best," Elodie laughed.

That evening, Elodie sat down to write a note to Giles. She decided that, perhaps, she should start writing in English and she found that 'yes' was the only word she needed.

On Monday week, Elodie stood on the platform at six forty-five, a small valise clutched in her hands. She was exceedingly grateful that the FANYs had cobbled together respectable clothing for her to take. The living conditions were harsh and their clothing, though it had been high-quality, was wearing out. The women had also tucked a list of desired items along with a small pile of francs into the valise. The top-most items were hand and face cream – luxurious necessities for life near the front lines.

"Elodie!" Giles strode toward her across the platform, kissing her on both cheeks. Elodie breathed in the smell of bay rum. He had not begun to grow back his mustache and she thought he looked younger.

"Do you like the clean-shaven look?" He rubbed his chin and grinned.

"I do. You look quite dashing."

"I am so glad you made it." He was wearing

his uniform and looked as if his new batman had spent hours pressing the cloth and shining every button.

"I don't think the girls would let me miss this. I have commissions to buy out the entire supply of hand and face creams in Paris."

"I've your ticket here, shall I hold it for you?" He held up two pasteboard stubs.

"Please."

The train arrived in a great cloud of steam and smoke. Giles helped her up the steps and they found seats facing forward as they pulled slowly out of the station. When the luggage was settled, the window adjusted perfectly, and a newspaper carefully folded, Elodie noticed Giles shifting uncomfortably in his seat.

"You act as if you were sitting on ants," she commented.

"Well, yes. Look, Elodie. I need to explain who we are going to stay with. If you change your mind, I will put you up at a hotel," Giles blurted out. Elodie sat back, eyes narrowed.

"Go on."

"These are very old family friends. I have known them for as long as I can remember." He paused. "They had a daughter, Gisele." His voice grew soft and Elodie had to strain to hear him over the noise of the train. Her heart was pounding and she felt almost sick. "We were married in 1910. She died three years later of pneumonia. She was so young."

Elodie sat frozen, uncertain what to do with

the information she had just been given. Giles looked miserably out the window and Elodie was not sure if it was the memory of his wife or embarrassment. She stood up, walking to the door at the end of the carriage.

Far from the Front, it was green and peaceful. The train whistled and began jostling over a switch onto a siding. It slowed to a stop and Elodie could smell ocean over the scent of grass. Giles was twenty-seven. A little thought might have suggested a possible wife in his past. At least it was not a divorce, her parents would never agree to marriage with a divorcé. Wedding bells did seem a bit presumptuous, but once thought, there was no taking it back. Another equally horrid idea occurred to her. Giles was not the only one with a secret. She walked back to their seats, from where Giles had been watching her. When she sat down beside him, he relaxed.

"I'm sorry, Giles," she said softly. He shook himself.

"It seems like a long time ago. This damned war."

"These people - your wife's parents - they are expecting me? And they want me to stay in their house?"

"Yes. I stayed with them on my last trip to Paris. They want to meet you." Giles looked out the window at the countryside, so peaceful and far from the trenches that it was hard to remember that behind them was a morass of blood and pain.

"Perhaps you should have told me you were a widower," Elodie said carefully.

"It seemed, I don't know. It seemed so far away and my life in Old Blighty - England, I mean - is like a dream I can barely remember. There is nothing but today in the trenches."

"What did you tell them about me?"

"That my first sight of you was standing in that damned muddy trench with a bag of woolen socks like some lady Father Christmas. And you were so polite about the rats. And then I danced the night away with you before a Zepp attacked. And that you ran towards where the bombs had fallen, not away like a sensible woman. I said you were remarkable."

Elodie flushed a bit and sat quietly. Giles left her to her thoughts, only glancing occasionally at her.

"Giles? I'm afraid I have a confession to make as well," Elodie said in a small voice. "But you can't tell anyone." Giles looked down at her as her cheeks turned bright pink.

"Will it put me at odds with my command?"

"I don't think so. Oh, dear. You see, Giles, the FANYs have a minimum age for volunteers. It's twenty-three."

"I've read that, yes."

"Well, I'm not twenty-three."

Giles studied her carefully. She had the slightly hard edges that women who served near the front lines developed, but under that? He suddenly realized she was definitely not twenty-three.

"How," he cleared a throat that had suddenly grown tight. "How old exactly are you?"

"Twenty."

"Thank God! I was afraid you were going to say sixteen and you'd be on the next train back to Calais. Or maybe straight to Le Havre and your mother." He sat back, taking her hand in his. "I suppose I shan't be calling you *mon bébé*. That might be a bit too close to the truth."

"You are silly, Giles."

"What shall I call you, then, *mon poupée*?"

"Not that. I don't want to be a doll." Elodie took a deep breath. "You are *l'amour de ma vie*." His lips moved as he translated the words.

"If we were alone, I would kiss you until…until you couldn't stand up."

"Perhaps later." Elodie smiled at him, shocked at her forwardness but relieved by his reaction. They sat silently savoring the moment.

Across the carriage from them were two French officers, engaged in conversation with an old man dressed in a double-breasted suit and carefully pressed trousers. His bowler hat rested on his knees and Elodie watched it jiggle with the impatient movement of his legs. The three were discussing the war and the old man seemed querulous about every point the others brought up. He also spent a fair amount of time grousing about the English on French soil.

A troop train thundered by outside the window. Very slowly, with a good deal of squealing and smoke, their train started up again, rattling back onto the main track. Giles and Elodie held hands as they talked with their heads close together. Giles described his life in London and Elodie talked about horses and wine and the farm.

They slowed to a stop at the next station and a fashionably dressed young woman, her hair carefully piled under a huge hat, boarded the train. Giles and Elodie looked in amazement at this fashion plate. In the mud and war of the last year, Elodie had forgotten that women wore something other than trousers and riding jackets or serviceable uniforms. The two officers immediately sprang to their feet, stowing the woman's wicker case on the luggage rack and inviting her to sit with them.

The train pulled out and the officers flirted outrageously with their new seat-mate. Elodie was about to look away when the older man suddenly returned to the topic of the war.

"What I would like to know is do the Scotch soldiers wear underpants or do they not?" His voice was very loud. The French officers glanced at him in some annoyance and shook their heads. The young woman seemed less than shocked.

"We do not see them much. Surely, they must

wear underwear in the trenches," one of the officers said. The fashion plate laughed a tinkly little laugh.

"Oh, Monsieur, they do not." She glanced around to be certain of her audience. By now, every passenger within earshot was listening. The woman smiled in pleasure.

"Madame, may I be permitted to know how it is that you know this?" The old man's voice was full of doubt.

"My rooms overlook the place where the Scotchmen play football. A good puff of wind and one sees. But I have not, of course, looked," she added modestly. Elodie felt a giggle starting to build in her chest. She did not dare look at Giles.

"Surely not," the old man grumped. "Nothing at all?" The young woman looked over at Giles and Elodie.

"Please, Monsieur. We will shock our English friends," she said coyly.

"Bah. The English never understand much of any language but their own."

Giles looked at Elodie questioningly and she whispered a quick translation into his ear. Giles got to his feet, his face turning scarlet as he tried to contain himself. He quickly walked toward the door between the carriages and Elodie followed him. Giles closed the door behind them and started to laugh. Elodie gave in to the giggles that had threatened to erupt. Finally, Giles straightened up, wiping his eyes.

"Oh, that hurt." He held his side and fanned his face with his hat.

"Giles, I would be happy to meet your in-laws," Elodie said suddenly. Giles looked at her and then wrapped his arms around her, leaning down for a long kiss. Since the three-hour journey to Paris took fifteen hours with delays and shunting aside for troop trains racing east, Giles almost succeeded in kissing her until she could no longer stand.

Chapter 11: August 1915

"Whenever you are in Paris at twilight in the early summer, return to the Seine and watch the evening sky close slowly on a last strand of daylight fading quietly, like a sigh." Paris: Places and Pleasures *by Kate Simon, 1967*

When the train arrived at Paris' *Gare-du-Nord*, Giles helped Elodie out of the carriage, tucking her hand securely under his elbow. He tried to carry both bags but found that he would have to let go of her arm. He finally gave up juggling the cases and Elodie took hers with a laugh. It was a peaceful night, and the skies above were clear. Occasionally, the Germans would send Traube bombers or hot air balloons to drop bombs on the City of Lights, but tonight was quiet. Elodie felt disorientated, partly from the lack of artillery and partly from giddiness.

"Twenty Rue de l'Université, Saint-Thomas d'Aquin," Giles told the female cab driver as he handed Elodie into the cab.

"Giles… Saint-Thomas d'Aquin? Who are these people?" Elodie whispered as he sat down beside her.

"Maurice and Maryam Bélanger. Maurice is the head of the School of Medicine. Maryam is curator of Oriental Art for the Louvre."

Elodie looked down at her worn skirt and ecru-colored blouse. It had been white until Madame Vincent had dyed it with coffee grounds to cover intractable stains. After months in a war zone, her clothing was shabby. Too shabby to be worn to a home in the second *arrondissement,* one of Paris' most prestigious neighborhoods. She looked doubtfully at Giles.

"You look fine, Elodie. The Bélangers will love you whether you are dressed in silk and lace or in trousers and kepi," Giles assured her. Elodie kept her thoughts to herself as the taxi traveled through the dark streets. It pulled to a stop beside a dark green door set into a cream-colored stone building. Elodie stepped out of the cab, taking the two valises with her while Giles paid. She was exhausted and apprehensive, desperately hoping there would be a bed in the near future. Even a stretcher or the corner of a room sounded appealing.

Giles took the bags and gestured for Elodie to ring the bell. He joined her at the top step and put the cases down, reaching out a hand for hers. She took it gratefully, hoping she was not clinging too tightly.

"Lieutenant Ellery, it is a pleasure." An old man in an impeccable suit opened the door. He glanced at Elodie, and his eyes crinkled with kindness.

"Good evening, Monsieur Roche. It's captain now. This is Mademoiselle Fabien."

The butler nodded a greeting. "Madame is awaiting your arrival."

"I hope we have not kept you up too late."

"It is a pleasure. Come with me, please."

A young woman in a black house dress and white apron took the valises from Giles and Elodie, darting away up the stairs. The door closed behind them and Elodie tried very hard not to gawk. She was used to the rustic elegance of their farmhouse and the Art Deco of her grandmother's home, but this was like stepping into a tiny slice of the Orient.

"It's a bit over the top. The Louvre in miniature," Giles whispered in her ear.

"It's beautiful," Elodie said, reprovingly.

The butler opened the door to a parlor that continued the Oriental theme with black lacquered chairs and divans; airy fabrics covering the windows were gossamer in the lamplight. Beyond the windows, nothing could be seen and Elodie realized they were covered with blackout curtains. The woman who stood to greet them was dressed in a gown that echoed the room's style. It was apricot with the tiniest Asian accent and hung elegantly on the woman's trim frame.

"Maryam, it is so good to see you." Giles' face seemed to lighten as he smiled at his mother-in-law. She gracefully moved toward Giles with her hands outstretched, then turned to Elodie.

"Elodie, may I present Madame Bélanger? Maryam, this is Elodie Fabien."

"Welcome to my home, my dear. Giles has told us so much about you that I feel as if I know you already." Her words were welcoming but Elodie thought she heard a touch of strain in them.

"Thank you, Madame. It is my pleasure." Elodie's voice was soft.

"I know train travel is dreadful and you must be exhausted. Perhaps a light meal and then bed?"

"Yes please, Madame."

She touched a bell and the same housemaid immediately brought in a tray with fruit, cheese, and bread neatly arranged on it. Elodie was very glad to see two small glasses of lemonade as well.

"Maurice apologizes for his absence. He must be awake very early in the morning. You will see him tomorrow evening. Now, Mademoiselle Fabien, Giles told me that you were traveling very light because of the dreadful conditions on the Front. I took the liberty of placing some gowns in your room. I hope you are not offended."

"You are more than generous. I should be honored, Madame." Elodie felt Giles' hand squeeze hers.

By the end of the short meal, Elodie found her eyes starting to droop. Maryam looked at her and smiled kindly.

"My dear, you are exhausted. Giles and I have been thoughtless. We can catch up tomorrow." She stood as the young maid entered. "Claudette, will you see Mademoiselle Fabien to her room?" The maid gestured for Elodie to follow her. Elodie left with a backward glance at Giles, who smiled encouragingly.

Her room was a light blue with white trimmings and delicate prints in the same colors decorated the walls. The furniture was painted white with blue drawer pulls and blue mats protecting the tops. Elodie felt as if she were stepping into a Japanese vase. Claudette opened the door to a bathing room and then the wardrobe. A rainbow of gowns met her stunned eyes. It was not stuffed full, but carefully curated. She itched to reach out to feel the material but was afraid the grime of the train would mar them.

"You needn't unpack for me," Elodie said hurriedly, to stop the maid from emptying the contents of her bag into the wardrobe. The maid looked at her for a moment and then seemed to understand.

"If you need anything, this is the bell. I am to attend you." Claudette pointed out a lever on the wall and then left, closing the door behind her. Elodie looked around once more. A real bath in a real bathing room. After months of washing in the train car or the sea, this was an almost unimaginable luxury. For a moment she was tempted, but she was too tired.

Tonight, a quick freshen-up would suffice, and tomorrow, a bath and one of those exquisite gowns. Elodie shivered in pleasure and went quickly to wash. She snuggled down in the comfortable bed, with soft sheets that smelled of flowers and not bleach.

In the morning, Elodie startled awake, feeling that she had missed something important. For a second, she wondered at the blue walls, comparing them to the grimy white of her tiny bedroom in Calais. Then she remembered. A bath. In a real bathtub.

The bathroom was pure white with a footed tub at the far end of the room. Someone had placed a robe and fluffy towels on a chair. The room was small and may have started life as a closet, but by the time the tub was full and lavender scent had been sprinkled in the water, it was heaven. She soaked and washed until the water grew cold.

Elodie wrapped herself in the robe and felt the stress of the last year melt away. Back in her room, she found the maid had brought a tray with coffee, fruit, and a pastry. The coffee steamed gently as Claudette made up the bed.

"Good morning, Mademoiselle. Shall I have your travel clothing cleaned?"

"Please." Elodie sat down to her tray.

"The captain said you would be in the bath. He said you have been at the Front for a year and a bath would be your first stop. Is it bad there, Mademoiselle?" Claudette was plumping the pillows. She stopped, looking at Elodie.

"Do you have someone there?"

"My brother. He is a *pouli*," the young woman said. Elodie turned her coffee cup in her hands, thinking. The papers reported on German atrocities but made no mention of the terrible conditions the French forced on their own men. She planned on platitudes, but the truth came out instead.

"It is terrible. It is muddy and noisy." She paused, searching for words. "Whatever you have imagined that hell is, the trenches are far worse."

"But the papers…"

"They lie. If the people knew what the Front is like, they would force the war to end tomorrow." The young woman's eyes welled up and Elodie immediately felt awful. She had not meant to be cruel, but the words had risen out of some dark murk before she could stop them.

"I'm sorry, Mademoiselle." Claudette wiped her tears with a corner of her apron. "I'll take these to the laundry. I'll be back in a few moments." The maid hurried out, closing the door behind her, and Elodie guiltily finished her coffee.

She dressed in her underthings, shabby in this fine room, and found a pair of silk stockings in a drawer. She had been wearing knitted wool or cotton stockings – the only materials that would stand up to hard use – and had dreamed of silk. Then she went to the closet to select a dress. Each one seemed prettier than the last and she sorted through them several times. She finally chose a pale pink one with flowers embroidered on the bodice and lace-capped elbow-length sleeves. It fell in long, graceful lines from the Empire waist. Elodie held it up to herself and looked in the mirror.

She had long admired the Directoire Revival style with the long flowing lines reminiscent of ancient Greece, and especially the lack of a corset. It had been deemed too immodest by her mother. But her mother was a long way away and this dress was exquisite. She found the designer's label and swallowed hard. This was a Paul Poiret dress. Surely Madame had not meant her to wear this. Quickly she sorted through the clothing to find each item bore a designer's label.

Finally, Elodie mustered the courage to put the gown on. The front crossed over itself, creating a deep neckline filled with lace. The underskirt fell to the ground in straight lines, while the overdress ended at mid-thigh. Elodie tugged gently at the low neckline, thinking that perhaps her mother had a point.

"Oh Mademoiselle, that suits you. May I do your hair?" The maid had slipped back into the room. Her eyes were red, but she had recovered her good cheer.

"Please. I am sorry I upset you, Claudette. Perhaps wherever your brother is, it's not too bad."

"Yes, Mademoiselle." She expertly began to

put Elodie's dark chestnut hair into a simple chignon and wrapped a pink ribbon around it.

Slipping through the hall, Elodie found Giles in the library with his feet up and uniform tunic put to one side. He was smoking a pipe and reading the newspaper. A cup of coffee sat on the side table. He looked up and did a double-take, climbing to his feet with a grin.

"Good Lord. You look fabulous, Elodie."

"This is a Paul Poiret." She smoothed down the fabric on her hips. "Are you certain Madame meant for me to wear it?"

"Of course. We must go out dancing after dinner." His eyes gleamed as he looked at her. Elodie's face flushed with pleasure.

"I'd love to." She twirled around, the top skirt flaring. Giles laughed and took her in his arms for a quick waltz around the room. Afterwards, he started to put on his tunic, but Elodie stopped him.

"Please, Giles, let's be comfortable. I won't be offended by your shirt sleeves and braces," she said, taking the tunic from him. Giles looked relieved.

"Now, I thought perhaps today we would take it easy here. Tomorrow we can see the sights and purchase all the face creams your friends could possibly want. Is there anywhere you'd like to visit?"

"Could we… I'd like to see the Sorbonne. My father promised me a year there, before the war broke out. I don't know if I will be able to go after the war, but I can dream."

"The Sorbonne it is. Does my plan agree with you?"

"Of course. Where are our hosts?"

"At work. They will be home later. Now, my dear, come sit with me and we can read all the lies the papers are printing." They snuggled down for a quiet day of rest.

By late afternoon, Elodie and Giles had read and napped, sometimes together, sometimes one at a time. Elodie discovered the exquisite pleasure of sitting on one end of a sofa with Giles' head in her lap and his feet propped on the far end. He slept soundly as she read to herself and occasionally looked down at him. The peace and quiet of the elegant room and the breeze drifting in through the open windows soothed souls made hard by the constant noise and stress of the Front.

Eventually, cheerful voices in the street below and the slamming of a door woke Giles. He sat up in confusion and laughed at himself.

"I was having the most wonderful dream. I had my head in the lap of a beautiful woman and there was no war. But then I felt and smelled my tunic, and I was back in the trenches and feeling miserable. And then I woke up. You cannot imagine how nice it was to find myself here with you," he said, leaning toward her for a kiss. Just then the door to the library opened and Giles straightened up like a guilty schoolboy.

Madame Bélanger smiled at them as Giles and Elodie got politely to their feet.

"Good evening, Giles, Mademoiselle Fabien. I see you have had a relaxing day." She took Giles' hands and pressed her cheek against his in greeting, then turned to Elodie.

"Good evening, Madame, thank you for the use of this beautiful dress. It is such a pleasure to wear," Elodie said quickly. Madame examined her with an artist's eye.

"It suits you. Leave the papers, Giles." She reached to stop Giles as he gathered up the stack of newspapers. "I hear Maurice in the street. Good. As soon as he joins us, shall we have a Dubonnet?" Maryam Bélanger took a seat in a delicate chair and the other two returned to the sofa.

Elodie had expected Dr. Bélanger to be tall and spare, to match the elegant room. The stout little man with the jolly smile seemed quite out of place and, for a moment, she was almost disappointed. Within minutes, she had forgotten that he did not fit the décor because his humor and kindness overwhelmed all else.

Soon he had handed out apéritifs, told three jokes, and plopped down in a seat with a sigh of relief.

"Now, Maurice, you are going to break the legs off that chair," Maryam scolded, but it seemed to be a long-standing joke between them.

"I'm quite certain Giles had his feet up on the

sofa's arms, eh, my boy." He chuckled at Giles' guilty face. "Your furniture is quite safe from me, my dear. I had Roche reinforce the chair not a month ago." He laughed cheerfully, and Maryam looked at him in fond exasperation.

By the time dinner was served, Elodie had fallen quite in love with the older man and was losing her shyness around Maryam. Giles smiled down at her, squeezing her hand gently as they went in to the dining room.

"What are your plans for the rest of your stay?" Maurice asked as they started on their cheese course.

"If I may, Elodie?" Giles asked, glancing over at her. She nodded. "We both need a long rest, so tonight we will stay in. Tomorrow, Elodie has commissions from her friends in Calais. After that, it will be seeing the sights and maybe a nightclub or two."

"Have you been to Paris before, my dear?" Maryam asked.

"Not often, Madame. I was to attend the Sorbonne, but with the war, my father felt it was not safe in Paris."

"But you are in Calais." The older woman looked puzzled.

"Without my father's permission."

"Ah. Well, then. You must go to *Les Invalides*. They are collecting war trophies there," Maryam suggested. Elodie looked down at her plate, not wanting to contradict her hostess. She had seen enough war trophies.

"We'll see what we can do," Giles said quickly and Elodie flashed him a smile.

In the morning, Elodie had the exquisite pleasure of selecting a walking dress from the magical trove in the wardrobe. Eventually, she settled on a dark blue twill skirt that fell to her ankles, a pale blue blouse with wide-spreading collar points, and a severely tailored military style jacket. Tassels hanging from the side seams saved it from being too masculine. She buttoned up a pair of tight boots in a matching color. She had been living in looser footwear for a year and found the constraint uncomfortable. She sighed for her feet but left them on as vanity prevailed over pain. As she tried on hats, the maid came in, watching with a frown.

"A moment, Mademoiselle. I have the perfect hat for you." Claudette rummaged through hat boxes in the wardrobe and emerged in triumph. The dark blue taffeta hat resembled the Adrian helmet worn by French troops, but was saved by a huge pleated ribbon in pale blue that fanned out like a peacock's tail. The whole ensemble was held on with a tight chin strap. Elodie looked at it hesitantly.

"If you will allow me?" Claudette's clever fingers fashioned Elodie's hair into a cluster just above the nape of her neck and soft waves to the front. She placed the hat carefully on top. Elodie blinked at herself in surprise. The very masculine hat and jacket were somehow transformed into something fresh and feminine.

"Oh, thank you," she breathed.

"My pleasure. The captain will be pleased, I think."

"I should hope so," Elodie agreed in delight.

Giles' face as she went down the stairs to join him was all that she could have wanted. He tucked her hand into his elbow and proudly led the way into the street.

As they approached the campus of the Sorbonne, Elodie looked around in excitement. The limestone buildings around a central courtyard were everything she had imagined. At the center, Elodie and Giles gazed up at the tall Astronomy Tower looming over campus, and the green cap at the top making it look as if the building were wearing a turban.

"It's one hundred twenty-nine feet high, Giles. Only the Eiffel Tower is taller," Elodie said. "I wonder if you are the very top, can you see the Front?"

"I'd rather look at the stars. Imagine what that might look like," Giles replied indulgently. "Let's go shop for your commissions. And maybe have something to drink."

By the end of the day, Giles was loaded down with two heavy bags filled with jars that clinked as they walked. As predicted, they had bought out several stores' worth of hand and face creams. They walked past a toy shop, the store looking a bit more tired and run down than the others. Elodie paused, looking at a toy horse in the window. It was not particularly well made. The ears were too short and hidden in the mane, and the brown of the nose had faded in the sun. Her eyes burned.

"Elodie, what's keeping you?" Giles suddenly realized she was no longer beside him and came back.

"It's… nothing."

"The horse?" he asked. Elodie nodded, trying not to cry.

"He looks like my horse. At our farm."

Giles looked down at her for a moment and then opened the shop door, packages clinking against the wood frame. A minute later, a hand reached into the window to pick up the horse. Soon after, Giles emerged, carrying the horse awkwardly.

"If I could find you the real thing, I would. But take him now, Elodie, before I drop these blasted creams." Giles juggled the horse into her hands.

Elodie hugged the toy to her chest and smoothed down the mane. It was perfect. She took a few skipping steps to catch up with Giles. She missed Brûlée dreadfully, but her heart sang at Giles' gesture. If she had not already been in love with Giles, this act of kindness would have pushed her over the edge.

The next day, they made the trip to look at the war trophies collected at the *Hôtel des Invalides*. This massive structure of interconnected buildings housed

Napoleon's Tomb at one end, while the former home for wounded soldiers graced the other. It looked out over six triangular gardens that pointed to the stone entrance. Following Madame Bélanger's suggestion, Giles and Elodie walked along the Avenue du Tourville towards the tomb.

It had become a pilgrimage site and women in black mourning dress made their way to the *Hôtel*. They placed votive candles at the foot of the tomb while their children – also somberly dressed - stood silently. Giles' uniform garnered glances and the occasional nod of appreciation.

The collection outside was diverse, dominated by several field-gray artillery pieces, their six-foot-long barrels pointed away from the tomb.

"Those are Feldkanone 96s," Giles whispered in her ear. "They aren't terribly accurate. The Germans fire them at us and sometimes they hit us and sometimes the shells land as much as five miles away from the trenches. Nasty things."

"I think I've heard them."

"Sometimes, it gets so loud it's hard to think or feel anything. There are two explosions, the round leaving the gun and then the blast when it hits. But then, like thunder, the sound rolls on and on. The ground shakes. Right before Festubert, we dropped one hundred thousand shells. I thought I would never hear again." His voice grew quieter. Elodie squeezed his elbow and rested her forehead on his arm for just a moment, remembering the anguish of those days.

Beyond the artillery pieces rested a wrecked airplane. Where fire had not scorched it, the plane was a cream color, and Elodie could make out part of the *Tatzenkreuz* decorating the tail and wings. She hoped it was the airplane that had shot down the French plane on the beach.

"This could be the Five-O'clock Taube that used to fly over Paris every day to drop bombs." Giles nodded toward the plane. "Maurice said that people would sit in cafés and take bets on where the bombs he dropped would fall. Maurice won a few francs on one bet." Giles said. Elodie laughed.

"That's one of the banners the Germans dropped when they almost invaded Paris," she said. "It reads, let's see, 'The German army stands before the gates of Paris. You have no choice but to surrender'. I felt so helpless." This time it was Giles' turn to comfort her.

"Do you want to see the helmets and such?" he asked.

"Not really. Would you mind if we walk along the river on the way back? And if we are going out dancing tonight, perhaps a rest?"

They walked back toward the Bélangers' home, stopping for a light lunch, watching the barges on the Seine as they ate. Back in her porcelain blue and white room, Elodie napped, dreaming of the handsome man in a room not far away.

After dinner, Giles escorted her to a nightclub to listen to jazz and dance the night away. The house was dark and all the inhabitants asleep when they returned. Once inside, Giles took Elodie in his arms, kissing her with passion. While she could think, Elodie thought about the stolen kiss with Lothar behind the barn and marveled at how much more magical a kiss was when shared with someone you loved.

"Ah, Elodie. Take yourself up to bed or we will embarrass our hosts," Giles managed in a rough voice. Elodie crossed lightly to the stairs and turned for a final glance. Then, her feet practically floating on air, she ran up the stairs to her room.

Toward the end of their stay, Maurice Bélanger took Giles away to his office for war talk, leaving the women in the salon. Maryam excused herself for a moment and Elodie went to the tiny balcony, pulling back the blackout curtains and stepping out to look over the dark city.

"You should see the view when the lights are on. It is magical," Maryam said softly, stepping out and pulling the drapes closed behind her.

"I would like that," Elodie said and clenched her hands on the railing. "Madame, thank you. For allowing me to come here and for being so gracious. I am very sorry about your daughter, and you have been so kind." There was a long silence and Elodie began to feel that she had somehow been rude or tactless.

"I miss Gisele every day, Elodie, but we knew that someday Giles would find a new love. I am happy that he found you and he loved Gisele enough to bring you here to meet us." A light on a bicycle twinkled below them as the rider wobbled over the cobblestones. The two women watched him until he turned the corner.

"His mother and I thought he had joined the infantry as a death wish. If you were the one who brought him safely out of the trenches, we are all grateful."

"Maryam? Elodie? Ah, there you are. Giles and I have settled the war and smoked fine cigars. Perhaps a nightcap?" Maurice's jovial voice called to them. Maryam turned, squeezing Elodie's hand as she went back into the bright room. Elodie followed, after she had taken time to compose herself.

The train to Calais left early in the morning. The Bélangers had hugged them both the night before and encouraged Elodie to visit again, with or without Giles. It was a bittersweet and fast journey. The passenger train made far better time since they were traveling the same direction as the troop and supply trains, and within three hours their sojourn was over.

Chapter 12: August - October 1915

"Sometimes, the most dangerous enemy is the one hiding in plain sight." *In* The Spy: A Novel of Mata Hari *by Paulo Coelho, 2017*

In Calais, Giles carried Elodie's heavy bag back to the hospital, while Elodie cuddled her toy horse. At the kitchen door, he smiled at her, his eyes crinkling.

"I shan't kiss you here in front of all your friends."

"Thank you, Giles. I had a wonderful time."

"I did as well. I'll see you in a week or two."

"I'll be here." The two looked at each other for a long moment. Elodie straightened Giles' tie, just as she had seen her mother do for her father. "Be careful, my love."

"Good heavens, Elodie," Lieutenant Richards flung open the door. "Thank God you are back.

Madame Vincent is threatening to quit, and Cook is sick. Oh, good evening, Captain." Her excited voice broke off when she saw Giles. "Come find me in five, please, Elodie. I hope you had a good holiday." She closed the door. Elodie looked at Giles shyly.

"Duty calls." She darted forward and kissed him, then opened the door and went back to work.

Calm returned to the hospital and autumn was making itself known in the cool evenings. Elodie turned from washing dishes to see Georges in the doorway. He was clean and his uniform newly washed, his face beaming from under his sunburnt patina. Elodie smiled back with pleasure. Her protégé looked as healthy and hale as she could wish.

"Georges, will you come in for coffee and a bun? I think Cook was expecting you because they are hot out of the oven." Elodie dried her hands and went to greet him with cheek kisses.

"Thank you, Mademoiselle." He stepped past Elodie, tipping his shoulder toward her, and took his place at the kitchen table. Elodie and the cook looked at him curiously. He drank his coffee and ate the bun with pleasure, but still with that odd posture. Elodie looked more closely. It took a moment to see the insignia on his shoulder: one narrow diagonal stripe and two wider ones.

"Georges! Cook, look, our Georges has made *Caporal*."

"Corporal Georges Laurent. I have my own fire team. I am the grenadier as my rifle is most accurate," he said proudly.

"Well done, Georges," the women exclaimed together. The young man beamed with pride.

"My father, he was an Apache." He used the slang for violent gangs roaming Paris streets. "I never thought I would be anything else. And look at my *médaille militaire.*" He pulled a leather pouch out of his pocket, shaking out a green and gold ribbon with crossed cannons and a medallion with a woman's profile on it. "I led an assault on a machine gun emplacement. And for this, I was given a medal." He handed it to Elodie, who admired it effusively before handing it to the cook. When they were finished poring over it, Georges carefully put it away.

"Mademoiselle, I must head back to my unit. Will you walk out with me to the station?" he asked shyly.

"Of course." She went to get her hat and jacket and the two walked toward the train station. There had been an influx of people who thronged in the street, pushing past Georges and Elodie.

"Mademoiselle, if it is not impertinent..." Georges began, but Elodie clutched at his arm.

"That man! In the British uniform up there. I know him."

"Which one?"

"In front of the woman in the red shawl.

Quickly, Georges, he is a German."

"Call him. In English," Georges commanded, no longer a boy but a leader from the trenches.

"Stephan. Stephan Rohr! Stop!" Elodie put all her lungs into the yell. Around her, people stopped to stare. The man paused and then started to walk more quickly away from them. "It's him, I know it."

Georges broke into a run, Elodie behind him, holding up her skirts so she was unencumbered. Stephan glanced behind him, and his walk became a sprint as he dodged down a side street. Georges pulled ahead of the slower Elodie as the streets narrowed around them.

Elodie cobbled together what little German she knew and yelled "Stephan, *ich kenne wo ist Lothar!*"

Stephan's feet slowed and he almost turned. In that instant, Georges caught up with him and reached out, grabbing the man's shoulder. Stephan dropped his hand to his belt, fumbling for something, and spun into his opponent. Georges let out a shriek that died suddenly. He collapsed as Elodie caught up, barreling into Stephan. They fell to the ground and Elodie felt fists driving into her face and stomach. She struggled to protect herself as hands clasped around her throat, pushing her face into a dank puddle.

This was no longer the boy she had dragged away from barn kittens: this was a soldier trained for war. Pain seared in her neck and darkness threatened her vision as she tried not to inhale filthy water. She gasped, then the hands ripped from her neck, and she drew a deep, painful breath, lifting herself up. One of the townsmen had knocked Stephan from her. With blurred vision, she saw the German haul himself up and race down the street.

Elodie threw up violently, trying to clear the foul water from her mouth. When her stomach had stopped heaving, she looked wearily over to the small crowd gathered around the still form. She crawled toward it.

Georges lay crumpled on the *pavé*, his face turned to one side, eyes open and shocked but no longer able to see. She rolled him over and he flopped to his back, a push knife protruding from his chest. Blood leaked out around the silver handle.

"No, Georges. Oh my God!" Elodie pulled the still form into her arms, bending over the young man and rocking back and forth.

In a few moments, men from the Belgian headquarters had joined the throng in the street, followed by French *gendarmes*. They were too late. Their solicitousness was unwelcome as they helped Elodie to her feet. Someone brought a piece of cloth to drape over Georges.

"Mademoiselle, you will come with us for questioning," one of the *gendarmes* said, taking her arm. On the other side, a Belgian officer pulled her toward him.

"What is going on?" A very proper British

voice silenced the crowd. Captain Wollert and Lieutenant Richards strode into the fray, accompanied by one of Madame Vincent's brood, his face alight with excitement. Elodie pulled away from the men, running to the captain who took her into her arms protectively. Elodie sobbed into her shoulder. Richards stood defensively next to the pair. The French and Belgians surrounded them, each trying to out-do the others in volume and vociferousness. Captain Wollert flung up her hand and the babble stopped.

"Elodie?" She asked gently. "What happened?" Elodie scrubbed at her face, shuddering.

"My friend Georges… he's there." She pointed at the still form. "I saw a German. He stabbed Georges." The captain looked uncertain and then took a firmer command over the situation. She kept her arm around Elodie and glared at the group of men who were beginning to shout at each other and at the British women.

"Ricky, tell them this: You will wish to interview my housekeeper. We shall conduct the interview in my office at Lemarcq Hospital." Captain Wollert said firmly. Richards stumbled through the sentences as Captain Wollert led Elodie away from the crowd. What seemed to be most of the city's residents followed in great excitement. Elodie staggered along, overwhelmed by shock and horror. The Belgians and *gendarmes* followed, still arguing.   The Belgian commander caught up with them, catching up in a quick conversation in Dutch.

The crowd thinned at the gates, leaving only the uniformed men to escort the three women into the hospital. The FANYs gathered on the stairs as the noisy group came into the building. Captain Wollert glanced around.

"Lottie, get tea, a towel, and something dry for Elodie to change into. Bring them to my office. Quick now."

The captain demanded that the officials wait until Elodie had changed out of her wet, blood-soaked clothing and was sat on a tattered couch, Lottie's arm protectively around her. The tea helped to wash the foul taste out of her mouth.

The questions came fast and hard in a bewildering mishmash of Dutch, French and English.

"Who was the French soldier?"

"Georges Laurent. I met him during the first gas attack," Elodie whispered, answering in English and depending on someone else to translate. "Oh, Captain Wollert, he was only fifteen. I didn't tell anyone because the *poilus* took care of him."

Lottie poured more tea, forcing Elodie to drink.

"What happened?" Captain Wollert asked.

"I saw a German I knew from before the war. His name is Stephan Rohr. He was in a British uniform."

There was general consternation. Spies were

always a concern, but this went far beyond the recent arrest of nurses gathering intelligence on both the German and Entente sides. The men looked at Elodie with greater suspicion.

"I think I saw him before today," Elodie said slowly. "I kept thinking I recognized a soldier but didn't think I could have. I don't know." She sat silently as the men raged questions at her. "I said nothing because I wasn't sure, I never got a good look at him."

"You shouted something in German at him."

"I said that I knew where his brother was. His brother Lothar is a prisoner of war in Guines. I drove him there."

"You speak German? Perhaps you are a German spy."

"I know about ten words."

The questioning went on as Elodie grew faint, sagging against her friend.

"Captain, with your permission, I am going to put Elodie to bed. She is all but out," Lottie announced sternly.

"Please do, Mullins. And stay with her until I come to see you," Captain Wollert said.

"No. She will come with us to the prison until we can question her further," the loudest of the *gendarmes* snapped, reaching for Elodie. Lottie pushed his hand away.

"No. The FANYs are under my protection. She

will stay here," the commandant said stiffly.

"She is a French citizen."

The tension in the room increased to almost unbearable levels. The Belgian commandant held up his hand to stop the interrogators.

"She stays here. I will post a guard. I suggest you find this German spy and leave this young woman alone."

Lottie helped Elodie to her feet and half carried her toward her room. She tucked Elodie into bed, sitting with her until Elodie fell asleep to tortured dreams.

The next day brought representatives from the French and British armies to join the Belgians. Giles stood in the background of the British group, his face at times white with fear then red with fury as Elodie was questioned over and over. The three groups began arguing over her head. Giles eased his way closer to her, his eyes full of anguish, and whispered to Lottie.

"Giles says he is doing what he can," Lottie whispered in Elodie's ear. "He says to be brave." Elodie bit her lip.

"Lottie? Where are…oh, I beg your pardon, Captain. There's a telegram for Lottie." Sally came into the room, glancing around curiously. Lottie took the envelope with shaking hands and tore it open. She read it and handed it to Captain Wollert with a triumphant grin.

"What is this, Mullins?"

"Elodie worked for a BEF veterinarian in Le Havre. I sent him a telegram. Well, we all pitched in the money because it was dear. Here's his answer."

"*EF not repeat not German spy. Could not read German documents. Letter to follow. Captain Oliver Harris DVM BEF.*" Captain Wollert read aloud. Giles crossed the room suddenly, taking the paper from her and reading it for himself. He handed it to the next man. Giles looked at Elodie, collapsed exhausted against her friend.

"Captain Ellery, will you assign a man to follow this up? I'll need a report." the British major said.

"Yes, sir," Giles replied. Elodie heard his footsteps clatter down the stairs.

"We'll soon get to the bottom of this. For now, I propose we adjourn until my man returns. I suggest we look for this spy, rather than trying to pin blame on this one girl."

Giles' major proceeded to usher the French and Belgians out of the room. "I'll reconvene this meeting when the investigator returns."

Angry complaints accompanied the men down the stairs, fading into the distance. The three women sat silently for a time.

"Well. Good thinking, Mullins. Even if it just gets them out of our hair for a week." Captain Wollert sighed. "Elodie, I promised the commandant that you would not leave, but I have no authority over you. If you choose to leave, I will understand." She fiddled with some papers on her desk. "You must realize that the Belgians are all that stand between you and being arrested. The French are looking for spies and they have you in their sights. I would stay in the hospital if I were you." She looked directly at Elodie.

"I understand, Captain," Elodie replied faintly. "May I be excused? I have duties I have shirked."

"Of course. And Mullins, I'll put a few francs toward the cost of the telegram."

Elodie left them deciding on the proper amount and went down to the kitchen to start her rounds. The cook immediately served her a cup of coffee and a commiserating glance.

In the days that followed, Elodie found herself dissolving into tears at nothing, wondering if two women laughing together were laughing at her or if odd looks from the townspeople were a condemnation. Only the quiet of her room gave her solace.

Days later, Giles returned triumphantly from an interview with Captain Harris. Once again, the concerned parties gathered in Captain Wollert's office. The French were suspicious, the Belgians irritated, and the British upset by a spy in their midst. Giles read aloud the affidavit from Dr. Harris.

"*To Whom it May Concern, Miss Elodie Fabien offered her help at my veterinary hospital just after the Battle of the Marne. She was excellent with the wounded and sick horses and provided translation services between the French workers and myself.*

I was sent documents found after the Marne, purportedly from a German veterinarian. The documents had been checked by Military Intelligence, but Miss Fabien did not know this. I asked her to translate these documents, but she could not. She recommended finding a Belgian refugee. I also left the papers where she could find them with a minimal amount of energy, but they were never disturbed.

As a result of this, I do not believe that Miss Fabien was in any way a German spy. If she were a spy, she would have taken the opportunity to ensure that the documents were not of importance to the German cause.

I have no qualms about accepting Miss Fabien back into my hospital and should her employment in Calais cease, I encourage her to return to Le Havre to work for me as I will create a place for her.'"

Giles looked at Elodie with the tiniest smile on his face as the Major finished reading the document for himself.

The discussion that followed meant nothing to Elodie. She recognized that each side wanted someone to blame for their failures and a single woman was an easy target. Lottie and Giles had poked a stick in their spokes. Elodie squeezed Lottie's hand in thanks.

"Captain Ellery, I'll give you ten minutes to finish your business here. Then find me," Giles' superior said. Captain Wollert herded everyone out of her office, leaving Elodie and Giles alone. Giles sat down beside her.

"You do have some adventures, Elodie," he said mildly. "I am sorry about your friend. It must have been an awful shock." Elodie nodded and Giles opened his arms. She burrowed into them, finding peace. He held her for a long time.

"Now, about this Captain Harris fellow. He was quite taken with you. You won't be leaving here to go work with him, will you?"

Elodie made a sound somewhere between a sob and a laugh. "No, Giles. Wherever you are, I will be." He chuckled deep in his chest and kissed her.

"Good. Now, I must go. Do try to stay out of trouble."

Elodie sat back and straightened his tie. "Wear your warm boots." He smiled at her and then was gone. This time, the cadence of his footsteps on the stairs was light and almost happy.

A week later, Elodie found herself rubbing her eyes, burning hot and itchy. Her stomach hurt and she was so very tired it seemed all she could do was to sit in a chair in the kitchen or run to the outhouse. The cook poured her a cup of coffee, but it tasted wrong. She cradled her head in her hands, feeling more wretched by the moment.

"Oh, Elodie, here you are. We need…" Lottie's voice trailed off as she looked at her friend. A cool hand rested on Elodie's aching forehead. "Oh, dear." She left the room. As if from a great distance, Elodie could hear Lottie calling for the doctor and the lieutenant. A few moments later, the doctor's thick fingers were holding her face, turning it this way and that.

"It is the typhoid," he pronounced gravely. Elodie felt a frisson of fear before the misery of her stomach and head overwhelmed her.

Hands lifted her, carrying her out of the kitchen and across the courtyard. While the disease was slowly waning, they still had a handful of unlucky soldiers in the typhoid wing. Elodie swayed for a few moments as FANYs and orderlies rushed about setting up a curtained-off bed. She tumbled into it and sat listlessly as Lottie undressed her and eased a nightgown on. The bed's softness soothed her aches. Her head pounded abominably. Someone brought in cool water and Elodie almost cried in relief. Impersonal hands helped her lay back. Over the next hour, the fever began in earnest.

It was not a light case. The emotional strain had taken its toll. Elodie was lost in a world where people came and went without explanation, appearing where they shouldn't be. Walls rose up in her dreams, leaving her exhausted from climbing them only to have them shrink when she was at the very top. Her mother was there sometimes, soothing her.

Giles came, his face thin and white. Behind him stood Stephan, eyes cold, still wearing a British uniform. Elodie shrunk from him, crying in fear. Giles looked even more distressed. She tried to speak, but the words were lodged somewhere in her fever dreams.

Someone spoke German to her, repeating something over and over. Try as she might, the words made no sense. Finally, the sounds went away, leaving silence.

Even Maurice Bélanger showed up in her dreams, looking down at her gravely and then turning away. She cried after him to come back. He had the key to make her well.

When the fever finally broke, Elodie lay on her bed, almost too weak to hold her eyes open. Her mother sat in a chair next to her, fiercely knitting. She looked older.

"Maman." Elodie managed a croak that she could barely hear, but her mother looked up, dropping her knitting.

"Oh, my darling," Isabeau cried, tears starting in her eyes.

"Water, Maman." Her lips were chapped and hurt dreadfully. When her mother brought a tin of cool water to her, Elodie found her arms would not lift off the bed. Her mother raised her gently. She held the tin to Elodie's lips.

"Don't drink too much. Just a few sips at first. Oh, Lottie," Isabeau looked up at the rustle of the curtain. "She's awake and making sense." Lottie came into focus just beyond the bed. Joy lit up her plain face.

Elodie tried to smile at her friend, but sleep overcame her, a peaceful sleep, not the nightmare-ridden slumber of the last three weeks.

Elodie awoke to a sunlit room. It hurt her eyes and she blinked, feeling the sting as tears wet what the fever had dried. Her arms lay like logs beside her. From far away, she could hear the sounds of the hospital – patients talking, footsteps on the wooden floors, the rattle of autos in the courtyard. A horse whinnied in the street, and she shrank away from the memory of horses dying in the battlefield shelling.

From somewhere, the smell of baking bread drifted in through the slightly open windows. Her stomach growled and she realized with surprise that she was hungry. She turned her head slightly. Giles sat in an armchair that she recognized from the FANY house, fast asleep with his head tilted back. His legs took up much of the space in the tiny curtained-off area and his booted feet looked enormous. His tunic was unbuttoned, revealing his khaki shirt underneath. One hand was tucked into the braces and the other hung over the edge of the chair. He looked very uncomfortable.

She watched him sleep, rediscovering his face, lean and tanned under dark brown hair. His lashes fanned over his cheeks. She wanted to get up and go to him, but she was too weak. Even the sheet felt too heavy to move. His fingers twitched and he came awake suddenly, eyes searching for danger before his body moved. His gaze fell on her and his face was lit with a smile. He folded up his legs and fell to kneel beside the bed, taking her in his arms. Bay rum and the clean smell of freshly washed clothing filled her nose as he cuddled her close to him. One of her hands managed to stroke his side.

"I thought I had lost you," he whispered. "Don't do that again, if you please."

"I'm sorry," Elodie whispered back. He kissed her gently and edged her over so he could lie down beside her on the bed. It was narrow and not very comfortable, but Elodie didn't mind. They snuggled together until it was time for Giles to go back to his unit. He left slowly; face drawn in thought.

The typhoid left Elodie weak and shaky, and nothing seemed to bring back her energy. Her heart seemed to race or sometimes not beat at all, and she was dizzy. Sitting was the limit of her endurance. There was not much she could do around the hospital. On one sunny day, the captain and lieutenant found her in a chair in the kitchen, absorbing the warm sun.

"Elodie. We need to ask you something," the captain said, pulling up a chair and leaning toward her. "We've heard that… Oh, bother, this is difficult." She drew a deep breath, marshaling her thoughts. "The FANYs are going to be absorbed into the Red Cross in January, if they can pass the driving and medical tests. That means there will be nowhere for you, my unofficial FANY. And you don't seem to be getting better. As a result, we are not certain what to do with you. Can you go back to your parents for a time, until you feel stronger, and we can find a place for you?"

Elodie looked at her, fatigued. Going home seemed like such a defeat, but she was so very tired. The too-ready tears leaked down her cheeks.

"I suppose so. I'm sorry. Sorry I am useless." The self-pity disgusted her.

"Oh, Elodie. You've not been useless. You are invaluable and the French and Belgians should give you medals for pitching in. You go home and rest. This damn war is going to carry on and we'll always welcome you back," Lieutenant Richards told her stoutly.

Elodie sent a letter to Giles detailing the conversation with Captain Wollert and Lieutenant Richards. As soon as he could, Giles visited her whilst on a quick trip to Calais. She sat on Jezebel's running board, resting. Giles stood, arms crossed and face impassive.

"They want me to go back to my parents in Le Havre. I'm too tired and weak to be of much help here," Elodie said softly. Giles calculated the distance between the British lines and Le Havre as he looked at the pale face in front of him. An idea occurred to him, and he sat down beside her.

"Not to worry, I have a plan and it won't

involve you going to Le Havre. That's simply too far away and I shan't be able to see you. You hold tight and let me see if I can get this going." He helped her back to her room where he sat beside her until she fell asleep.

The plan took two weeks to put into motion. Eventually, it resulted in a warm invitation from the Bélangers to join them in Paris until she was stronger. Her parents were pleased that she would be under the direct care of a doctor. Elodie accepted the invitation gratefully.

Elodie and Lottie packed her few belongings. On her last day, the Belgian command showed up in full force and in dress uniforms, Cook prepared as fancy a treat as her provisions would allow and the FANYs escorted Elodie to a seat in the main ward. Here, the FANYs and the Belgians shared tiny cakes and good cheer with the patients.

The commandant offered Elodie an envelope with her name written on the front in elegant copperplate. She opened it, pulling out a fine piece of paper with the royal arms of Belgium as a header. The short paragraph thanked her for her service to the country, signed King Albert of Belgium. Elodie read the letter over in awe, passing it around before Lottie tucked it away in Elodie's bag. The commandant hugged her tightly, thanking her for her work to save his countrymen. The Belgian doctor and nurses covered her with ardent cheek kisses and well wishes.

At last, there were hugs from the FANYs and Lottie walked Elodie to the train station.

"I'm going to miss you. It's been jolly having you here. I'm glad I ran into you at the wharf." Lottie tried to smile.

"You can come to Paris. And perhaps I will be back."

"There's the whistle. Hurry now." The two women hugged each other.

Just as Elodie was getting ready to step onto the train, one last well-wisher came to the station. The coffin man in his rusty black made his way quickly to her. He was no less terrifying than the first time she had seen him, but his face was kind and worn with sorrow. He took her hand, pressing something into it, then helped her up the steps to the train carriage. Elodie waved goodbye to Lottie and the coffin man. Lottie's face was streaked with tears.

The train slowly pulled out of the station and Elodie sank into her seat, looking down at what the man had given her. It was a leather pouch. Inside, Elodie found the green and yellow medal that had belonged to Georges. She held it close to her heart and stared blindly out the window.

Chapter 13:
October to December 1915

"Let woman choose her own vocation just as man does his. Let her go into business, let her make money, let her become independent, if possible, of man." In *Let Woman Choose Her Own Vocation, Maggie Lena Walker, 1912*

The Bélangers met Elodie at the *Gare-du-Nord*. She practically collapsed in exhaustion, grateful to be off the train. She barely remembered the trip to their home and was asleep before someone dimmed the lamps in the blue and white room.

Late in the morning, Elodie sat up in bed, panicked and disoriented. Her heart pounded and the room seemed to spin. She clutched her head and slowly things righted themselves. She was in Paris. Through that door was the bathroom. Slowly, she slid out of bed and went to bathe.

"Good morning, Mademoiselle," the maid,

Claudette, said cheerfully as Elodie came out of the bathroom.

"Good morning."

"Your breakfast is here. Monsieur the doctor wishes to speak with you when you have dressed and eaten. He says there is no hurry, he is working on a paper. I took the liberty of taking your clothes last night for a good cleaning. Madame has left you a selection. May I pick out an outfit for you?"

"Please." Elodie sat down to drink her coffee. She felt as if she could crawl back into the bed Claudette was making. Talking of nothing in particular, the maid laid out a gray wool skirt and a pale green blouse. Elodie noted with pleasure that fashionable collars were no longer worn high on the neck. Wearing high, tight collars while working in hospitals, aid stations, and trenches was often uncomfortable, and when they were alone, the FANYs had often unbuttoned them. Elodie had grown used to the freedom.

The fine wool stockings felt so light on her legs and comfortable in her shoes. Her old stockings had been darned until there was nothing left of the original foot, and they rubbed painfully inside her boots. Claudette worked Elodie's hair into a low chignon that was brushed severely back from her face.

"The pompadour is passé, Mademoiselle. The new styles are low and smooth."

"I like it, but it seems rather plain."

"Not to worry. When the captain comes to visit, I shall dress it far more elaborately."

"Thank you. Now, the doctor is waiting for me?"

"In his office."

Elodie went out into the hallway and walked slowly down the stairs. She tapped gently at the closed door of Maurice's study.

"Come in." Elodie entered to find Maurice putting on his jacket and stubbing out a smelly cigar.

"Ah, good, Elodie. You look far better than last night. I want to give you the once-over, to see how you are recovering." His voice was cheerful as always, but Elodie felt as if she was a prospective horse. He asked questions and then listened to her heart and lungs with a wooden stethoscope.

"Lightheaded and your heart is racing? Hmmm. You had a bad bout of typhoid and it's going to take a while to recuperate. Spend as much time as you need sleeping and eating for the next month or so. I'll check you then."

"I haven't much appetite."

"Make the most of what you do eat, and I will speak with Cook. And rest. I've heard from Giles that he will be here in three weeks. Let's get some flesh on you and the gray out of your face."

"Yes, Doctor. And thank you for taking me in and for, well, for everything."

"Of course. I quite enjoyed meeting your

mother. She and Maryam were thick as thieves when your mother passed through on her way to Calais. Now, off you go and get some rest. Read, sleep, knit, or whatever you ladies do to relax."

Elodie went to the library and picked out a few books, then returned to her room and settled down to read and nap. Claudette appeared periodically with a tiny cup of soup or a small snack, watching to make certain that Elodie ate her offerings. Elodie did, smiling to herself because she felt like a pig being fattened for market.

For the first week, she slept most of the day, supported by a stack of pillows since lying flat made it hard to breathe. Eventually, Elodie started to feel better, sleeping only half the day away. She worried she was being selfish and lazy, but just as those guilty feelings would threaten her, she would fall asleep.

By the end of the second week, she was knitting socks for the trenches and Claudette had found the softest wool in the market for Elodie to crochet an afghan for Giles. Winter had come and, while he was rarely in the trenches, this might provide a bit of comfort for him. As she crocheted, she thought about the letter she had received from Lottie in the morning mail.

November 1, 1915
Dear Elodie,
It is rather hard to believe that we have been here for an

entire year. On some days, it seems to be just yesterday, and on others, I think I have been here forever. We've had some major changes at the hospital. The British Red Cross is now providing the ambulances and any FANY who passes their driving test will transfer over.

The hospital is left with a skeleton staff. It pretty much runs itself – Lieutenant Richards says it is your good organization that we are running on – and the Belgians aren't doing a lot of fighting. I stayed on with the hospital. It was rather selfish of me, but I have a better chance of getting to England to see Siôn with the FANYs than the Red Cross.

I do miss our chats. I hope to get to Paris over Christmas and will look you up. You take care and get healthy and all that.
Love, Lottie

Elodie missed the other women and the feeling that she was contributing, but she was so worn out that it was almost painful to think of going back to the terror of the Front.

The doorbell rang and Elodie set down her crocheting. She might as well answer the door. Monsieur Roche moved so slowly these days that sometimes the person was gone before the old man could get there. She opened the door to find Giles on the step. His eyes crinkled and he gave a whoop of delight.

"Just the person I wanted to see. Where's old Roche? Did they draft him for the war?" Giles stepped into the house and dropped his valise with a thud. He wrapped Elodie in a hug and kissed her with great enthusiasm that Elodie returned in equal measure. His trench coat was cold and damp from the snow. He finally stepped back, looking down at her seriously.

"You look better, but still a bit peaky. *Bon après-midi*, Monsieur Roche." Giles grinned at the butler, who greeted him warmly.

"Are you tired, Giles?" Elodie asked.

"A bit. I shall probably crash later, but for now, a drink and sitting on something that isn't thumping over fishplates will do."

"I am so glad you're here. I've got a comfortable nest in the sitting room, and it's warm there."

Once in the room, Giles took off his uniform tunic with an apology for sitting in his shirt sleeves. Elodie snuggled up beside him, pushing the crochet work to one side.

"What's this?" he asked.

"An afghan. For you." Elodie held it up and laughed. It was only a foot long. Giles took it, draping it carefully over his shoulders.

"It's rather short, but too wide for a scarf. I could be your grandmother." He flipped it over his head, peering out at her.

"Goose. My grandmother would not be caught dead in a headscarf. Hand it over and I'll put a few more feet on it," Elodie commanded. Giles complied happily. The afternoon passed pleasantly, in warmth and comfort and desultory talk about nothing and everything.

The Bélangers returned in the evening with hugs for Giles. After dinner, Maurice took him into his office. When they emerged an hour later, Giles' face was pale, and he looked at Elodie searchingly. She smiled at him, wondering about the sudden change.

In the morning, he proposed a day of resting.

"Would you take me for a walk, Giles, a very short one? I should enjoy the fresh air," Elodie suggested instead.

"Do you really think we should?"

"When I watched the nurses do the Kenny exercises, they sometimes had to bully the men into doing them, but once they started, they got better. I am tired of being tired, Giles, and walking is the best thing I can do," Elodie insisted.

Giles relented and Elodie found her warmest coat. Giles waited for her in his trench coat. Elodie wrapped his scarf around his neck, trying to cover up his ears.

"It doesn't look very dignified," Giles complained, easing it down. Elodie laughed at him. He opened the door for her and together they went into the bright winter sunlight. She managed the four hundred feet to Rue Gaston Gallimard, stopping several times to catch her breath. Giles looked at her in concern.

Once they were back in the house and ensconced on the sofa in the sitting room, Elodie questioned him.

"What on earth is going on? You are fussing." Giles looked guilty.

"You should ask Maurice. He'd be better at explaining."

"I'm asking you." This was followed by an uncomfortable silence. Giles got up and poured himself a drink, tossing it back. He filled the glass again and brought one for Elodie. She sniffed, making a face, but sipped at it anyway.

"Maurice said that sometimes a typhoid case develops myo… myocarditis. It affects the heart and makes the patient very tired and their heart beat oddly. He's afraid you may have it. There is nothing to do for it." His voice was shaky. Elodie sat for a few minutes, absorbing the news.

"And why did he tell you and not me?" she asked. Her voice was low, but there was a sharpness in it that surprised Giles. He fidgeted under her glare.

"Because, well, because of Gisele," he finally said.

"That makes no sense."

"He is worried about you. And about me too, losing another wife. I told him I was going to marry you." Giles was turning bright red. Elodie closed her eyes and realized that her fingernails were driving into her palms. She felt betrayed by both men.

"It seems as if there is a lot of gossip and planning going on behind my back. Perhaps I should talk to Maurice and perhaps you should ask me to marry you yourself, instead of all this whispering about it." Her voice was cold. There was a long silence.

"Elodie?"

"Yes, Giles?"

"Will you marry me?"

"No," Elodie said shortly. Giles stood up abruptly.

"But… but Elodie," he managed to stammer. "Have you been toying with me? I thought we had an understanding." When she had judged he had suffered enough, Elodie took pity on him.

"I'm only twenty, Giles. My father wishes me to be twenty-one before I marry. I turn twenty-one in June. You can ask again then and perhaps I will give you a different answer. And I want my father's blessing. I don't think you have time to travel to Le Havre to get it." She gave him a smile that was only partially forgiving. Giles collapsed back onto the sofa.

"Minx." He tucked his arm around her and drew her in. "You gave me a turn."

"Good." Elodie cuddled against him, feeling that odd heartbeat that seemed to rush and pound at the same time. She said nothing to Giles.

When Giles returned to the Front, Elodie went to speak to Maurice. He examined her again and frowned.

"Are you having many palpitations? Lightheadedness?"

"Not really. Not so much," Elodie lied cheerfully. "I felt better when Giles and I were out walking. It seemed calming." The doctor fiddled with his stethoscope.

"Then I encourage you to keep walking. I do not believe that any harm will come from it."

"Thank you, Doctor. I will start on your recommendation." Elodie went to the door. For a moment, she paused, wanting to tell him not to speak to anyone about her, but it felt awkward and rude. She closed the office door behind her and went up to her room.

Taking the stuffed horse in her arms, she sat down in a chair where she could look out into the pocket garden behind the house. It was snowing gently, and the scene was peaceful. Thoughts swirled through her head. There were so many things she wanted, and so many that were impractical.

She detailed them carefully, examining each. First and foremost was the desire for revenge. No, she shook her head. She did not want revenge, she wanted to personally destroy Stephan. That was the most impractical thing she wished for. Surely, having been brought to the attention of the Entente, Stephan was back in Germany. She allowed herself a moment to daydream about meeting him again. She moved him firmly into the 'Someday' category.

Second, the FANYs were a closed door. They had been a good thing, but there was no going back. She still wanted to help with the war effort, but that meant looking for other opportunities.

Going to Le Havre was out of the question. She loved her family dearly, but she had outgrown them. She laughed to herself. Perhaps that was why people did not let their daughters leave home. It kept them from branching out and up and growing away from their parents. Here she was, infinitely older than she had been a year ago, and grown too much to go back home.

Staying in Paris was equally problematic. The Bélangers were kind and generous and had opened their house to her, but she craved privacy and the ability to make her own decisions without consulting her hosts.

Elodie could not keep asking her parents for money. With the farm inoperable for the foreseeable future, they would be short of funds. The situation was worse because her father could not work as a judge in his district. She needed to make her own money and pay her own way.

Perhaps she had been a fool to turn Giles down. With his income, they could find a tiny apartment in Paris or even a rooming house. That would mean trading her dependency on her parents and the Bélangers for dependency on Giles, also not the solution she was looking for. Elodie held the horse up to eye level and growled at it.

"You are becoming a Modern Woman," she said in a high-pitched voice, as if the horse was speaking. The horse had a point. Modern Women had jobs and places to live that were not with their parents.

Elodie smiled in triumph as her plan fell into place. A job to start, and then she was only a mile from the Sorbonne. Her first step was to recover enough to be able to work. She hugged the horse and put it back on her table before dressing warmly and going out into the snowfall to walk a little farther each day.

Chapter 14:
December 1915 - May 1916

"When radium was discovered, no one knew that it would prove useful in hospitals. The work was one of pure science. And this is a proof that scientific work must not be considered from the point of view of the direct usefulness of it." *Marie Curie, 1921*

The cold brought roses to Elodie's cheeks and an appetite that fed her improving health. She still felt the odd heartbeat, but the episodes seemed fewer. She had rediscovered the Jardin du Luxembourg, not far from the Bélanger's home. She and Giles had strolled through the expansive gardens in August. Now the plants lay under thick blankets of snow and children, shrieking with laughter, ice skated on the Grand Bassin.

Beyond lay the campus of the Sorbonne, and as she grew stronger, Elodie walked through the grounds, wondering if she would ever attend even a single class.

Female students outnumbered male students. Most French male students had joined in the early days of the war, fighting and dying in disproportionate numbers. Any not in the trenches were recruited to work in factories. The university was not generally interested in educating women but had to make up funding shortfalls, so women were allowed to enroll in greater numbers.

"You'll find the administration puts as many roadblocks in our way as they can," one female student told Elodie, irritably. "You must prove literacy in Latin before you can graduate. That knocks most of us out of degrees. After all, the girls' lycées are about training us to be cultured, not educated."

Elodie walked back to the Bélanger's thinking that she did not need to graduate, she just wanted the experience. A job was still the next step.

In the early days of the war, Paris had closed down, businesses shuttered and streets unoccupied, but at the end of 1915, life had crept back because women could not wait for men who might never return. It was no longer unusual to find women in every job from sweeping streets to working as government officials.

Here she discovered her next hurdle. Clothing that had come with her from the Front was hard-worn and immediately marked her as provincial. Clothing borrowed from Maryam Bélanger was far too grand for a shop girl. Elodie gritted her teeth after yet another refusal and stalked back to the house.

Christmas came and went quietly. Elodie sent Giles a box of tea and the afghan. He sent a letter.

On February 21, 1916, the Germans attacked the city of Verdun. Elodie read the frenzied reports in the paper. Verdun represented France's military strength and destroying the town would symbolically devastate the French army. Verdun could not fall, the politicians and military leaders declared. In March, when it became clear that this was going to be a battle like no other, the French government set up the *Voie Sacrée*, a road that ran from Bar-le-Duc to Verdun. The only purpose of the road and the rail line beside it was to transport men and material to this one battle. Verdun would not fall.

Unable to sit still, Elodie went out for a walk. The peace of the city felt wrong. With the battle raging a mere one hundred sixty miles away, it seemed obscene that life in Paris went on. She walked down the Quai Voltaire, idly watching the Seine and the boat traffic that never ceased. It was peaceful by the river, and she could feel quiet descend over her.

As Quai Voltaire became Quai de Montebello, she paused, looking at Notre Dame across the Seine. The great stone towers stood to her left while the stained-glass window glinted dully at her. Perhaps walking down to this place in the evening when she could see the window in all its glory would bring some solace. The Bélangers would probably object. The Latin Quarter spread out behind her was not a place for a respectable young woman. Defiantly, she walked through that storied neighborhood.

Next to one of the gate posts of the Pantheon, Elodie noticed a woman leaning against the bricks, fanning herself despite the cold weather. She was tiny, and her black overcoat almost dwarfed her. Her hair under her black hat was gray and fly-away. Elodie noted the pallor of her thin, somber face. She had seen that look on the faces of the wounded. The woman's eyes were closed, pinched in pain, and one hand pressed to her side. For a moment, Elodie made to step around her, but the humanity that the front lines had not managed to kill rose in her chest.

"Pardon me, Madame, may I be of assistance?" she asked kindly. Sad, dark brown eyes fluttered open and looked up at her.

"Perhaps… yes. My offices are only minutes from here, but I find myself very tired." Her French was vaguely accented. Elodie offered her hand to help the woman up. She tottered for a moment and then gestured down the road. "I have been very ill and sometimes walking catches up with me."

"I understand, Madame. I am walking for my health and often find I must sit for a time." They walked the few blocks, exchanging polite pleasantries.

"These are my offices." The woman waved her

hand toward a large, four-story, yellow brick building fronted with windows on every level. At the very top of the third story, just under the mansard stonework, were the words '*Université du Paris*'. Just under the rain cap above the main door, carved in stone was '*Institut du Radium Pavillion Curie*'.

Elodie glanced down at the woman in surprise. Everyone knew of the brilliant physicist Marie Curie and her work with invisible bits of matter. Now that Elodie knew who this was, she could see the resemblance to Irène Curie in the set mouth and the determined dark eyes.

"Come, my dear, we shall use the private entrance and perhaps you will allow me to serve you refreshments." Marie Curie led the way to the right side of the building and up a few stairs.

Immediately inside the door to the right was a simple office, filled with books, an oak desk, and filing cabinets. There was a cheerful messiness to the room. To the left of the door was a small but comfortable room filled with overstuffed chairs and a low sofa. The woman gestured Elodie into the room and unpinned her hat, her hair now even more untidy. She wore a black pinstriped dress, utilitarian in its cut and with no bows or ribbons. It was well-tailored to her slight frame.

"Are you… are you Madame Curie?" Elodie asked.

"Maman, where have you been? The workmen

are setting up… oh, you have company." Irène Curie, attired in the same simple style of dress, rushed into the room. She looked at Elodie curiously and then her face lit up. "Oh! Mademoiselle Fabien. What are you doing here?" She crossed to Elodie, holding out her hands to catch Elodie's and kissing her on each cheek.

"I met your mother on the street, and she was kind enough to ask me in," Elodie smiled at her former room-mate.

"Maman, this is Mademoiselle Fabien. She was most kind to me when I was setting up the X-ray room at Lamarq Hospital in Calais," Irène told her mother. "Mademoiselle Fabien was the housekeeper for the hospital and shared her room with me."

"Ah, I am doubly in your debt for your kindness not only to me but to Irène." Marie gestured Elodie to the sofa and sank tiredly into an armchair. "Irène, would you ask Juliette to bring coffee and cakes, and perhaps you would join us."

"Of course, Maman."

In moments, a maid brought in a tray filled with tiny madeleines and a steaming pot of coffee. She set it down and left the room with a curious glance at Elodie.

The coffee was welcome, and Madame Curie seemed to recover some of her color as she sipped at the cup and nibbled on the cakes.

"You have been ill, Mademoiselle?" Marie asked Elodie.

"Yes. I had a severe case of typhoid."

"Are you still working at the hospital?" Irène asked.

"No. Most of the FANYs are with the Red Cross now. The few that remain in the hospital can manage without me."

"The FANYs sang her praises to me," Irène added. Elodie blushed with pleasure.

"How did you come to be with the English?" Marie asked.

"I met them in Le Havre where I was staying with my grandmother. They needed a driver and someone who could speak a bit of Dutch." Elodie replied. Marie looked at her speculatively.

"Irène and I are training young women to take X-rays at the Front. If you are well enough, perhaps you would consider training," Marie Curie offered. Elodie considered the proposal. The X-ray cars, dubbed *Petit Curies* by the *poilus*, were often just behind the trenches in the clearing stations. During battles, they might see thousands of patients. The hours were long and difficult, and she was not certain that she was strong enough, but this was, perhaps, a chance to help.

"Madame, I want to go back, especially now with Verdun. But I am not strong enough yet. Is there something else I can do to help you?" Elodie asked. Marie looked keenly at her for a few moments, sizing her up. Irène sat quietly but gave Elodie a tiny nod of encouragement.

"I'm not sure. You say you can drive?"

"Yes, Madame. My father's chauffeur taught me, and I learned maintenance with the FANYs."

"Hmmm. I may have an idea. Allow me to think it over. How shall I contact you?"

"I am staying with Doctor and Madame Bélanger on Rue de l'Université." Elodie said as a man in rough work clothing appeared in the doorway.

"Madame, I must have your input on these installations," he said insistently.

"Very well. I will be there in a moment."

"I must be going as well, Madame. It was a pleasure to meet you and thank you for the coffee," Elodie stood politely as the older woman left the room. Irène took Elodie's hands, squeezing them gently.

"It's been wonderful to see you. Perhaps we will see each other again."

"I would like that." The women pressed cheeks and then Irène was off after her mother. Elodie went out to the street, looking up at the building in awe. Then she turned for the Bélanger home.

It took a week for Marie Curie to write Elodie. When the letter did come, she accepted it from Claudette, for a moment excited to think it was from Giles. The thrill faded when she realized the envelope was much too clean to have traveled all the way from the Front or Montreuil-sur-Mer, where the legal teams were stationed. She thanked the maid and went to her room, sliding her finger under the flap to open it. The handwriting was forceful, the black ink seeming to carry the writer's personality.

April 12, 1916
My dear Miss Fabien,
I enjoyed our meeting and am taking this opportunity to write you. I sense that your experiences at the Front have left you with a feeling of emptiness at being here in Paris and not serving. To this end, I would like to speak with you about a service you can perform for France.

Please come to the Institute on Friday at one p.m. so that I may explain in person.
Sincerely,
Marie Curie

Filled with excitement, Elodie read the letter through several times and then placed it back in the envelope.

At dinner that evening, Dr. Bélanger nodded at her news.

"I met Madame Curie a few days ago and she outlined her plans for you, which I believe you are healthy enough to undertake. I did caution her that you are not ready to stand for hours on end in a radiologic car," Maurice answered. "I think it will be more to your liking than working as a shop girl."

"What will Giles think? He sent you here for safe-keeping," Madame Bélanger objected. Maurice laughed.

"Now Maryam, you should be the last person to stand in Elodie's way," he chided gently. "Giles is not her husband and I do recall you being rather frustrated with a brash young medical student who attempted to control your destiny." Maryam laughed, but her breath caught.

"I have come to think of Elodie as a daughter. I just do not wish to lose another." Tears brightened the older woman's eyes. Elodie took her hand.

"You honor me, Madame, and I could not have asked for a better stand-in for my parents. But I want to do something, and I think Giles will understand."

The side door of the Institute was open, letting in fresh air and letting out the stink of chemicals. Elodie wrinkled her nose and walked into the narrow hallway, peering into Madame Curie's office. The gray-haired woman was bent over her desk, her pen scratching loudly. She glanced up at Elodie's gentle knock.

"Ah, you are prompt. Come with me to the sitting room." When they were seated, Marie smiled at her.

"Pardon me for being direct, but I am very busy today."

"Of course," Elodie said faintly.

"I understand you know the Front well."

"I know the area between Calais and Ypres, and the region around Reims. And I can read a map."

"Excellent. You see, I have managed to equip two hundred front-line hospitals with radiological machines. Each of those X-ray machines takes a special type of vapor to run it. Irène has been taking this vapor to the front lines, but I need her to help me here. I want someone to take over from her, transporting the vapor, photographic chemicals, and X-ray plates. I will pay you, of course. It's not much, but it is something. You'll have a van." Marie looked at Elodie, her eyes suddenly twinkling. "And, of course, a map. Your job will be to take this equipment to each hospital, pick up old vapor tubes, and return them to me."

"I think I should be able to do that." Elodie said, mentally planning her route.

"Irène also tells me that you wish to attend the Sorbonne. I have a small influence there and may be able to assist you."

"Oh, Madame, that would be amazing and so kind!" Elodie jittered with excitement. "When shall I start?" The two women looked at each other in satisfaction.

"I thought you would do. I will have the next batch of tubes filled by Monday. Come by at noon and you can pick up the chemicals, vapor, and plates. You can leave on Tuesday."

"Oh, Madame. Thank you. I shall be ready."

"The matrons at the hospitals allowed Irène to sleep in the nurses' quarters, so you will have somewhere warm and relatively safe. And they will generally feed you. I'll advance you some money so you can buy food."

"Yes, Madame. I'll be back on Monday." Elodie said. As she walked home, she planned a letter to Giles.

April 14, 1916

My dearest Giles,

I hope this letter finds you well and your duties will allow you to write me. I have exciting news. As you know, when I was in Calais, I met Irène Curie. In an odd circumstance, I met her again, as well as Madame Curie, here in Paris. Madame has offered me a position taking X-ray supplies to French and Belgian hospitals.

Irène has been doing this task, but Madame Curie requires her assistance elsewhere. I shall be able to stay in the hospitals at night and will not be any closer to the Front than the front-line hospitals. In addition, I will be earning some money for my efforts. I had decided, before this opportunity, to try for a year at the Sorbonne, but lacked the funding. This job will make that possible.

I will let you know what my schedule is so that I can see you either in Paris or in Montreuil-sur-Mer.

Yours faithfully and forever,

Elodie

She posted the letter, knowing it would take at least a week to reach Giles and a week for any return letter. She would be on the road by the time he received it, and possibly not back in Paris before any response could arrive.

Chapter 15: May to June 1916

"(World War I) soldiers rode in on horseback and flew out on airplanes" *Libby O'Connell, historian, 2018*

The task itself was simple. A minuscule lump of radium gave off radon gas that collected in a glass box. Madame Curie siphoned it off every forty-eight hours, injecting the radon into a tube that fit within the X-ray machine. With electricity, radon made a light that special photographic plates captured and turned into pictures of broken bones and shrapnel. It seemed like some fantastic magic.

Marie showed Elodie the tiny piece of silvery metal in its box. Elodie peered at it, unimpressed. Radium was used in everything from glow-in-the-dark watch faces men wore in the trenches to children's toys, and from women's makeup to medicines.

"The tube lasts roughly a month. When you get to a hospital, the technician will replace the old tube with a new one and you bring the old one back. Most of what you'll be transporting are the plates and chemicals to develop them. You'll start with the hospitals around Verdun where the fighting is heaviest, then travel to the areas without heavy fighting. You'll have to return here to pick up more tubes and plates as you run low. Irène has been returning each week or so, depending on demand. It's not the most efficient system, but it is the best I can do with one piece of radium. At the moment, most of the easily accessible radium is underneath the battlefields."

"It seems rather complicated."

"Just be careful not to break the tubes."

"Will it hurt me if that happens?"

"It does seem to be harmless. I carry the tubes in my apron," Marie said, opening a pocket so that Elodie could see them. "It will give you rough, itchy skin if you handle it too often. The radiologic girls get burns on their arms when they work too long in the *Petit Curies*, so we've given them lead-lined aprons and gloves."

"Do I need anything special?"

"No, I put the tubes in a lead box. It makes it heavy, but they are safer if you have a road accident."

"Do I visit the *Petit Curies*?"

"No, they return to Paris to rotate staff and pick up supplies."

"I expect I'm ready."

"Tomorrow, you leave for Bar-le-Duc. I'll have

a pass for you. At first, they refused to let Irène through on the *Voie Sacrée*. I had to petition General Pétain for permission."

Elodie had been to tiny Bar-le-Duc before the war. The sleepy farm town was seventy miles from Reims. Now, it was filled with troops, vehicles, repair shops, and depots for materials heading to Verdun. Twenty-four hours a day, trucks and trains traveled north, with a truck leaving every fourteen seconds. Elodie was gestured aside as she reached a guard post on the *Voie Sacrée*.

She stepped out of the van and smoothed her skirt. Two guards manning the road gate looked at her suspiciously.

"I work for Madame Curie, taking important medical supplies to the front-line hospitals. These are my identity papers and a letter from General Pétain," she said, handing over the all-important documents.

One of the guards read through them and called for an officer, the other continually waved loaded vehicles through the gate.

"You are a different girl," the officer said, glancing at Elodie.

"Yes sir. Mademoiselle Curie had other duties assigned to her."

"Very well, check the back of the van and let her go," he said to the guards. Elodie retrieved her papers and was waved through. The road was heavily guarded and tow trucks patrolled the route, looking for broken down vehicles. There was nothing more important than continually resupplying the lines that held Verdun.

Elodie made the drive and delivery in record time and spent the night in the nurses' quarters. She was on the road early in the morning, heading northwest to where the fighting remained fierce. After six days on the road, she turned at Compiègne for the long trip back to Paris. Once resupplied, she headed out on another run, repeating this pattern over and over.

At the Bélangers several weeks later, she found a letter from Giles on her dressing table and opened it with shaking fingers.

April 26, 1916
Dearest Elodie,
You are not to take this position. You are to stay at the Bélangers where I know you are safe. You have already given so much to the effort, you do not need to do more.
Yours,
Giles

Elodie read the letter over, noting where Giles had pressed so hard that his pencil lead had gouged the paper. Her new assignment was boring but, for the most part, safe. Far safer, she reflected, than Giles' job, and there was nothing suggesting that men had the sole right to do dangerous work. She suspected that she needed to quell this over-protective streak that Giles occasionally displayed.

May 2, 1916
My dearest Giles
No.
Lovingly,
Elodie

Before a letter could arrive, Madame Curie had another shipment ready for Elodie to take toward Calais. It would be at least two weeks before she would be back in Paris, as the front-line hospitals required a constant supply of plates and chemicals.

When Elodie returned to Paris, there was no letter waiting for her. Unhappily, she sat down to write a note to Giles.

May 20, 1916
Dearest Giles,
I'll be in Dury on May 27. If you can, meet me there. I'll stay at the French hospital's nursing quarters – it is in the old Lunatic Hospital.
If you can't, please send a letter in care of the Matron with "Hold for Courier for Madame Curie" on it.
I miss you terribly,
Elodie

To her disappointment, there was no letter waiting for her in Dury.

"I'll let the orderlies know you have arrived. Go to your van and I'll have them unload our supplies. You are in good time. The X-ray people were saying that the quality of X-rays is fading and that means that whatever makes them is old," the matron said kindly, noting Elodie's downcast appearance.

"It does. Once I deliver the radon, I think I shall take a walk before dinner. May I sleep in the nurses' quarters?"

"Of course. There's a bed made up for you."

The hospital was in an old asylum, surrounded by tall red walls. The grounds included the hospital, dormitories, and a convalescent home. Ambulances were parked with precision in one parking area and Elodie looked over them with professional interest. Once the supplies were unloaded and the precious radon tube turned over to the X-ray staff, Elodie walked into the large gardens to sit in a comfortable chair. Men in uniform strolled around the grounds, some pushing their comrades in wheelchairs.

Elodie drew her legs up, draping her skirts around them. Her mother would have tart things to say about this unladylike comportment, but Elodie did not care. Curling up into a little ball felt comforting. Her heart fluttered and raced for a few moments and then slowed.

Gradually, the peace of the grounds settled

around her. If she closed her eyes, she might be sitting underneath the oak tree at home. What an odd journey it had been from that July morning in 1914. There had been so much pain and fear since then, yet there were bright spots that seemed to take away some of the anxiety. Lottie and the women. And Giles. She probed that thought as she would a sore tooth.

Had he taken exception to her defiance? He was worried about her, certainly, but he was not her parent to put controls on her behavior. And, regardless of French attitudes towards women, she was perfectly capable of making her own decisions. But the memory of his black hair dropping over his forehead and the brilliant green of his eyes ached in her heart. A tear escaped and trickled uncomfortably down to rest under her nose. She sniffed and rubbed it away on her knees.

Why had he not written her? Surely, his pride was not so fragile. But if it was... She would have to move out of the Bélanger's house. The Bélangers were his family, not hers, despite their kindness to her. Perhaps Madame Curie would know of a room for rent. She would not be a nuisance because she would hardly be there. Then she would give herself a year at university. What came next? The revelation she experienced when Giles was missing still held true: without him, all the things she wanted to do held no appeal. Elodie supposed she would go back to the farm and live there. Perhaps Theo's eventual wife would not mind his spinster sister living in the attic.

The gentle gray of dusk started to settle across the gardens and Elodie suddenly realized all the men and their attendants had gone inside. Dinner and bed.

Tomorrow, she had a long drive to Soissons. She stood up, brushing down her skirt and started across the lawn toward the hospital. A uniformed man came out of the building in front of her, moving quickly but with the slightest hitch from an injured knee. Elodie stopped. The man saw her and then held out his arms. Elodie ran toward him, wrapping an embrace around his neck.

"I thought you were angry with me," she said, partly muffled by the rough wool of his uniform.

"Even if I am angry with you, that doesn't mean I don't love you," he said. His breath tickled her ear. "Come on, Matron said I could eat with you in the convalescent home, and they are serving - well - probably well-cooked horse. God, I'm tired of horsemeat. Please don't serve it in our house. Ever."

"Of course not, Giles," Elodie said meekly. They turned toward the convalescent home, holding hands since it was dark, and no one was around to see.

Once in the dining room, Elodie passed on the casserole and nibbled on bread and cucumbers with a side of new peas. Giles picked at his bowl of stew, eating with a resigned expression.

"I got your letter, and I was so angry that I wanted to come to Paris immediately. 'No' was your only response?"

"It's a small word. And pretty much the same in both French and English." Elodie smiled sweetly.

"Luckily for you, before I could get to Paris, I was sent to England to get some depositions for a court martial. I just got back this morning. I drove over here as quickly as I could. What were you doing in the garden?"

"Making plans for life without you." All her worries fell away, and she felt her heart lift.

"Perish the thought." They ate in silence for a few moments.

"What is your court martial?" Elodie asked. Giles put down his fork and rubbed his face.

"It's a bad one. Officer said he got lost in No-Man's-Land. Brass says he deserted, and General Haig, our commander-in-chief, is a martinet. 'We aren't shooting enough officers', he says. Oh God, Elodie, it's vile. I'm supposed to be his 'prisoner's friend,' his defending officer, and it's not going well." He picked up a knife and unconsciously stabbed at the tabletop with it. Elodie took it away. Giles picked up his napkin and twisted it into a tortured mass.

"Haig likes something called Field Punishment Number One. The men call it crucifixion. You get some poor chap whose only crime is being scared and then you tie him to a post for two hours a day. If you get a bad officer or NCO, they tie them up in sight of enemy lines. The prisoners don't last long." Giles' voice trailed off. He put his head down on the table, covering it with his arms. Elodie thought she saw his shoulders shaking. Hesitantly, she reached out, resting her hand on his. After a few moments, he tucked his face into the crook of his elbow before sitting upright. He took Elodie's outstretched hand.

"Where are you off to tomorrow?" he asked.

"Soissons. Then back to Paris to resupply for a run to Verdun. Then back to Paris again. I'll have some time there before a fast run to Épinal. There're only a handful of hospitals southeast of Verdun with X-ray machines, so I bring all the supplies they need in one go."

"Then back to Paris?"

"Yet again."

"Send a telegram if you can, to let me know when you head back. I'll try to meet you there."

Elodie smiled at him. "I'd like that."

"I have to get back to Montreuil-sur-Mer. I had to beg for this time off." Giles stood up and helped Elodie to her feet. "Be careful." Elodie straightened his tie.

"I will. You be careful as well. My heart won't stand another scare like this last one." Her words were meant to be teasing but Giles looked almost frightened.

"Of course. I'll see you in Paris."

Elodie drove to Soissons to replenish their chemicals and plates. In the hospital grounds, she sat in the driver's seat, deliberating, looking westward. She should start back to Paris, but Reims was only thirty miles away and no longer behind enemy lines. The region was relatively calm and in French hands. She suddenly wanted to see her home. She could make the drive to Reims and then turn to Paris without losing a great deal of time.

The road was in poor shape from the shelling and fighting, and she rattled over it. The destruction began on the western edge of Reims, and Elodie barely recognized her beautiful city as it lay in ruins. In the early days of the war, the German army had shelled the town, beginning with the Cathedral and working outward to knock out the five forts that had protected the city since the 1880s. The forts had been constructed to hold out against an army on foot or horseback, perhaps with cannons. They had not been built to withstand the barrage of modern artillery.

On Reims' streets, people with blank, pale faces stared at her as she motored past. The buildings had been blasted into nothing but the barest of foundations. Homes constructed out of duck cloth and timbers rose shakily out of the ruins. The tree-lined avenue leading to the cathedral was no more, not even stumps remained. To Elodie, it seemed as if the entire town was gray. Inexpertly filled shell craters made the streets rough and created soggy bogs that threatened to suck down her van.

Elodie drove up to the cathedral in a silent fog of despair. Only the twin towers still stood, raggedly pointing up to the sky. The square where she had heard the declaration of war was filled with the debris of the church, blown outward by direct hits. Her father's offices across the street were gone. Elodie peered at the ruins. Someone had constructed a wooden shack, and the French flag flew bravely above the structure. She turned off her car and walked toward it.

A hand-painted sign reading *'Bureau du Procureur de la République'* hung next to the entrance. Elodie knocked and opened the door at the response. Her father sat at a cobbled-together desk, a lantern casting a dim light over the papers stacked on every available surface. He looked up.

"Mon Dieu, Elodie! What are you… is your mother well?"

"Oh, Papa. Yes." Elodie gasped as she flung herself across the office to hug him. "I'm sorry, Papa. I didn't mean to frighten you. Perhaps you don't know. I work for Madame Curie and I was delivering supplies to Soissons. I had to see how Reims was."

"That was a very foolish thing to do, Elodie." He shook his head.

"I know, Papa. I wanted so badly to see what survived."

"The farm stands. Barely," her father said, tiredly. "My vines are gone. It is going to take a lot of work to rebuild." He sat down. Elodie looked at him, suddenly realizing that his hair was liberally sprinkled with white, and his face was aged.

"What are you doing here, Papa?"

"I came back when the Germans retreated from Reims. I have my duties, now more than ever."

"Are you living at the farm?"

"No. There are a few of us to run the town and we have a tent we share. It is safer." He looked up at Elodie, his face creased with worry. "You need to leave soon. The looting… there is nothing left to loot, but there are people desperate enough to steal anything. Go to Paris and don't come back until the war is over."

"Maman and Theo?"

"With my mother, like sensible people." He smiled at her to take the sting out of the words. "When you write her next, tell her the oak tree survived." Elodie almost laughed.

"I will. And Papa, I miss you so much."

"This is good training for me to live without you and Theo. Your Maman told me about the English captain. I assume he will be taking you away from us at the end of the war?" Tears glistened in his eyes. Elodie blushed.

"Would you mind, Papa?"

"Not too much. Maman said he is a fine man," he sighed and hugged her again. "You'd better go."

Elodie kissed her father. He was slighter than she remembered and perhaps shorter. The war had worn all of them down. She let herself out of the shack and walked quickly to her car, turning back once to wave. Her father stood in the doorway; hand raised in farewell.

Elodie drove away from Reims, checking the time on her watch with the radium face. Paris was only ninety miles away. She would arrive after dark, but still in good time. Only ninety miles. Elodie shook her head. Two years ago, Paris had seemed as if it were on the moon, and to travel there was an occurrence.

Elodie celebrated her twenty-first birthday in Verdun. It wasn't much of a day. She thought about her twentieth birthday in Calais. Lottie, Sally, and Dora had taken her to the beach and given her a tiny cake that Cook had prepared, after the women had saved up sugar from their tea rations. They had split the cake in quarters, each having just enough to remind them of better times. At this front-line hospital, there was no celebrating, especially not with a battle that had dragged on since February.

She finished her deliveries as efficiently as possible. Madame Curie would need time to fill the glass tubes and Elodie could expect a week off. She and Giles would meet in Paris. Elodie daydreamed on her drive back to the city.

Giles and Elodie sat on the banks of the Seine,

watching the barges go by and sipping coffee. He had arrived the evening before with a huge smile and an air of mystery. The day had been spent in the Louvre, with long discussions about art and the practicalities of dusting fancy woodwork. Giles grinned at her over his coffee cup, and Elodie felt her heart thump, but in a good way.

"Happy birthday, Elodie." He set down a small box in front of her. It was a dark green leather box with gilt lacework painted around the edges. Elodie caught her breath, picking it up and opening the clamshell top. Inside, nestled in the cream-colored silk, was a ring set with three emeralds. The central emerald was the largest and, on either side, two small diamonds were set in flower clusters. Next to these were smaller emeralds. She looked up at him, her heart full to the brim.

"Will you marry me? I can get down on one knee. But I will have a devil of a time getting back up." Elodie closed the box and held it against her chest, eyes filling with tears. Giles frowned in consternation.

"Here now, if it's not the right ring, I can get another," he stammered, but Elodie shook her head.

"It's not that…"

"You don't want to marry me? I thought we had an understanding."

"Oh, Giles. We do. And I will. The ring is beautiful," she managed. Giles sat back looking relieved.

"Right-oh, then what is it?"

"I never really expected to find someone that I wanted to marry. I mean, I supposed that I would eventually, but I had so many other things I wanted to do first. Then came the war, and you, and I am ready to chuck it all in just to be with you. I am afraid of this war."

"You are the one driving all over the Front like a madwoman. Here, hand over the box." He took it from her and picked out the ring with slightly shaking hands to slide it over her ring finger.

"Do you like the emeralds?"

"I do. They match your eyes."

"That's what the sales chappie said. I fancy he was flirting with me."

"Giles," Elodie giggled. She settled the ring on her finger more comfortably.

"I've been carrying that around with me for months. I haven't been able to ask your father yet. I suppose we could go to Le Havre, and I can ask."

"I saw him in Reims in May. He gave me his blessing. Maman told him you were a good man."

"I say. Well then," Giles let out a deep breath, clapping his hands on his knees. "When shall we get married?"

"We can skip the banns and have a proxy wedding whenever we want. We've fulfilled all the requirements, except the living together part. Perhaps staying in the same house counts." Elodie found herself blushing.

"Tomorrow. We shall find the *mairie* and make this all official." Giles said and they stared at each other in anticipation, excitement, and a touch of trepidation.

"Shall I move to Montreuil-sur-Mer? I should like a small cottage or even an apartment to live in."

"That might be an issue," Giles mused. "They call us the Monks of Montreuil because there are almost no women there. And our hours are long, it's every day from sun-up to midnight. You'd be spending a lot of time alone without much to do."

"I can stay here. Madame Curie still needs me," Elodie said, disappointed.

"I'd rather you give up your work for Madame."

"But then I will be spending long hours alone here with nothing to do. That doesn't seem much better," Elodie protested. They looked out over the river.

"Here. Staying with Maurice and Maryam was good while you were ill, but," Giles said slowly, "I think it's time for something different. Let's find a place here, a rooming house or something. You do your year at the Sorbonne. After that, surely, this war will be over."

Elodie felt a weight lifted from her without even knowing it had been there. She could still find places to help the war effort while she studied, even small jobs like volunteering at a school or convalescent home would be a possibility. Those looked toward the future, not wallowing in the pain of today, and after the war would be a new adventure with Giles in England.

"Tomorrow it is," Elodie nodded to Giles. He stood up, taking her hand.

"Let's go tell the Bélangers and, perhaps, write letters to your parents and mine."

Together, they walked toward their future in the warm summer twilight.

Chapter 16: June to July 1916

"They had no choice" *Engraved on the Animals in War Memorial, Hyde Park, London.*

Elodie knocked on Madame Curie's door, waiting until the older woman had set down her pen and blotted her work before she entered the office.

"Good morning, Mademoiselle Fabien. You are early today."

"Good morning, Madame. And it is now Madame Ellery," Elodie said shyly. "I was married on Friday."

"To your British captain? Congratulations!" Madame Curie stood up and clasped Elodie's hands.

"He wishes for me to stay in Paris and attend my year at the Sorbonne. I can drive for you until the end of August."

"I will be sorry to lose you. When I find a replacement, can you train them?"

"Of course, Madame."

"And you, are you all right with this decision?

I know how keen you've been to help."

"I will find somewhere to volunteer, perhaps in a convalescent home. They always need extra hands and I have the experience."

"I will provide a reference for you."

"I am sorry to leave."

"I understand. Your van should be ready to go. I'll bring out the radon and you can be on your way." Marie shooed Elodie out and went to collect the lead box.

The run to Verdun had gone smoothly and Elodie returned to Paris in high spirits on the evening of July 2, 1916. She could take a week to settle into her new home, a set of rooms in a house near the Sorbonne. On Friday, she would board the train for Le Touquet for the weekend. She and Giles could enjoy the beach and spend some time away from the war in the seaside town. Her feet were light as she danced up the stairs to Madame Curie's office.

"Madame Ellery!" It took a hand on her arm to get Elodie's attention. She was not used to the sound of her new name. Madame Curie looked up at her, more fly-away than usual.

"Are you quite well?" Elodie asked in concern.

"Yes, yes. Do you have time for another run? I must have someone to take as many plates and chemicals to the Front as possible."

"To Verdun?" Elodie asked in surprise and

some trepidation.

"No, to the Somme. The French and British went over the top yesterday and it has been terrible. There are thousands of casualties. I am having all the radiologic cars move to Verdun and the Somme because the hospitals are overwhelmed." Marie's voice was strained. Elodie felt a quake of horror followed by desperation.

"Of course, Madame. If you'll lend me paper and an envelope, I can write my husband to let him know." Elodie felt a thrill at that new phrase.

"I will have the men load your van. It will take all the plates and chemicals I can find." She hurried off while Elodie sat down to write a quick note.

The trips to and from the Somme and Verdun became endless repeats. Where the radiographic plates came from, Elodie never learned. All she knew was that on each return trip to Paris, there was another shipment waiting for her, some destined for Verdun, to maintain the constant demand there, and some to the Somme as the British and French tried to drive the Germans back. By the time both the Battles of the Somme and Verdun drew to an exhausted close in the dead of winter 1916, more than a million French, Canadian, and British men had been wounded and one hundred fifty thousand killed. The trench lines themselves had not changed much despite all the deaths. But for Elodie, the war ended a month after the Somme had started.

In August 1916, the hospital at Dury was overwhelmed and the grounds where Elodie and Giles had met were no longer quiet. The influx of patients meant a continual flow of Red Cross ambulances rotating men to hospitals as far away as Paris. Trains carried still more injured to farther flung cities, and barges made constant trips up and down the river. So many died on the barges that bodies floated down the Somme River, washing up near Calais or being swept out to the ocean.

Elodie dropped off much-needed supplies and turned toward Paris again to collect material for another run. She was very tired, but Madame Curie had found two new delivery people to take over from her. One person could not keep up with the demand in the aftermath of two huge, never-ending battles. Some days, Elodie thought she drove the roads asleep, dodging shell holes and troops by sheer luck.

A loud pop brought Elodie to startled awareness and she jerked the wheel as her van veered wildly. She stepped on the brake. The vehicle limped to a stop, the front end sagging ominously to the right. Elodie gripped the steering wheel, shaking it violently. Not another flat tire.

"Fait chier," Elodie cursed the car in terms that would have made her mother faint and opened the door. She walked around to verify what she already knew and gave the offending tire a swift kick. Then she went to the rear of the van to get the jack and tire iron.

She knelt in the ever-present mud and began to work. From down the road to the south, the distinct sound of harness rings and hooves on hard-packed dirt and *pavé* came closer. Elodie stood up to watch. The first team of artillery horses hauling guns to the Front passed her, the mounted drivers looking at her curiously. She lifted a hand in greeting to her countrymen and the gunner seated on the limber waved back.

"Do you need help?" The artillery officer on his horse paused to ask, the horse jigging at the change in pace.

"No, thank you," Elodie replied, and the man nodded, turning his attention to the road ahead. He trotted on to catch up with the lead team. Elodie automatically eyed the next team, her heart going out to them. Conditions were hard, food was scarce, and the French did not provide their charges with veterinary care. She could tell that this group was suffering, the right wheel horse especially.

His too-short ears under the heavy mane brought her to a stop. Seal-brown with a mealy mouth under the mud, the horse barely resembled the fiery jumper she loved. This horse was ruined, bones sticking up under a coat rough with illness. Her mouth trembled. She bit her lip, watching as the caisson rattled past.

Elodie said nothing, glad the slight breeze blew her scent away from the horses. Brûlée would recognize her voice and her smell. Whether either would penetrate his misery, she could not guess, but she refused to give him false hope. When the last of the gunners walked past, Elodie sat down on the running board of her car, throwing down her tools and sobbing into her fist.

This hurt more than all the deaths of all the men. Brûlée should be at home, well-fed and lovingly groomed, not out here where horse lives counted for even less than the expendable human troops. There was not enough flesh left on him to provide the soldiers with a good meal when he finally fell. She cried for her beloved horse, for herself, for the countless men she had cared for, and for the fog of pain that seemed to lay over the Front. Eventually, the tears had to stop.

Elodie picked up the tire iron and tried to break one of the nuts loose. It slipped, smashing her fingers painfully into the ground. She sprang up, rage boiling in her chest. She wanted to hit something. Anything. A tree standing just off the road made a perfect target. She swung the tire iron as hard as she could, over and over, crying and swearing and screaming her pain. When the fit wore off, she stood winded. Her head and hands hurt. Her throat felt as if she had swallowed rocks. The tree was missing bark and smaller limbs. Elodie immediately felt guilty, and her tire was still flat.

She pulled herself erect and turned around.

The road was filled with French infantrymen, all staring at her in silence. More fodder on their way to the Front, she thought bitterly. The officer on his horse glanced at one of his men and nodded towards Elodie. The man edged over, watching her as one might a mad dog. He carefully took the tire iron from her and broke loose the nuts, changing the tire expertly. When he had finished and put the tools away, he smiled uncertainly. Elodie rubbed her face on her jacket sleeve.

She was about to thank him when a terrific explosion north of them knocked Elodie and the soldiers off their feet. Elodie curled into a ball as the shockwaves and the stink of explosives washed over them. Her ears hurt and she worked her jaw to clear them. The soldiers were already running toward the blast. Through her fogged ears, she heard the screams of wounded men and horses. Scrambling up, she started the car and reversed it, following the men.

The van chugged around a corner in the road and Elodie gripped the wheel hard, staring at the complete devastation littering the ground. A shell launched from somewhere in Germany had missed the front lines, traveling far off course to explode in the middle of the artillery horses. Dead and dying horses lay in crumpled heaps, the living ones trying to stand and screaming in pain. Men lay everywhere, over caissons, under them, or in pieces. It took a moment to steel herself, her knuckles growing white under the strength of her grip.

Elodie grabbed what served as her first aid kit – a few rolls of gauze and some blankets -- and joined the soldiers who were trying to help. Her headlong rush slowed to a walk and then a stumble as she looked around. The shell had hit the middle of the road and the shockwave had torn apart anything close to it. Those were the lucky ones. They died immediately. The explosion had peppered the survivors with shrapnel, ripping through bodies and joints. She could smell guts and blood and her stomach heaved.

The artillery officer who had offered help lay in a heap, partially under his dead horse. So dashing minutes before, horse and rider were now just carrion. The sound of the screaming horses was unbearable. The men were being helped. She could help the horses. She rubbed her ears that rang from the noise.

Elodie fumbled at the dead officer's belt, taking out his revolver. She opened the cylinder. Six rounds. There would be more bullets in his pouches. She opened each pouch she could reach, shoving the rounds she found into her pockets.

"Here, what are you doing?" A man grabbed her arm, pulling her up and away. "Dirty thief."

"Let go," Elodie ordered harshly. "There are wounded horses. I am going to put them out of their misery."

"Leave them," the man demanded, reaching

for the pistol. Elodie slapped his hand away and moved out of his reach. She had never considered shooting a human before, but she could see herself lifting the revolver, pointing it at him, pulling the trigger. He would spin, and fall... With effort, she lowered the pistol.

"One of them is my horse, from my farm. I will put him down. Get out of my way." Her voice was cold. The man looked from her to the dead officer at her feet and to the pistol in her hand. Madness and desperation emanated from her. He had witnessed her beating the tree and had seen battle insanity in the trenches. He stepped out of her way.

Elodie went to the first horse, cataloging not only the horrific injuries but, as any horseman would, picking out the characteristics that told her about this animal -- a fine horse with a good pedigree. She pulled the head into position and held it there by standing on the broken reins. Mentally, she drew a line between the eyes and from the center of the head down. Where the lines crossed, she aimed the pistol. When the horse paused in its struggles, she pulled the trigger. The movement stopped and the fine head was no more. Elodie did not realize that she was liberally spattered with blood and tissue.

She moved on to the next horse. With each loud report, the sound of screaming lessened. Around her, she could see men running, carrying bodies, looking at her, saying things, but she could hear nothing. Her ears had ceased to work, and she moved in an eerie silence. She did not question it. By the time she had reached the center of the explosion, she knew what she would find.

Brûlée lay in a heap on the ground, lips drawn back and neck tendons straining. Elodie stood for a long moment, looking down at his gaunt frame and the once bright and inquisitive eyes that were filming over. She sat down next to him, laying her head on his shoulder behind the collar. His coat was rough, but he smelled of horse sweat and leather. The pistol lay beside her, and she touched the handle. This could make everything silent. How odd that she could no longer hear. She picked up the gun.

A hand reached down, taking it from her. Elodie looked up, angered by the intrusion. The infantry officer shook his head. His lips moved. Then he pointed to her van and toward Dury. Elodie stared at him before laying her head on her horse's shoulder. The hand came back and lifted her, forcing her to walk toward the van. Her van sagged under the weight of wounded men. The few walking wounded leaned on the infantrymen. To one side of the road was a pile of bodies.

Elodie climbed into the van automatically, following a pattern that had been set for months, and drove toward Dury, still enveloped in that absolute silence. In the trenches and the hospitals, Elodie had seen men with shell shock and the myriad different forms that it could take. Some men lost the ability to see or hear; some saw and heard only terrible things. Some lost the ability to move despite having no injuries. For others, shell shock rose up like a foul, dark monster at night, or under stress, or if a sudden smell swirled past them, bringing back old memories. She never imagined that shell shock could affect a woman.

Elodie floated through the drive. The world seemed to be drawn in colored pencils and she felt as if she were looking at a book where the pictures made no sense.

In Dury, she stood in dumb silence as the wounded were unloaded from the van, waiting for a thought to filter through her brain. It took a long time. Men walked past her, but if they spoke, she was unaware of it. The image of a gray-haired woman drifted across her mind, and Elodie studied her intensely before deciding that she needed to see this woman. Again, automatic reflexes carried her into her van.

Elodie's eyes were resolutely focused on the road as she passed the shell crater where men and horses still lay. Ravens and feral dogs scavenged among the bodies. The silence continued in Paris as she drove without care down streets and through intersections, leaving cursing drivers and traffic snarls behind her.

She parked the van near the Institute and

found Marie Curie sitting at her desk. Marie looked up in horror. Elodie's dress, soaked with blood and flesh, had dried and hung stiff. She left behind a trail of dark flakes of blood as she moved. Elodie stood for a few moments until the need to see this gray-haired woman left her. Jerkily, she turned and left the Institute.

On the street, she walked directly to the Bélanger's, following the path that her feet had traced many times. Someone ran up beside her. Elodie looked dispassionately down at Irène Curie's worried face. Her friend's mouth moved but no sound penetrated the silence. Elodie wondered without caring if she was deaf. Irène took her arm, gently guiding her steps to the Bélanger's.

Here, Elodie stood again, knowing that this was not her home, but uncertain where to go. Irène tried to urge her up the steps, but Elodie resisted. Finally, Irène rang the bell. Elodie stood as her friend held a frantic conversation with the servants who answered. Her feet began to take her down the street. Before she was too far from the front door, a hand, Claudette's this time, took her under the elbow and gently guided her back the way they had come. Elodie was so tired that she went passively.

Claudette led her toward the rooms that Elodie and Giles had rented in June. Elodie felt warmth seep through her. This was a good place. The maid helped her up the stairs with the landlady, Madame Corbin, fussing after them. Once in the bedroom, Elodie fell onto the bed, unconsciousness claiming her instantly.

In the morning, she woke suddenly, wondering where she was. It took a few moments before reality set in. These were the rooms where she and Giles had spent their first nights as a married couple. But she had been in Dury. She probed her memory, but there was nothing there. A muffled snore made her sit up and draw the sheets around her. She was dressed in a very dirty shirtwaist and not much else. There was a pile of clothing near the door that looked vaguely familiar. The snore came again, and she saw Claudette under a blanket in the armchair, uncomfortably curled up and sound asleep. Elodie wondered at her presence for a moment, then she fell asleep again.

When she awoke, Claudette was making a cup of tea from Giles' stash, heavily sweetening it with sugar. She brought it to Elodie who took it with thanks. Elodie sipped at the drink, the sugar giving her a jolt of energy. She still wondered at how she had arrived at the apartment. Her last clear memory had been dropping off X-ray plates in Dury, and then nothing until she had awoken to Claudette snoring in the armchair.

The maid kept glancing at her out of the corner of her eye, as if expecting some odd reaction. After a few minutes, she vanished downstairs, eventually returning with hot water. Deftly, she helped Elodie clean up and dress in fresh clothing. Elodie could not remember how her blouse had gotten so dirty. Claudette assured her that it would come clean.

Heavy steps came down the hallway, followed by the rustle of her landlady's skirts. Someone knocked and Claudette opened the door to Dr. Bélanger.

"Elodie, my dear. Can you hear me?"

"Of course. Why shouldn't I be able to hear you?" Elodie asked. Doctor and maid exchanged glances. He held a piece of paper in his hand, glancing down at it and then back at Elodie. He put the telegram in his pocket.

"Giles says he won't be able to join you but hopes you are well. He says he'll write."

"Oh bother. We were supposed to spend the weekend together," Elodie said, disappointedly. The doctor frowned, realizing there were several lost days in Elodie's memory. The landlady gathered up Elodie's filthy clothing, carrying it away. The rank smell of dried blood and rotting flesh went with her.

Claudette and Dr. Bélanger left later, both promising to come back. Elodie watched them go. Silence settled, faint sounds from the street the only distraction. The silence grew, pressing on her ears until they ached. Flashes of memory began to intrude. Noise filled the room as shells exploded around her. Screams of injured horses. Sunlight flickering and flashing through leaves. Men running. The smell of blood. The kick of a pistol in her hand. Elodie covered her ears, screaming.

"Madame Ellery, what is the matter?" Madame Corbin ran into the room. She looked around wildly. Seeing nothing out of the ordinary, she sat down next to Elodie, wrapping her arms around her. With kindness borne of uncommon sense, she soothed Elodie and encouraged her to talk.

The story of the artillery horses flooded out, followed by the men Elodie had been powerless to help, the typhoid patients coughing away their lives, the rats in the mud, the terror of the trench raid, Georges dying in the street and the sheer horridness that she had experienced. Madame Corbin listened as she talked, held Elodie as she cried, and allowed her to rage at the ineptitude of the armies. When the story had poured out, Elodie sank in an exhausted heap, crying gently. Madame Corbin fixed her a hot drink.

"Oh, Madame, I am so sorry. I did not mean to burden you with this," Elodie garbled out through gentle sobs.

"It is not a burden, my dear. I discovered that it is better to talk about the bad things than hold them in. You see, I had three boys. I lost one to whooping cough, one to a runaway delivery wagon, and one is in the trenches. If I tried to hold all that in, I would have died many times. Now, you lay down and sleep. I will be downstairs, and I will hear you if you need me." She took the cup away from Elodie and covered her with a light blanket, then she opened the windows so a gentle breeze flooded in. Elodie drifted off to the cheerful sound of birds outside.

The next day, Elodie had moved from the room that served as a bedroom to the sitting room, trying to convince herself to start a new pair of socks. As she cast on, knitted, unraveled and cast on again, she heard her landlady coming up the stairs, speaking in very slow French, almost as if she were speaking to a child. She knocked briskly on Elodie's door and opened it at her call.

"Madame Ellery, you have a visitor. A Doctor Myers." Madame Corbin stepped aside to admit a small, dapper man with dark hair and a luxuriant mustache. His face was gentle and his eyes held a kindly expression.

"How do you do, Madame Ellery? I am Doctor Myers from the Duchess of Winchester Hospital in Le Touquet. I am a professional associate of Doctor Bélanger," he said in English, holding out an envelope. Elodie took it, quickly reading the note of introduction from Dr. Bélanger.

"What can I do for you, Dr. Myers?" she asked.

"I understand you've had a bout of what we call shell shock. My hospital specializes in treating shell shock. Current thinking is that the condition is found only in men, and cowards at that. I'm trying to prove otherwise and am very interested in speaking with you. It could help other women in this damned war."

"Please sit down," Elodie gestured to a chair and the doctor sat across from her. Elodie glanced at her landlady and the good woman seated herself out of the way. She pulled a ball of yarn and a crochet hook out of her apron pocket and began to work.

The doctor questioned Elodie closely, offering a clean handkerchief when emotion overwhelmed her, but not stepping in to hush her or dismiss the emotions.

"In my experience, you have been most fortunate, Madame Ellery. I've found that the best treatment for shell shock is promptness of action, not letting the person suffer on and on. We follow this with a suitable environment such as you have here, with quiet and peaceful surroundings. I am what the French call an *aliéniste,* so I always recommend psychotherapy."

Elodie's face paled at the word. "You believe I am insane?"

"I don't like that term, I prefer traumatized. And it can be overcome," he reassured her. "Your French psychotherapists agree with me. It's my countrymen who I have problems with." He sighed. "Who was it that took action and encouraged you to talk through your ordeal?"

"Madame Corbin, my landlady." Elodie glanced over at the woman and smiled gently. Dr. Myers turned to study her.

"Amazing. She is a native *aliéniste.* Those are

rare indeed. Would you ask her if she would be interested in volunteering at one of the French shell shock hospitals? I can give her a letter of introduction."

Elodie translated for Madame Corbin, watching as her face expressed doubt and then grew bright in excitement.

"Madame says yes, she would be honored," Elodie told Dr. Myers.

"Most excellent. I will send a letter for her to take to the hospital. Now, I recommend that you take time to recover. This is not a quick process. Allow yourself to cry or be angry or frightened when you need to and talk to your landlady. I'll be in Paris periodically to see you and we can, of course, write. I will be most interested in your progress." He shook Elodie's hand and then left, escorted by Madame Corbin.

Several days later, Elodie sat down at the writing desk to send Giles a quick note.

August 21, 1916
My dearest Giles,
Please do not distress yourself about not being able to get to Paris to see me. I am fine. It is more important to me that you take care of yourself.

Our choice of landladies proved most auspicious. Madame Corbin has been wonderful to me and has taken up volunteering with shell shocked French soldiers. Her intuition is truly amazing, and Dr. Myers says that it is due to her that I am a good distance down the road to recovery.

I went to visit Madame Curie to apologize for my abrupt departure. She was most gracious and has found new drivers. She also was able to help me enroll in the College of Arts. I start in September and am taking a light class of French Composition and French Literature. As I do not wish to graduate, they have been most accommodating. Thank you for my year at the Sorbonne. I love you so and this just makes me love you even more.

When this year is over, perhaps…

Elodie raised her head, hearing an uneven stride in the hallway. She threw down her pen and ran to the door to find Giles on the other side, flowers in one hand and a huge smile on his face. She laughed delightedly and pulled him into their rooms, shutting the door on the world and the war.

Epilogue: 1918

"At eleven o'clock this morning came to an end the cruellest (sic) and most terrible War that has ever scourged mankind. I hope we may say that thus, this fateful morning, came to an end all wars." *David Lloyd George, British prime minister, November 11, 1918*

November 14, 1918
London, England

Dearest Maman and Papa and of course (Uncle) Theo,
I hope this letter finds you well and you have received the telegram that both mother and daughter are doing well. Imagine the welcome Honora Victorine received on the eleventh hour of the eleventh day of the eleventh month of this year when she slipped into this world. The entire world went crazy welcoming her!

I see you looking at each other in consternation. Do not worry! I am not so far gone with love for Honora that I disregard the real meaning of the celebration. Although when I am with her the entire world can go hang — that's an

American expression. It's not very nice. She is sleeping in a cradle that belonged to Giles – his father and mother brought it over last week. Her eyes are still blue, but I have hopes they will turn green like her father's.

Lottie is coming to help me. Thank you for your kindness to her in Le Havre. The Spanish Flu left her so weak that without you, she may not have made it home to Siôn and me. Siôn, her husband, was also hit hard by the flu. I'm afraid he will not be able to go back to work as a teacher, but I need Lottie, so they can make do that way.

As you know, the doctor thinks my heart will not withstand another pregnancy, so Honora may be our only child. I have not discussed that with Giles, so please do not say anything to him if you should see him before I do.

The last year has been terrible, although how it could be worse than the first three years I do not know. The only good thing is that Giles will be coming home soon and will meet Honora. She is sucking her tiny fist right now and is possibly the most precious thing you have ever seen.

Dr. Myers has been in touch and is expecting to be terribly busy in England. He thought perhaps I could work with him, but the arrival of Honora precludes that. I just want to be in a small world with my husband and my daughter. What a thrilling word. Daughter. I love her so.

Lottie volunteered with Dr. Myers on her days off and understands the process he is using to help shell shock victims. While I am recovering, there are still some events that bring back that awful time - like driving a car. Lottie can help me to deal with my memories when they return to overwhelm me.

I do beg of you, once Honora is old enough to visit, please do not tell her of the war or my part in it. I do not think I could bear her questions or having to relive those days. Surely in this new world she will inherit, there will be no more wars.

I hear Lottie's key in the door. I will write again and send a photograph of Honora, although it will not capture her delicate pink cheeks or faint fuzz of hair. Take care and let me know if the oak tree is still standing in the farmyard.
Love,
Elodie

Real Individuals Mentioned

Edward Baker - I was not able to figure out which, if any, of the ten Edward Bakers with the 21st Lancers this Edward Baker was. Regardless, he was a real person whose story is at the heart of this one. In 1898, Warrant Officer Edward Baker was in the Battle of Omdurman. As he waited for rescue, he dreamed about a group of women who would gallop onto the battlefield, provide first aid, and then remove the wounded to casualty stations. In 1907, Sergeant Major Edward Baker formed the First Aid Nursing Yeomanry (FANY), a group that played a huge role in both *An Unorthodox War* and *A Woman's War*. The FANYs are still in existence and provide emergency services in Great Britain. Edward Baker ended his military career as a captain.

Coralie Levy Cahen (21 June 1832 – 12 March 1899) was a French-Jewish philanthropist and sculptor. She married a doctor in 1851 and was instrumental in founding an orphanage for Jewish girls that focused on helping young sex workers. When the Franco-Prussian War broke out in 1870, she became a central committee member of the *Dames de la Société de Secours aux Blessés Militaires* (Ladies Committee of the Society to Aid the War-Wounded) and created an ambulance service dedicated to non-officer ranks. She later became manager of the hospital at Vendôme. After the war, she visited French prisoners held in Prussia and negotiated with Empress Augusta for their release. During this time, she discovered thousands of files pertaining to these prisoners and was able to have them sent to France, providing the first word of these prisoners. Cahen later became the Vice-President of the Association of French Women within the French Red Cross. Toward the end of her life, she was an advocate for child protection and education.

Edith Louisa Cavell (4 December 1865 – 12 October 1915) was a British nurse working in Belgium as an instructor. When WWI broke out, she treated any wounded soldiers regardless of nationality and assisted more than two hundred Entente soldiers to escape German-occupied Belgium. This brought her to the attention of the German military. She was tried for espionage and willingly admitted to the crime of helping soldiers escape. She was executed as a spy and her death was used as propaganda against the Germans. In recent years, evidence has arisen suggesting that she was indeed a spy. Spying was a relatively common occupation by nurses in military hospitals and the French executed at least four women for spying for Germany. In 1919, Cavell's body was one of only three to be repatriated to Britain.

Irène Curie (Joliot-Curie) (12 September 1897 – 17 March 1956) was only seventeen when WWI broke out. She was pressed into service as a trainer of X-ray technicians, an X-ray equipment installer, and trainer of the American Military Medical Corps. After the war, she earned a PhD in Chemistry. She and her husband, Fredric Joliot, were awarded the 1935 Nobel Prize for Chemistry. According to some sources, Irène blamed her fatal illness on X-ray exposure during the war. Her life story is not well known, but she deserves to be remembered.

Marie Skłodowska-Curie (7 November 1867 – 4 July 1934) was born in Poland. She later moved to France, where she and her husband, Pierre Curie, undertook research into the brand-new field of radioactivity. For this work, Marie was awarded two Nobel prizes. When war broke out, Marie realized that X-rays were going to be critical medical care in battlefield hospitals. She figured out how to turn a car engine into a dynamo to provide electricity to the X-ray equipment and raised money to outfit twenty radiographic cars. She did offer to sell her Nobel Medals to generate funds, but this was unnecessary. Once the radiographic cars were up and running, Marie decided to put X-ray machines into every French and Belgian battlefield hospital. She managed to outfit two-thirds of the seven hundred hospitals, saving thousands of lives. Her work continued with harvesting radon for the X-ray machines and in training the American Military Medical Corps. Like her daughter, Marie blamed her fatal illness on X-ray exposure.

Field Marshal Douglas Haig (19 June 1861 – 29 January 1928) was a military officer with a brilliant career. In late 1915, he was named the commander of the British Expeditionary Force and oversaw major actions including the Battle of the Somme. In the 1960s, his reputation underwent criticism for the two million British casualties that occurred under his leadership. He was by all accounts a strict leader. Unlike many commanders on all sides during WWI, he was able to adopt new tactics and respond to the rapidly changing face of war. After the war, Haig dedicated his life to the welfare of ex-servicemen throughout the Commonwealth.

Sister Elizabeth Kenny (20 September 1880 – 30 November 1952) was a self-trained nurse who developed techniques to relieve "spasm" in either polio or meningitis patients. Her techniques became the basis for modern physical therapy. The title "Sister" is traditionally given to a senior nurse and Kenny earned that title during her service on troop ships during WWI. I did take some liberty with her timeline, but according to sources from the day, convalescent soldiers were put through similar exercises.

Dr. Charles S. Myers (13 March 1873 – 12 October 1946) was an English physician who specialized in psychology. In 1909, Myers became the first lecturer at Cambridge to teach experimental psychology. In 1915, he authored a paper where he used the term "shell shock," although he did not coin the term. In 1916, he was named consultant psychologist to the British armies in Le Touquet, France. He came into conflict with the military for his assertion that shell shock was treatable and not a reason to execute a man suffering from PTSD. Shortly before his death, he refused to testify about "shell shock" because he was too traumatized to relive those experiences.

Acknowledgments

Writing a book is never a solo endeavor. I'd like to thank the individuals who made this book possible. And, as always, all mistakes are mine alone!

Family members are my first and foremost supporters:

Bob Green for listening to my ideas and the very rough first drafts, and always providing support.

Madora Daley-Green for going down rabbit holes with me on the hunt for random facts. Madora also created the cover artwork as well as the silhouettes.

My Marine, Will, for advising on proper military etiquette.

My sister, Robin Daley, for reading, proofing, fact checking, and supporting me through thick and thin.

My friends, whether they are named here or not! A special thank you to:

My beta readers, Debby Blanck Wiltse and Rick and Betsy Moore, read the first manuscript and provided valuable feedback. Deborah Kassner was the final set of eyes to ensure it was as clean as possible.

And to Jennie Lawrence who read all the versions and encouraged me to keep going.

This book stands on the shoulders of giants who have either lived the events or researched them, \. A special thanks to:

Indy Niedell's *Great War* series on YouTube. His documentation is outstanding, and his narration is excellent.

From his recommendations, I discovered *Poilu: The World War I Notebooks of Corporal Louis Barthas, Barrelmaker, 1914-1918*.   I only made it halfway through the book because of the horrors he described. The scene that Georges described to Elodie was drawn from Barthas' experience.

Two books available through the Gutenberg Project were invaluable. These were the sources for many of the scenes. *A Fanny Goes to War* by Pat Beauchamp Washington was a fabulous resource for the lives of FANYs in WWI. Major Frank Fox's book *G.H.Q.* provided background for general staff officers during WWI.

From Google Books, I read *A Nurse at the War* by Grace McDougall, another firsthand account of FANYs in WWI by a woman who served with Beauchamp.

I spent a good deal of time on Google maps for distances and locations and used BatchGeo as the basis for the map at the front of this book.

Author's Note

When I finished *An Unorthodox War*, I wanted to move forward in time to see what happened with Ellie's children or grandchildren. My military advisers told me it was inappropriate to tell stories of women who were still able to detail their own experiences. It could be considered a form of stolen valor. Since I want to highlight women's service, not to steal it, I looked back in history.

I decided to explore World War One and the role of women in that war. I had several choices given my (then limited) knowledge of the Great War. Nurses, ambulance drivers, and refugees were the most obvious but, on the whole, are very decently documented. The next choice was spying. Mata Hari, Edith Cavell, the White Ladies spy ring in Belgium, and the Girl Guides who were the backbone of the British intelligence were pretty obvious story points. However, rewriting *An Unorthodox War* but with Gibson Girls in corsets was not very appealing.

At first, my heroine was to go to East Africa and provide witness to the military actions and tribal warfare that was World War One on that continent. I got the protagonist as far as landing in Mombasa, but she wanted to return to France. It was then I discovered *A Fanny Goes to War* by Pat Beauchamp Washington. The story of Ellie's parents, Giles and Elodie, blossomed.

About the Author

 Marjorie's interest in historical fiction about ordinary women living extraordinary lives was inspired by the reality of women's achievements and the frustration about how their achievements and lives are ignored.

Marjorie is a Wyoming native but grew up overseas. This exposure resulted in a love of travel, complete bewilderment between English and American spelling, and an appreciation for other cultures.

Marjorie lives in Wyoming with her husband Bob, horse Miss Penny, and rescue dogs Diesel and Tira. Her two children and stepson are grown and making their own history.

Email: daleymarjorie@yahoo.com

Facebook/Instagram: MarjorieDaleyauthor

Website: marjoriedaley.com

Also by Marjorie Daley

Fiction Books

An Unorthodox War - the story of Elodie and Giles' daughter as a secret agent in France during World War II

Fire Ground - a female firefighter investigates a murder mystery

Non-Fiction Books

The New Adults' Guide to Basic Finances

Naughty Dogs: Identifying, Diagnosing, Understanding, and Correcting Your Dog's Unwanted Behaviors

The Ultimate Guide to Wild Canines, Primitive Dogs, and Pariah Dogs: An Owner's Guidebook for Wolfdogs, Coydogs, and Other Hereditarily Wild Dog Breeds